For Dan,
bard of nothingness

Arugula

And Other Stories

Jon Wesick

Gnome On Pig Productions

Written by: Jon Wesick
Edited by: Jessica Lami
Cover art by: Danielle Kisch

Copyright©2017

ISBN:978-1-387-00520-8

www.gnomeonpigproductions.com

Acknowledgments

The stories in this collection have appeared or will appear in Berkeley Fiction Review, Binnacle, Bracelet Charm, CC&D, Clockwise Cat, Contemporary World Literature, Cynic Online, Everyday Weirdness, Hipster Fight, Hot Air Quarterly, Jersey Devil Press, Journal of Experimental Fiction, Medulla Review, The MiniMag.com, The Missing Slate, Samizdada, Sangam Magazine, Smashed Cat, Space and Time, Tabard Inn, Tales of the Talisman, Words of Wisdom, Writers Post Journal, and Zahir.

Several people helped with the creation of this collection. I want to thank Sam Hamod, Kristen Scott, R.T. Sedgewick, Gwyn Henry, and Ishmael von Heidrick-Barnes for their constructive comments on my stories. I'd also like to thank Jessica Lami for making the text presentable.

~Jon Wesick

Arugula

Contents

Arugula

Jon Wesick

Moon of a Divided Heart

I'd made all the preparations. Stephanie had four days off (one of the few perks of working for Amtrak), we had reservations at Chez Jacques, and the emerald engagement ring rested in its velvet box in my pocket. I fought the urge to rehearse some grand speech that would no doubt come out stilted and corny like the guys getting on their knees in those 1940s movies. No, better to stay in the moment and say something honest like, "Stephanie, this past year of living together has been the best in my life. Will you marry me?"

Traffic on the I-8 slowed as soon as I got to Hotel Circle. I tuned the radio to "All Things Considered" and settled in for a long wait. The sun had set by the time I got home but we still had twenty minutes to get to the restaurant. I pulled into the parking spot, grabbed my laptop from the backseat, and dashed toward the courtyard. Only then did I notice the full moon rising over the eucalyptus trees by the fence. Damn! Why hadn't I realized it? Up the stairs two at a time. I burst into our second-story apartment just as Stephanie began the change. Already thick, black fur covered her skin and her body's altered shape was stretching her clothes to the point of ripping.

The conventional wisdom about werewolves simply isn't true. Stephanie doesn't change into a snarling, vicious beast but into an affectionate Newfoundland dog with floppy ears and warm, friendly eyes. Werewolves transform into larger breeds, because a one-hundred-thirty-pound human turning into a Chihuahua would violate the conservation of mass. Then there's the myth about becoming a werewolf when one bites you. First of all, Stephanie would never bite anyone, though she drools like Victoria Falls in her dog state. Secondly, this doesn't explain how her father Max, who doubles as a two-hundred-pound mastiff, passed the condition to Stephanie but not her six sisters. Finally, there's that hokum about killing werewolves with a silver bullet. Anybody who points a gun at my Steph is in for a serious ass kicking! Enough said?

"Come on, Steph. Get off the couch."

Steph, her metamorphosis complete, whined and complied. I helped her out of her torn running shorts and halter-top. Honestly, I don't know why she puts on lingerie on the nights of her change. Perhaps she finds the thought of me unhooking the bra from a dog's torso amusing.

"Woof!" Steph stretched out her front paws to lower her head and shoulders below the level of her hips.

"Quiet! You want the manager to hear?"

"Woof!"

I reached for her nose to hold her jaws shut, but she danced out of my grasp and began romping around the apartment. You'd be surprised how fast a big dog can move, but agility was never Steph's strong suit. She bounded toward the couch, turned, and cleared a pile of New Yorkers from the end table with her tail. I dove to catch a half-full glass of red wine before it ruined the carpet but could only watch in horror as momentum carried Steph's massive body into the TV stand. The TV tipped off its support and tumbled to the floor with a heart-wrenching crunch. The downstairs neighbor began banging on the ceiling with a broom handle.

"Bad dog!"

Hanging her head, Steph crawled away. She returned moments later with a chew toy, dropped the rubber mouse at my feet, and gazed at me with sorrowful eyes.

"Don't give me that look!"

Steph pushed the toy mouse closer to my feet with her nose.

"Oh, all right." I bent and reached for the toy.

Steph snatched it with her teeth for a game of tug-of-war. I played a few minutes for form's sake but had little motivation to hold on to the slobbery mouse. After Steph's victory I wiped my damp hand on my pants and felt the outline of the velvet box through the fabric. Was it too late for a refund? I mean, after she changes back to human and wants to be romantic, it's hard to forget cleaning Steph's messes off the sidewalk with a plastic bag the night before. And what if, like her dad, she starts spending more than a few nights a month as a dog? What if she stays that way forever? The glass inside the broken TV rattled as I lifted it off the carpet and set it back on its stand. I sat down to read. Steph collapsed on the carpet with a snort and rested her chin on my foot. She started growling before I made it through two pages of Pride of Baghdad. Someone knocked on the door.

"Just a minute!"

I dragged Steph into the bedroom and closed the door behind her. What I wouldn't give for a good choke chain at times! I opened the front door and found my apartment manager standing on the welcome mat.

"Ah, Mrs. McGarrigle, how are you, tonight?"

"Mr. Thomson in number twelve complained about the noise," she said. Mrs. McGarrigle was a shrewish, gray-haired woman with a face like a hatchet and a personality to match. To my knowledge, no one in the apartment complex knew her first name.

"Yes, I'm sorry about that. The TV fell off its stand."

"He said he heard barking."

"I was watching 101 Dalmatians, not the Glenn Close version but the original animation. Have you seen it?"

Cruella's eyes shifted. I followed her gaze to the pink rubber mouse lying on the carpet.

"Stephanie's niece." I leaned closer. "Teething."

"You are aware that your lease forbids pets and that violations are grounds for eviction."

I nodded. Steph started scratching at the bedroom door.

"What a friend we have in Jesus!" I belted out to cover the noise. "It's 7:15, time for my nightly hymns," I explained. "All our sins and griefs to bear!"

The scowling Mrs. McGarrigle turned on her heels and walked away. I sang a few more verses for good measure before releasing Steph from the bedroom and returning to my graphic novel. Steph ambled up to me and stood panting with breath that could knock down a charging rhino.

"What do you want?"

I stared into her dark, brown eyes. Was my Stephanie in there or did the change transform her mind into a dog's too? I'd never learned the answer because Stephanie forgot everything that happened in her altered state on her return to human form. I got her a dog biscuit and read until 9:30 when Steph scratched at the door. She gnawed my sleeves and batted my hand with her paw as I put on her collar and attached the leash. I peeked to make sure no one was looking and snuck her through the parking lot and out the side gate to the wooded area on the edge of the canyon.

Steph squatted almost immediately. I turned away and examined an old, gnarled juniper. With its mass of dead branches that lay like Carol Kane's frizzy hair atop its listing trunk, the tree could have inspired a thousand classical Chinese poets. I recited a few lines from Tu Fu's "Ballad of the Army Carts" from memory. Lost in contemplation I must have loosened my grip on the leash, because Steph broke free and dashed down the sloping canyon wall.

"Steph, come back here!"

Tongue lolling out of her mouth, she looked back with an expression of pure joy and loped up the other side to the street beyond.

"Damn it! I don't have time for this. I have to work, tomorrow."

I descended into the canyon, made my way through the brush, and climbed to the neighborhood on the other side. Fortunately, the street lamps lit the scene with enough mercury-vapor glow for me to make out Steph's receding form. Careful not to run and turn this into a game, I tracked her past a house with a torn sofa on the porch and down a side street. I walked by more homes and an apartment building with techno music coming out of one of the windows. I froze in front of an auto shop. There, horror of horrors, I found her. Lit by spotlights she and another dog were coupling. Having climbed onto her back, the German shepherd clung to her with his front legs while pumping his hips for all he was worth. Of course, she couldn't help it, but the hurt cut to my spleen.

"Steph! How could you?"

She stared at me with uncomprehending eyes.

"Get away from there!"

Boiling with rage, I shoved the other dog aside and dragged Steph toward home. I was so furious that I didn't check the courtyard for witnesses. Once inside I slammed the door and went to bed without checking her fur for burrs.

Around daybreak Stephanie, now in human form, climbed into bed. She draped an arm around me and snuggled close pressing her warm flesh against my back. She was always randy after a transformation. As her fingers toyed with the elastic on my boxer shorts, I tossed off the blanket and sat up.

"Is something the matter?" She raised herself on to one elbow. The sheet fell away from her olive-skinned torso exposing her pear-sized breasts.

"No, nothing," was all I could force out of my tightened chest. She was such a beauty with her raven hair and thin lips that curved in a perpetual smile, but I couldn't bear to look. I turned and fumbled into the pants I'd left on the chair the night before. "I have an early meeting this morning."

I got to the office before my coworkers, placed the Yellow Pages on my desk, and opened it to the section on marriage and family therapists. Three were within a few miles of home. Would they believe I was jealous of a German shepherd? If they did would they report Stephanie's condition to her employer? Even though the change happened at precisely predicable times, Amtrak wouldn't let someone who had blackouts continue driving their locomotives. I put the phone book back on the shelf and stared at the blank computer screen while the others arrived. Only one person could help me.

"Stan." I rested a hand against the door frame of my supervisor's office. "I'm not feeling well, today. Is it all right if I go home?"

Stephanie's parents had moved to a small house in Normal Heights after the girls went off to college. I parked on the street in front of it, entered through the gate in the chain-link fence, followed the walkway to the red concrete porch, and rang the bell. A dog barked from inside the house. Stephanie's mother answered.

"Kyle, I was expecting you." She held the door for me. "Come in."

A mastiff waited in the hallway.

"Hello, Max." I scratched Stephanie's father behind the ear and followed Mrs. Peterson into the living room.

She wore faded jeans and a tight pullover that showed off a figure that was mostly unchanged since her days as a campus protester in the sixties. With her full breasts, dark eyes, and shoulder-length black hair she radiated a mature beauty that even eighteen-year-olds would find hard to resist.

"Would you like some tea?"

"All right." I sat on an Early-American armchair with a white doily draped over its back.

Stephanie's mother returned with a porcelain tea service that was decorated with tiny flowers.

"Milk?"

I nodded. She poured the milk into my cup before adding the tea and handing it to me. I carried the delicate cup to my chair and sat balancing the saucer on my lap. Mrs. Peterson took the seat across the coffee table. Max sat on his haunches and stared at her as if expecting a treat.

"How do you manage?" I stammered.

"It was hard at first. We dated for almost six months before I found out. Max's family had money so he could rent a house instead of living in a college dorm." Mrs. Peterson sipped her tea and left a lipstick smudge on the rim of the cup. "I guess living with a werewolf is like anything else. You get used to it."

"But one minute he could be discussing Mendelssohn and a few hours later eating garbage off the sidewalk."

"I have to accept him the way he is." She patted her husband on the head. "Isn't that right, Max?"

The mastiff thumped his tail on the floor.

"The hardest part for me is…" I swallowed to get the words out. "I'm afraid she won't be there for me when I need her."

"Their mental state is what it is, even if it's not what you want it to be at the time. But though their brains change with the transformation, their love for you remains the same." She placed a card on the table. "POW – Partners of Werewolves. It's our support group. Only you can decide if you can commit to a life with Stephanie, Kyle. Whatever you choose, I'll help however I can."

Max lay down and rested his chin on his paw. The whites of his eyes made tiny crescent moons as he kept his gaze on his companion of thirty years. This look did more to make up my mind than all Mrs. Peterson's talk of heroic love. Stephanie and I would have to get a house with a fenced yard but the housing bubble was going to burst and it was time to get out of that apartment complex, anyway. I excused myself and walked keys-in-hand to my car. Traffic was light this time of day. I'd be home in a half hour. That would give Stephanie and me plenty of time to celebrate before dark.

Political Correctness

I unlocked the apartment door, tossed the letters from Planned Parenthood and NOW on the counter, and rushed to the back room, where I switched on the computer. It was 6:30 and Stephanie wouldn't be back from her Samba class until after 9:00. With luck I could get close to three hours of writing done. While the computer was booting up, I went to the refrigerator and got the One-Hand-Clapping sandwich I'd bought at the Diamond Sutra Deli. The edge of the cling wrap was harder to get a grip on than the faces of my parents before I was born. Eventually due to the merit of thousands of past lives, I got it open. Just as I took a bite, the doorbell rang.

"Hey, don't get upset. I'm not here to mug you or anything," said a black teenager whose grin revealed a diamond-inlaid tooth. "How you doin', tonight?"

"Urrph," I said.

"I hear you, man. I belong to an organization that helps kids say no to gangs and drugs." He flashed a plastic-covered sheet in front of my eyes. "Care to help us out by buying some candy?" He pointed to the cardboard box at his feet. It was filled with peanut butter cups and licorice strips.

I swallowed the mouthful I'd been chewing. "No thanks."

I slammed the door, carried the sandwich to the computer and began typing.

The election of Ronald Reagan ushered in an era that saw increasing attacks on reproductive rights. In 1982…

The doorbell rang.

"Damn!" I went to the other room and answered. It was a cholo in a plaid shirt.

"Do you want to buy some table grapes or iceberg lettuce to help the orphans in Michoacan?"

"No!" I slammed the door, returned to my computer, and picked up my sandwich.

The doorbell rang.

"I'm Brittany. The Trout Foundation gives young people like me an opportunity to win a scholarship." The blonde girl in a plaid skirt, knee socks, and penny loafers extended her arm, straight as a ten-inch gun on an Aegis class cruiser, to hand me a brochure. "You can help by subscribing to our DVD of the month club."

I sighed and made no move toward the brochure.

Her smile collapsed into a moue. "You do like movies. Don't you?"

"I guess." I took the brochure from her hand.

"Great!" The perky smile returned. "If you subscribe to our Sappho series, not only will you get twelve months of girl-on-girl action, but we'll throw in 'Amy's First Anal' for free!"

After I sent her away, I was visited by Native Americans offering samples of the new Bill W. Beer, two men selling shares in Smith & Wesson to support a Christian drug treatment center, red-robed Tibetan monks lugging Ann Coulter books, a woman in an electric wheelchair selling pâté de foie gras, and a bald cancer kid dragging a rolling IV pole and several tins of chewing tobacco. I slammed the door and rested my back against the cool metal. After several deep breaths my pulse rate slowed. I stepped away from the door and the bell rang again.

I looked through the peephole and saw a six-foot dolphin balancing on its tail atop the welcome mat. It began to toss its head and chatter, as soon as I opened the door. With its snout it gestured to the box of Phospho Clean Laundry Detergent swinging from its flipper.

"Get the hell out of here!" I yelled.

The dolphin made a rude gesture with its free flipper and began hopping down the stairs. I retrieved the Mag-Lite from the bedroom and set it by the door. The next peddler to disturb me would get a nasty surprise. I didn't have long to wait. The doorbell rang in less than five minutes. I snatched the heavy flashlight, lifted it over my head, and yanked the door open. The familiar aquiline nose and beefy face of the man in a black tuxedo halted my downward strike in mid-swing.

"Dick Cheney!" I let the Mag-Lite drop from my hand.

"Hello, Tim. I'm here to collect for the most endangered minority in America, the straight, white male. Mind if I come in?"

"Not at all." I ushered him inside, and he sat at the kitchen table.

I retrieved a damp sponge from the sink and began wiping the table's wooden surface.

"What the hell are you doing?" Cheney asked.

"Oh this?" I looked at the sponge. "There's scientific proof that women have more sex, when their partners do their share of the housework. My wife showed me an article in Jane."

"And how is that working for you?"

I dropped my eyes to stare at the crumbs I'd swept into my palm. My silence was answer enough.

Cheney struck a wooden match on the sole of his shoe, lit a cigar, and shook out the flame. He tossed the match at the wastebasket, but it bounced off the wall and landed on the linoleum.

"Where is the little woman, tonight?" he asked.

"Oh, she's at Samba class with her dance partner, Raul."

"Raul. Raul." Cheney's expression grew pensive as the clouds of cigar smoke enveloped his head. "Let me check with Homeland Security and see if we have anything on this Raul." He jotted a reminder in a small spiral notebook and returned it to his jacket pocket.

"All those door-to-door peddlers, you sent them. Didn't you?"

"That's right, Tim." Cheney blew a stream of smoke toward the ceiling. "I've had my eye on you for quite some time, and I knew the only way I could get you to stand up for yourself was through subterfuge."

We talked for another half hour. Before he left, Dick Cheney visited both bathrooms and lifted the toilet seats in each. After all his help what else could I do but make out a large check to the RNC?

I sat on the couch and looked at the campaign pamphlets he'd left behind. When Stephanie got back, we'd have a long talk. I was scared but excited too. I looked at the clock. It was 8:45. I had fifteen minutes before she returned, fifteen minutes before the start of my new life.

The Slender Thread

My insurance agent sent me a birthday card. It was a cheap, disposable thing with the company logo inside along with a preprinted message thanking me for my business. It was the only card I received but I was okay with that. I'm past the age where women view me as a sexual being so no wife or girlfriend remembered the date. If I'd told them, the guys at work would have taken me to lunch but I kept quiet. Why spend an extra hour making small talk with people I have little in common with?

I left work early on my birthday and despite the traffic by the Del Mar Fair got home at 4:30. The card was where I'd left it on the blond-wood table. I picked it up, carried it to the garbage can, and paused to examine the greeting written in faux gold cursive on the rainbow cover. Somehow, I couldn't throw it away. It was as if the card had become the last slender thread connecting me with the rest of humanity. I checked my watch. It was 4:38. I had just enough time.

I dashed to my blue Honda Civic leaving the front door unlocked in my haste. I backed out of the stall, slammed the car into gear, and burned rubber in the parking lot. At the exit I stopped while a pregnant woman pushed a baby carriage in front of me at the speed of continental drift. Once she cleared my path, I rocketed down the street, took the right of way from a white van, and fought my way through the traffic by the mini mart. I took a left, barreled down Tamarack, and got on the freeway. Bad idea! Traffic was going nowhere. It was 4:52. Desperate measures were called for if I wanted to make it before closing time. I jerked the wheel to the right and passed the others on the shoulder. Sadly for me, a guy in a silver Toyota Tundra had the same idea and cut me off. I followed him onto the exit and into the left-turn lane where he stopped even though the light was green.

"Damn it!" I laid on the horn, passed him on the right, and only then saw a line of cars had blocked him too.

By the time I got to my insurance agent's location on El Camino Real, the office was closed. I pounded on the glass door with my palms and was about to leave when a man with gray, curly hair came from the back. Even in the warm, California weather he wore a tan cardigan. I placed the birthday card flat against the glass. He tilted his head back to look through the reading glasses riding low on his nose, gave a smile of recognition, and unlocked the door.

"Thank you for the card," I said. "I had to come."

"You're welcome. Won't you come inside?" He stepped out of the way to let me pass and locked the door behind me. "I've been meaning to talk to you about life insurance. We offer whole life policies as well as term insurance for as little as a dollar a day."

I followed him to his office where we talked until long after dark. As we discussed my age, medical condition, and whether I smoked or took part in risky activities, I felt a deep, human connection with him. Around 8:00 I left feeling refreshed, renewed, and secure in the knowledge that for just a few thousand dollars a year I would make some distant relative very happy when I died.

The Quest – A Postmodern Retelling of the Gandavyuha1

I'd had it with white lies, polite fictions that lubricated hurt feelings, the 10-W-30 fracked by mendacious corporations of social convenience at the expense of the ground water of personal integrity. No more! From now on I'd tell people exactly what I felt. Radical honesty, baby! That's how I'd roll.

My first chance to put my resolution into practice came that very afternoon. As usual my rusty Volvo 240 stalled at the corner of Bleaker and Alvarado blocks from the Potemkin Village Apartments where I rented a 200 square foot efficiency for just $3000 a month. And as usual my Republican congressman neighbor was patrolling his 30-acre property's fence line on horseback. Like a guard at a Louisiana prison farm he wore a cowboy hat and carried a pump-action shotgun barrel to the sky, its stock held comfortably against his hip.

"How's it going?" He spit a plug of chewing tobacco onto the grass.

"Not so well." I stopped pushing against my Volvo's door frame and let it coast to a stop. "My mother had a stroke. Whenever I look at her bedridden, mute, and blind, I see myself in twenty years. I worked for decades and my big reward will be being stuck in a diaper in some nursing home! What's the point?"

"I hear you." The congressman rested the shotgun across his knees and leaned forward in the saddle to look down at me. "That's why it's crucial to lower corporate taxes and eliminate all government regulations. Yessir." He sat up again. "God, guns, and free enterprise made this country great!"

When I got to work the next day, a synthesized voice message was waiting on my teleputer.

"Mister … Nutter … would like to see you at … 8:30 AM Pacific Standard Time."

Anderson Nutter had risen to the senior ranks of Applied Applications Corporation at the unheard of age of twenty-nine. Since then the hair at his temples has grayed giving him an air of maturity and wisdom. After filling him in on the status of the Myers account, I asked him about the malaise caused by my mother's affliction.

"When I was your age, advertising analytics was an immature field." Nutter waved his 18-karat-gold, Cross pen like a conductor's baton. "I worked hard for my success and deserve everything I have." He set the pen down on his mahogany desk. "I'll need you to come in on Saturday."

I'd already talked to a Republican. To get a Democratic perspective I phoned my senator's help line. Strangely enough, she answered in person so I described my feelings of dissatisfaction brought on by my mother's illness. Since the senator seemed sympathetic I elaborated.

"Despite spending ten years in college, I could only get a job at a glorified ad agency. I didn't study basket weaving or some other nonsense. I got a Ph.D. in physics. Maybe I'm not the best example but if we're spending all this time and effort educating our smartest people and then throwing their careers away, doesn't that seem like a waste of talent?"

"I hear you." The senator's voice came loud and strong through the phone line. "Like you I share your concern about science and technology. That's why I voted to raise the number of H1-B visas to compensate for the lack of American scientists and engineers."

"Didn't you hear what I said?" I screamed into the phone. "I'm an American scientist who can't find a job and you let in a bunch of foreigners to make it even harder! Oh, never mind."

"Hey, before you go, I have another idea. How about putting Social Security in a lock box?"

The E.W.O.T. Giga-Church occupied eight city blocks in a mountainous valley east of West Orange. After sensing my problems were spiritual, I contacted Pastor Ron who graciously agreed to meet me in his study after his 8:00 AM Pacific Standard Time Pilates for Jesus class. He offered me a complimentary protein bar and asked what my problem was. From his purple leotards and sweat dripping from his blonde ringlets, I intuited he was no stodgy preacher but a hip, happening man o' God so I had little difficulty telling him about my ailing mother and stagnant career. Then since he seemed sympathetic, I elaborated.

"Robin Williams' suicide troubles me. He had everything I'm working for – money, success, a beautiful wife. People loved him but that wasn't enough. I've been thinking that if everything I'd searched for didn't make Robin happy, maybe I should be searching for something else."

"Son," Pastor Ron called me son even though I was older than him. "God has a plan for you." He took my hand in both of his. "And it involves denying women access to contraception! We'll be picketing the Kearny Villa Planned Parenthood office this Sunday. Be there!"

I attended but did not stand with the Pro-Life protesters who held photos of dead fetuses along with AR-15 assault rifles loaded with Red Tooth and Claw Wad Cutter Ammo featuring projectiles that shatter into dozens of jagged, impossible-to-remove fragments on impact and are guaranteed to cause a cascade of internal mayhem leading to death 33% faster than Brand X bullets. Though tempted by Pastor Ron's one-armed push-ups, I chose instead to stand with a dozen tattooed women in Birkenstocks under an oval-and-plus-sign, female banner with the image of a clenched fist inside its angry uterus. After the Pro-Lifers left to lobby for defunding childhood nutrition programs and increased use of the death penalty, I fell into a conversation with a woman who'd shaved her head. As I gazed at her armpit hair ruffling in the gentle breeze, I intuited that she was not bound by social convention or other people's expectations. Sensing I would benefit from her counter-culture perspective, I told her about my invalid mother, stagnant career, and Robin Williams. Then since she seemed sympathetic, I elaborated.

"I used to date but the whole scene has gotten stale – making a nice-guy first impression, going to dance clubs even though I'd prefer a power drill to my testicles, and biting my tongue when my date expounds on fad diets and pseudoscience. I'm fed up with the pretense and even though I haven't felt intimacy since the days of love beads, Nehru jackets, and woolly mammoths, I can't make the effort to phone a woman after meeting her. Somehow, I don't feel the same way with you. I can talk from my heart and feel a real, human-to-human connection."

She turned her pierced eyebrow to me and said, "I want a baby and a house." As I walked away she yelled, "You need therapy!"

The less spoken about my therapist the better. Let's just say that after spending 13.25 minutes and $4000, I learned more about Selective Serotonin Reuptake Inhibitors than I care to know. Since therapy was a bust, I decided to ask my karate teacher. Harold Okinawa was a thin man with a voice big as Arnold Schwarzenegger's. His explanations of awareness during sparring led me to believe he was more than a brute fighter. He was a man with a keen perception and intellect so I asked him about my invalid mother, stagnant career, Robin Williams, and moribund love life.

"You know," he stroked his chin, "I could kill a man with my roundhouse kick. If you dedicate your body, mind, and spirit to the practice for eight hours a day, you can be like me."

Wondering if Zen held the answer, I phoned Zen Master Ron who graciously agreed to see me the following day. The Aging Bosatsu Zen Center is located just north of South Carlsbad. I arrived after the 7:29 AM Pacific Standard Time ritual and Zen Master Ron ushered me into his study. He was a youthful man in a purple rakusu.2

"You seem familiar." I looked at the sweat dripping from his blonde ringlets. "Have we met before?"

"Your question is meaningless because the past is an illusion and the future has not yet arrived," Zen Master Ron bellowed. "What brings you here?"

I told him about my bedridden mother playing checkers with Death, stagnant career, Robin Williams (adding a similar tale about David Foster Wallace for emphasis), and moribund love life.

Zen Master Ron removed a Reese's Peanut Butter Cup from the folds of his brown robe and held it up for me to see.

"Understand?" he asked.

I shook my head.

"Your spiritual dis-ease is like the sickness of a prepubescent boy who gorges on Reese's Peanut Butter Cups." Zen Master Ron removed the orange wrapper, bit into the confection, and closed his eyes as if swooning with pleasure. "The tantalizing marriage of milk chocolate and peanut butter! No matter how I try, I can never replicate the texture of the center." Zen Master Ron popped the rest of the Reese's Peanut Butter Cup in his mouth and tossed the wrapper under the altar with the others. "While the other boys learn to drive motor bikes and pick up girls, this boy attends fat camp to cure his addiction to sugar, cacao mass, and peanuts. The Zen koan3 is like a fat camp for the mind. What is black and white and red all over?"

"A newspaper."

Whack! Zen Master Ron hit me in the head with a stick.

"Ow! A bloody nun."

Whack!

"Ow!"

"What walks on four legs in the morning, two legs at noon, and three legs in the night?"

Whack!

Arugula

"Ow!"

"A train leaves Philadelphia heading west at 22 miles per hour at 5:15 AM Eastern Daylight Savings Time. Another train leaves Tucson heading east at 67 miles per hour at 7:29 AM Mountain Standard Time. Assuming the cities are 2384 miles apart, when will the trains meet?"

"Your question is meaningless because the past is an illusion and the future has not yet arrived." I snatched the Buddha statue from the altar and clocked Zen Master Ron in the head.

After leaving Zen Master Ron's unconscious body lying in a pile of Reese's Peanut Butter Cups, I concluded that people are crazy and best avoided whenever possible. But all is not lost. My newly empty social calendar freed my evenings for the activities I like best – reading science fiction novels and binge watching Danish cop shows. Just the other day I saw a man lift a caterpillar from the sidewalk and place it in the grass where it would be safe. There is one thing I miss, though. When I was little, my mother bought several folding, aluminum trays that let us eat frozen dinners right in front of the TV. I'd love one of those.

1. a Buddhist sutra that describes a pilgrim's meetings with various enlightened workers who practice
   different professions
2. the bib like garment worn by Zen teachers and students
3. Zen riddle like "What is the sound of one hand clapping?"

Necessary Precautions

The intel boys reported the Safeway on Garby Street was friendly. Those same ivory tower eggheads, who'd never faced a crazed stock boy wielding a nine-inch bayonet or a store manager with an RPG, had said the same thing before Tet.

I donned my jungle fatigues, smeared my face green and tan, and drove my rusty magenta Honda Civic to a secure Wal-Mart. After a twenty-minute hike I set up in the bushes atop a hill overlooking the Safeway's parking lot. I raised my field glasses and scanned the building's perimeter. I scouted entrances, emergency exits, and lines of fire. Nothing looked suspicious, just the usual minivan traffic. I watched for over an hour. Periodically, the teenager, I'd code-named Echo One, collected shopping carts from between parked cars and wheeled them back toward the entrance. I pegged him as a noncombatant but would keep an eye on him just in case.

I tightened the straps on my Kevlar vest, sheathed the K-bar knife on my ankle, and chambered a round in my AR-15. I was going in.

My watch read 4:19. I pressed the buttons on the side to set the countdown timer for five minutes, the amount of time Charlie would need to send reinforcements.

I shouldered my forty-pound pack, ran down the hill, and took cover behind a beige SUV. Next came the hard part. Eighty yards of open asphalt separated me from the entrance. If there were snipers in the hills, I'd be riddled with more holes than a piñata at a porcupine's birthday party.

Knowing each step could be my last I set off in a zigzag pattern. Somehow I made it. I flattened against the wall by the doors and sucked air. My breath came in ragged gasps. I checked my watch – two minutes down. Already I was behind schedule.

My AR-15 leveled, I burst through the sliding glass doors and swung the barrel in an arc from left to right.

"I'm not out to hurt you," I announced. "Just keep your hands where I can see 'em and go about your business."

For some reason the shoppers hustled their carts out of my way. I grabbed one of the orange plastic baskets and set off.

Resting my finger on the rifle's trigger guard I followed my topo map past candy bars and feminine hygiene products. When I turned down aisle six I froze. The black rubber soles of my jungle boots left skid marks on the blanched almond linoleum.

A display of tortilla chips blocked half the aisle. That wasn't on my map! I strained to make out any nylon fishing line that could indicate a booby trap.

Should I go back? I checked my watch - three minutes forty seconds. By now trucks full of men with AK 47s could have been bearing down on my position. I had to risk it.

I inched past the tub of azure bags. Once I got to the other side, I realized I'd held my breath and exhaled. I continued to the end of the aisle and peered around the jars of Tucson Jake's Pineapple Salsa at the dairy section.

Things seemed quiet – too quiet. Fearing an ambush I ducked back behind the salsa and watched the dairy section's reflection in my hand-held mirror. A woman wearing a forest green fleece jacket parked her cart in front of the yogurt and began scanning labels. Some would call her arrival a coincidence, but I don't believe in coincidences. Her purse could have concealed a 9mm pistol or a fragmentation grenade.

I slowed my breathing, while precious seconds ticked away. Eventually she selected a 32-ounce tub of piña colada and moved off.

In a fraction of a second I ran to the butter display, dived behind a wheel of Manchego cheese, and looked for muzzles protruding from the seafood section.

I turned around and realized I'd made a potentially fatal mistake.

"My God!" I whispered.

Nothing could have prepared me for the plethora of margarines each touting competing health claims with words like polyunsaturated and partially hydrogenated. I contemplated butter, worse for your heart but with fewer cancer-causing free radicals.

The alarm on my watch sounded like a death knell. I had to get out, before Charlie surrounded the building. I grabbed a yellow tub and raced toward the checkout. An entire retirement home of grannies blocked the express lane. I skirted the line of blue hair and dowager humps to squeeze into lane three and cut off a woman reaching for the checkbook in her purse.

"Don't try anything funny." I leveled my AR-15 at the cashier, while she rang up my purchase.

The moment she handed me my change I knew the intel boys had been wrong. Her glare reflected Lenin's goatee, SS-19 missiles rolling past Red Square, the cheerleader who'd snubbed me at the senior prom, and Ricki Green who'd stolen my lunch when I was six. She cared nothing about the democracy and fair play you and I hold sacred. The only way to deal with such people is through the threat of superior force.

I made it back to my car at the Wal-Mart, drove through yellow lights, and took a circuitous route back to my hooch to lose any unwanted followers. I was looking forward to a cold beer and a long hot shower to wash away the stench of adrenaline, when I realized I'd forgotten the eggs.

Angola

Life couldn't be better! In Angola's capital, despite the presence of our Cuban comrades, the war with the UNITA counterrevolutionaries and their South African allies was far away. I drove through a Luanda shantytown, where a crowd dug through garbage for food, and turned the Volkswagen Rabbit onto February 4th Avenue. I was doing much better than them. Lieutenant Javier Olime, two girls, and I were on our way to the Zambia Hotel, where the night manager would accept some Soviet vodka for a few hours in private rooms. These girls didn't hide their bodies in colorful cloth like most African women. Instead they wore short skirts and thin tops that showed off their womanly charms. Aiyah! I tapped my fingers on the steering wheel to the rhythm of the twangy bass coming from the boom box in the back seat. Yes, it was definitely a good night, and I owed it all to Lieutenant Olime.

I glanced in the rear-view mirror at my benefactor. Lieutenant Olime's tall, rangy frame sprawled in the backseat. One arm rested over the shoulder of his girl so his hand dangled at her breast. He lifted a Cuban cigar to his lips, puffed until the tip glowed orange, and met my eyes in the mirror. Ordinarily, an officer wouldn't consort with an enlisted man like me, but we were cousins. When we first slipped away from our village to join the MPLA and fight the Portuguese colonizers, my aunt made him promise to look after me. And when Angola gained independence in 1975, I followed him into the Angolan Armed Forces. Tonight, we had vodka, cigars, two willing girls, and even a car, admittedly borrowed from Major Ribera who was due back from Havana on Tuesday. My girl ran a finger around my kneecap and up the inside of my thigh. My urge to get to the hotel grew.

I pressed on the gas pedal, but the car began slowing. I pressed harder. The VW continued to lose power. A dashboard warning light came on and the motor quit. I coasted to the side of the road.

"Why are we stopping, Gonçalvo?" Lieutenant Olime asked.

"The motor died."

"That's not good."

No, it certainly was not good . The major had left instructions that absolutely no one was to drive his car while he was away. If he found out we ruined it, we'd be in very big trouble. The last man to get on the major's bad side was transferred to a platoon of transvestites defusing land mines on the Namibian border. I got out, lifted the hood, and stared at the mass of wires and metal underneath. A cluster of men with untucked shirttails gathered like flies on giraffe dung and tried to sell me trinkets they'd plucked from the trash.

"Be quiet!" I said. "Can't you see I'm busy?"

They stayed and barked about their wares, so I got back in the car and turned the key. As the starter motor groaned, my hopes for a fine evening vanished. My girl turned her back and began tapping the same fingernail that had stroked my thigh on the window frame.

"The Santos Club isn't too far from here," she told her friend. "You want to go?"

"Just wait a few minutes to fix the car, and we can have our own party," Lieutenant Olime said, but the girls were already out the door.

It was a very bad night. I can't begin to describe my humiliation at asking that crowd of hawkers for directions to the garage. No, I won't tell you of my journey on foot to that place nor of my shameful pleading with the mechanic. The good news was that he could fix the car, if only he had a fuel pump. That was a problem! With the imperialist boycott of our newly independent nation there were none to be had in all of Luanda.

Desperation tests a man's character. A lesser individual would have paid someone to steal the part from another VW, but my lieutenant located a fuel pump in Lucala. All we had to do was travel 150 miles of dirt roads to get it.

"Corporal Okilbe, in my office!"

I left my squad cleaning their AK-47s in our quarters and followed Lieutenant Olime to the parade ground of red dirt surrounded by a concrete wall. A red and black Angolan flag, with its emblem of a machete and broken gear, fluttered on a flagpole.

"Good news," he said. "A Cuban camera crew is going to Dondo to film the sisal harvest, and I got us assigned to be their interpreters and bodyguards."

"But how will we get them to make the thirty-mile side trip to Lucala so we can pick up the part, Javier?"

"We'll offer to introduce them to some girls there." Lieutenant Olime smiled. "I've never met a Cuban who'd pass up some hot African pussy."

But my lieutenant had never met Comrade Dolores Alvarez Blanco. We took a crowded bus through Luanda's slums to the Fortress Hotel to meet the Cuban news crew. Comrade Blanco was tall and thin and wore a black beret like the one in that picture of Che Guevara. The sleeves of her fatigues only came down to the middle of her forearms. The cameraman, Ramon Gutierrez, was short and heavy. Standing together in front of a Russian GAZ-69 staff car in the parking lot, the two looked like the number 10.

"Comrades." Dolores Alvarez Blanco spoke in Spanish-accented Portuguese. "Thank you for joining us. We're filming stories about how Marxism has brought prosperity to the Angolan people. I must say I admire your courage. No others would risk the journey knowing of the recent UNITA attacks in the area. Rumor has it this bunch castrates all their prisoners."

My hands moved of their own volition to cover my privates. How I longed to be with my squad cleaning weapons and policing the compound for cigarette butts. At least they'd all be fathers and grandfathers someday. Lieutenant Olime met my eyes and nodded. He was more afraid of Major Ribera than of the invaders.

"No sacrifice is too great for the revolution," he said. "There is one other matter. My superiors have ordered me to retrieve some medical supplies from Lucala. After filming, could we perhaps take a slight detour and pick them up?"

"Absolutely not," Comrade Blanco said. "We need to get the footage to Havana as soon as possible. Fidel himself wants it aired on TV to inspire the workers for the sugar harvest."

"I'm afraid that without the side trip to Lucala we can't accompany you."

"That's not what Colonel Beltrão said." Comrade Blanco placed her fists on her hips. "Besides don't the Soviets send all the medical supplies you need through the port right here in Luanda? Comrades, your belief in witchcraft is keeping your country backward. Put your trust in dialectical materialism and modern Socialist medicine. This quest of yours for magic spells and talismans is a waste of time."

My lieutenant's eyes got the same look he had as a child when the teacher asked a question he couldn't answer. I had to help him.

"It's a heart," I blurted, "for a transplant."

Lieutenant Olime glared at me with eyes that blazed like flamethrowers.

"But no one has transplanted a heart in black Africa before." Comrade Blanco stroked her chin. "And a Socialist country would be the first." Her stony face broke into something resembling a smile.

"Exactly!" Lieutenant Olime quenched his rage and grinned. "You white people think we Africans are backward, but in ancient times we performed brain surgery in the great city of Zimbabwe. And now we're even using laser beams for scalpels."

"Why haven't I heard of this before?"

"If the UNITA counterrevolutionaries got wind of this project, they'd do anything to stop it. The recipient is a very important man. I can't tell you who he is, but let's just say you'd recognize his name."

"President Neto?"

Lieutenant Olime held a finger to his lips.

"This could be an inspiration for the masses," Comrade Blanco said. "All right, Lieutenant. We'll take you to Lucala. But if you're lying to me, you'll wish the South Africans had captured you instead. Now, put our bags in the car and we'll be off."

Lieutenant Olime showed his white teeth like an angry dog and ordered me to fetch the Cubans' luggage from their rooms. The Russian camera equipment was as large as a small refrigerator and required the lieutenant's help to move. This put him in an even worse mood. We traveled in the heat of the day, when UNITA soldiers would be too tired to bother with ambushes. Ramon drove and Comrade Blanco sat in front. As usual the Africans were stuck in back. Lieutenant Olime scowled while the Cubans jabbered in Spanish. I could follow what they were saying with difficulty, but then my head began to hurt. I looked at the acacia and tamarisk growing out of the red earth and eventually dozed.

We arrived in Dondo in late afternoon. The plantation was a deserted field of plants with thick, machete-shaped leaves. Shoots that looked like giant asparagus sprouted from some. Ramon parked in front of a concrete shed with a corrugated-tin roof. A one-legged African with yellowed eyes sat on a rusty folding chair inside. He was so thin you could almost see his ribs through his back. A mattress and threadbare blanket lay in the corner.

"Greetings, comrade," Dolores Alvarez Blanco said in her heavily accented Portuguese. "I bring warm greetings from your Cuban allies."

"Who is this hideous woman?" the man asked in Kimbundu. "And what is she shrieking about?"

"She's a Cuban reporter here to film the sisal harvest," Lieutenant Olime replied in the native language the Cubans could not understand.

"Harvest? There hasn't been a harvest in years. Since the fields were mined, nobody goes out there anymore. All the other workers have left. I only sleep in this shack. Hey!" The squatter's eyes widened. "Did you have sex with her?"

"Why, yes!" Lieutenant Olime grinned. "Several times."

"How was it?"

"Like eating a starved chicken." Lieutenant Olime and the squatter laughed.

"What is he saying?" Comrade Blanco asked.

"He welcomes his Cuban comrades on behalf of the Angolan proletariat and thanks you from the bottom of his heart for standing shoulder to shoulder with us to resist the capitalist aggressors." Lieutenant Olime then switched back to Kimbundu. "Do you want to sleep with her too?"

"She's not much to look at," the squatter said, "but her legs are nice. How much do you want for her?"

"What about the harvest?" Comrade Blanco asked.

"He says the workers left two days ago to fight the UNITA counterrevolutionaries," Lieutenant Olime told her. "Even though poorly armed, they've already won a major victory."

"If we can't film the harvest, maybe we should travel to the front and interview the fighters," Comrade Blanco said.

"How far is it?" Ramon asked.

Lieutenant Olime addressed the squatter. "That is not the way it is with white women. She says she finds you very handsome and will pay you twenty Kwanza to pose without your shirt in the sisal fields."

"Anything to make her happy," the squatter said.

My lieutenant switched back to Portuguese. "The roads are mined. We wouldn't make it. However, he says he'll demonstrate how he harvests sisal. All he asks is a donation of two thousand Kwanza to help feed the families, the heroic workers left behind to fight on the front-lines."

And so my lieutenant made everybody happy. The Cubans got their film, the squatter got to believe a white woman found him sexy, I earned two hundred Kwanza for joining the harvest, and the lieutenant pocketed the rest of the money so he could make even more people happy someday. Fortunately no one stepped on a land mine. After filming, we stopped to eat at a café in town. A handful of Angolans sat at rickety tables and watched the news on an old black-and-white television set. The waiter brought us aluminum bowls of gray stew, gumbo, and mealie meal. What a delightful dinner! The stew even had meat. Right away the lieutenant and I extended our hands into the communal bowl of cornmeal. The Cubans gasped as if we were handling anacondas at the table.

"Eat! Eat! It's good." Lieutenant Olime waved his hand smeared with cornmeal.

They reached toward the bowl as if to pet a rabid jackal, but after the first taste they got used to eating the African way. Comrade Blanco seemed very fond of the stew. I've never seen a skinny girl eat like she did.

"So." Ramon wiped his mouth with the scrap of brown paper that served as his napkin. "There's one thing I don't understand about this heart transplant. Why are you doing the first one on President Neto? Wouldn't it be better to try it out on someone less important?"

"We have no choice," my lieutenant said. "Our president is very ill."

Comrade Blanco formed a ball of cornmeal, dipped it into the stew, and stuffed it in her mouth.

"If that's true, why not send him to the Soviet Union?" Ramon asked. "They have surgeons to rival those in the West. Even Fidel went to Moscow when he needed his gall bladder removed."

"If only we could," Lieutenant Olime mused. "But now he's too sick to travel." The Angolans cheered the soccer scores on TV. "Comrades, I wish you could see how bravely he goes about his duties from his hospital bed," the lieutenant continued. "It's an inspiration, let me tell you. When I asked if he worried about his upcoming surgery, he told me he'd place his life in the hands of our Angolan doctors any day."

Comrade Blanco swallowed her plug of food. "This is really delicious. What is it?"

"Monkey," I said.

Comrade Blanco's face turned the same shade of pale green as the walls. She clasped her hands over her mouth and ran from the room, just before the television showed President Neto stepping out of a Tupolev airliner at the Moscow airport. The camera focused on the dignitaries assembled on the tarmac and zoomed in on Leonid Brezhnev's thick eyebrows. When President Neto made it to the foot of the stairs, the general secretary embraced our leader in a strong bear hug. Lieutenant Olime looked like he'd swallowed a rat.

"I know what you're doing," Ramon said. "You're smuggling diamonds, aren't you?"

Lieutenant Olime opened his mouth, but only a squeaking sound like a rusty hinge came out.

"Don't worry, comrades. I'll keep your secret," Ramon said, "for a share of the diamonds."

What else could my lieutenant do, but agree? The Cubans booked hotel rooms and left us to our own devices, but we still had the cash we'd earned that day. All that beautiful pink and blue money, depicting heroic workers and soldiers, went for a cramped room with mildewed walls. I peeled back the blanket of my bed and found a handful of cockroaches waiting for me.

"Move over, brothers." I crawled into bed with my companions and went to sleep.

"What do you know about the organ donor?" Comrade Blanco asked during the drive to Lucala the following day.

"Ah, the donor." Lieutenant Olime looked heavenward for inspiration. "The donor was a newlywed who died fighting UNITA counterrevolutionaries. As a new father, he could have delayed military service, but he insisted it was his duty. It is said Jonas Savimbi himself fired the shot that killed him."

"To the head?" Ramon asked.

"I'm sorry?"

"It would have to be a head shot, so as not to damage the heart." Ramon shifted gears.

"Quite so," Lieutenant Olime said. "It's ironic that the UNITA leader's shot will keep his arch-rival alive, don't you think? Of course, there is a fund to help the widow and baby, if you'd like to make a donation."

Lucala's dozens of pink and turquoise two-story buildings huddled around the roads of broken pavement and potholes. Yellow dogs, nothing more than famine stretched over a frame of bones, roamed the sidewalks and poked their muzzles into garbage dumped by the road. Comrade Blanco wanted to interview the doctors at the local clinic, so we parked in the town square flanked by flagpoles. Lieutenant Olime sent me ahead to check the clinic out. On the way in I stepped past a drunk sprawled by the entrance. He had a pale birthmark the size of a fist on his cheek. Its shape seemed somehow familiar, but I couldn't place it. The clinic smelled of urine and disinfectant. A handful of patients sat on folding chairs. One had an ax protruding from his forehead. He smiled and played cards with the others. A doctor leaned over a nurse at the desk at just the right angle to see down her blouse. They were speaking Spanish! Eyes wide in shock, I dashed outside and ran into our party carrying the camera from the car.

"What is it, Corporal Okilbe?" Lieutenant Olime asked.

I opened my mouth but not a sound came out.

"Speak up, man!"

"Cubans," I croaked in Kimbundu. "They'll tell Comrade Blanco there's no transplant!"

"What's he saying?" Comrade Blanco asked.

"You must excuse Corporal Okilbe. He speaks Kimbundu when he gets excited." Lieutenant Olime said. "It seems the doctors want us to pay for the interview. Shameful!"

"We'll see about that!" Comrade Blanco made for the door.

"No!" I cried.

Lieutenant Olime moved to block her path. "If they know you're Cuban, they'll ask for more money. Corporal Okilbe, why don't you find our friends a nice café and then come back by way of Kuanga Boulevard to help negotiate?"

I escorted the Cubans across the square and dropped them off at a café. In my haste to get to the garage, I ignored the television antenna on the café's roof. My only thought was to buy the fuel pump and leave this town before anything else went wrong. Once the Cubans were safely stowed, I set off on foot toward the garage. I hurried past a barbershop. Its owner in a white smock leaned idly against the door frame His uneven hair looked like it had been yanked from his scalp by overzealous chimps. My route took me through a market with piles of anemic yams and raw, fly-speckled meat hanging from iron hooks. I turned the corner, passed a snarling dog, and nodded to a group of dirty children playing with an old tire. Down the alley a stocky woman listened to a transistor radio while grinding cassava. Somber music played.

"It is with deep sadness that we report the death of Agostinho Neto," the announcer said. "Our beloved president passed away in Moscow earlier this morning."

I stopped in my tracks. The Cubans! The television! If they found out the president was dead, our whole plan would collapse! Then Comrade Blanco would make good on her threat. I started to sweat. What could be worse than being castrated by UNITA terrorists? I'd never been in an

Angolan prison, but few who enter ever come out alive. I turned and ran past the children. The dog barked and lunged only to be yanked off his feet by the thick chain attached to his collar. I dodged through the crowd at the market, sprinted past the puzzled barber, and burst panting into the café. The Cubans turned from watching a Zambian soccer game on the television.

"Is something wrong, comrade?" Ramon asked.

I struggled to catch my breath. "Did you see my wallet?"

"No."

"Must have left it with my gear at the clinic." I raced out the door.

Outside I sliced the antenna cable with my pocketknife and retraced my steps past the lazy barber and into the market, where I had an inspiration. I haggled with the butcher for a goat heart. The man accepted three Kwanza and placed the bloody organ in a leaky plastic bag. With my arms held out to keep my prize from dripping on my slacks, I proceeded past the barking dog, the playing children, and the cassava woman to the garage. It was closed.

I banged on the metal door in frustration. This was too much. How would we keep the Cubans in town long enough to get the fuel pump? I ran toward the clinic and came to a halt in front of a newsstand. A hundred newspaper headlines screamed, "President Neto Dead." My pulse pounded and I began to shake. A customer took a paper from the rack. I snatched it from his hands.

"Military emergency! Get out of here!"

He gave me the puzzled look of a beaten dog and slouched away.

"How much for all the papers?" I asked the attendant.

He scratched his chin. "Twenty-five Kwanza."

I didn't have enough money to buy the papers and pay for the fuel pump too. "Look, I'll give you fifteen Kwanza and return with the rest later. You can keep this goat heart until I come back."

I made the trade, threw the papers in the trash bin, and ran the rest of the way to the clinic. The patients and Cuban medical staff were gone. Only Lieutenant Olime and a man in a white lab coat, whose skin was so black it looked purple, remained.

"Ah, Corporal Okilbe," my lieutenant said. "The Cuban staff evacuated the patients after I warned them of a rumored UNITA attack. Despite his lack of medical training, Mr. Wabiri has agreed to stand in until they return. Did you get the fuel pump?"

"The garage is closed," I said. "But there's worse. President Neto is dead."

Lieutenant Olime collapsed into a chair.

"I never liked him, anyway," Mr. Wabiri said.

"Watch your tongue." Lieutenant Olime stood and began pacing. "We need an excuse to keep Comrade Blanco and Ramon here. Ah!" He stopped in place. "We'll tell them the donor hasn't died yet."

"I thought you told me he was a newlywed." Comrade Blanco sniffed at the reek of alcohol coming from the drunk impersonating the donor.

The Cubans had already filmed their interview with the sham doctor. Lieutenant Olime had translated, of course. We stood around the drunk's bedside. He'd accepted a bottle of vodka in exchange for having his head wrapped in bandages and pretending to be in a coma.

"Well, yes," my lieutenant said. "They get married late out in the countryside."

"It's a pity we can't film him," Comrade Blanco said.

"Why not?"

"Look at his birthmark. It's shaped like South Africa. Poor man!" Comrade Blanco moved toward the doorway. "At least his suffering will be over soon."

The Cubans returned to the café. I walked toward the garage. With luck things would stay under control long enough for me to buy the pump and leave, but it wasn't to be. Once again the newspapers with their horrible headline were on display at the newsstand. I approached the smirking attendant with the urge to twist his head off like the cap from a cheap bottle of vodka.

"Hey! Those are mine!" I yelled.

"You threw them away, which means anybody can claim them."

Violence would do no good. I took out my wallet. "Here's twenty-five Kwanza for the papers and another ten for the heart."

"I traded it to the old lady in the alley for some cassava." The attendant handed me back the ten and pointed to the papers.

This time I tore off all the front pages before throwing them away. Fortunately, when I arrived at the garage, a man in grease-stained overalls was unlocking the door. I bought the fuel pump and headed up the alley to the old woman's bungalow.

"Hello, auntie," I said when she opened the door. "I'm here to buy back the goat heart."

"You can't have it." She crossed her arms over her ample bosom. "I need it to cast a love spell."

"The pride of African womanhood like you?" I dropped my mouth open in mock disbelief.

"With the war on, there are few suitable men around. I'm tired of waiting. I want to have a love affair just like on Coronation Street on the BBC."

"Sell me back the heart, auntie, and I promise you'll get your man. Just don't let him go for forty-eight hours when he arrives."

She plucked a hair from my head and returned moments later with the bag. "See that you send him, or I'll have the witch doctor put some bad juju on you."

As planned I delivered the heart and fuel pump to Mr. Wabiri at the clinic and went to the café where Lieutenant Olime sat at the table with the Cubans.

"May I speak with you in private, sir?" I asked my lieutenant.

Ramon pretended not to be interested, but his eyes shifted like those of a hyena witnessing a lion's kill. Confident that Ramon would follow, I led Lieutenant Olime to the men's room.

"The diamonds will be ready in an hour." I winked. "The old cassava woman in the alley past the market is packing two bags. That way we can share only from the smaller one with Ramon."

"Well done." Lieutenant Olime flushed the urinal, and we returned to the table.

"I need some air." Ramon stood and stretched before stepping outside. Little did he know that he would soon be meeting his African bride.

Fifteen minutes later Mr. Wabiri carried in a Styrofoam cooler and lifted the lid. Inside the reddish-purple goat heart lay on a bed of ice. Veins spread like the branches of a baobab tree over the thin layer of yellow fat that covered part of the organ.

"That's disgusting!" Comrade Blanco turned away. "Can't you see this is a restaurant? Get it out of here!"

Mr. Wabiri looked puzzled until Lieutenant Olime told him in Kimbundu to place the cooler in the car.

"How that man got to be a doctor without learning Portuguese is beyond me," Comrade Blanco said.

A half hour passed.

"Where is that Ramon?" Comrade Blanco asked.

"If he doesn't return soon, we'll have to leave without him. We must get the heart back to Luanda immediately." Lieutenant Olime pounded the table for effect.

"Let's look outside." Comrade Blanco led us out the door.

All the flags in the town square flew at half-mast. Comrade Blanco asked why.

"Oh, they're honoring the brave organ donor," Lieutenant Olime said.

As soon as my lieutenant had spoken, the drunk with the unfortunate birthmark walked behind the lieutenant's back and waved at Comrade Blanco. My heart seemed to freeze in my chest. I tugged at Lieutenant Olime's sleeve.

"Not now, Corporal Okilbe. Of course the townspeople know nothing of the organ transplant yet." Lieutenant Olime continued. "Just think how proud they will be when they find out."

One of the stray dogs had jumped in the car and was gnawing at the cooler in the backseat. He retrieved the goat heart and ran away with the bloody prize in his jaws. The wind blew a sheet of paper into Comrade Blanco's face. She snatched it away and was about to crumple it up when she read the headline announcing the president's death. Her face grew red as a baboon's behind. Before her anger could explode, the sound of a racing motor came from up the road. An olive drab truck marked with a red cross sped into the town square and slammed on its brakes raising a cloud of dust. The Cuban doctor jumped from the cab and ran toward us.

"UNITA counterrevolutionaries!" he yelled. "They're five miles east and are heading toward town!"

Gunfire echoed in the distance. A mortar round landed in the town square and showered us with dirt. We ran back to the café, where we'd seen a telephone. Lieutenant Olime placed a call to headquarters in Luanda.

"I need to speak with Colonel Beltrão! Lucala is under attack!" He paused. "I don't care if the colonel is with his wife! This is an emergency!"

Comrade Blanco snatched the phone from the lieutenant's hands. "This is Dolores Alvarez Blanco from Television Cubana. I'm sure you'd hate to see the story of how you shirked your duty broadcast in Havana." She held the phone away from her face and stared at it. "The line is dead."

We went out to the town square to await our fate. I thought of all the sons and daughters I'd never have and murmured a silent apology to my dead father for not carrying on the Okilbe line. Then three Mi-24 helicopter gunships rumbled overhead. The sound of their rotors cutting the air shook windows and vibrated my lungs.

"Hooray!" We jumped and waved at the pilots. The helicopters hung like giant steel locusts in the sky and fired rockets and machine guns into the trees outside of town.

Comrade Blanco wrapped her arms around me and gave me a kiss on the cheek. Once she realized what she was doing, she let go. "Comrades, you're in serious trouble for lying to me."

"May I offer a word of advice, comrade? Admitting you believed a country with practically no doctors could perform a heart transplant would be bad for your career. Even Television Cubana could not tolerate a reporter so gullible." Lieutenant Olime cocked his eyebrow.

"The heart transplant would have been a good story, but my report on saving the town will be even better." Comrade Blanco took off her beret and shook out her long dark hair. "Where do you suppose Ramon went?"

"Perhaps the UNITA counterrevolutionaries captured him."

"Poor man! I'll mention him in my story. His name will live forever as a martyr to the revolution." Comrade Blanco tossed the Styrofoam container out of the car and drove away, leaving us behind.

I walked over to where it lay on the ground and retrieved the plastic-wrapped fuel pump from the spilled ice. We had twenty-four hours to get it back to Luanda. Knowing my lieutenant, we would find a way.

Golden Delicious

Now that the cancer has spread through my liver and bones, and I've no loved ones to threaten, there's nothing they can hold over me. For at 73 I've survived two wives and an older sister. I have no children due to a genetic abnormality. My vast fortune has paid for a private room at the Sunnyvale Hospice that looks out on the glittering waters of Thunder Bay. In the late afternoon the sunlight paints the walls of my room in honey-colored light. The nurses are kind and solicitous. Little do they know the private shame I've carried all these years.

The events began in September 1982. True, a child of seven cannot be expected to single-handedly bring down a conspiracy that like cedar rust fungus has reached its malignant spores into every American home. Still, my disgust at what I've become gnaws through my soul like the larva of the codling moth through ripe fruit.

We'd recently moved from Eastern Washington to Chicago, so my father could take a job as director of the Advanced Spallation Neutron Facility at the Argonne National Laboratory. Owing to my artistic nature, my parents opted for a private school, so despite the considerable expense they enrolled my sister and me in the Acorn Academy in Oak Park. The school's philosophy was to break down gender stereotypes while fostering the child's positive self-image. I learned this to be the case on my first day, when Story Glück stood from the math circle to object to an entry in the times table.

"It's not! It's not!" He stomped his Reeboks on the rubberized tile. "Eight times nine is sixty-seven."

Mrs. Hughes merely smiled. How insignificant a few paltry numbers were when compared with a child's self esteem. Ah Mrs. Hughes, I remember her long skirts, thick-soled shoes, and how her over-sized glasses magnified her soulful eyes. Who would have thought such a sweet, old lady could be capable of such duplicity?

Snack time came after self esteem through numbers, the theory being that children learned better when their blood sugar is within bounds. The Acorn Academy did not serve dairy, for that lent legitimacy to the exploitation of animals. Nor did they serve high-sugar, processed foods. No, all food had to be healthy, vegan fare. One could be forgiven for imagining this food was organic, but the added expense would have cut into the bottom line. All produce came from the local supermarket.

"I have a special treat for you, today." Mrs. Hughes set a brown shopping bag in the middle of the circle and withdrew a handful of apples.

My classmates rushed forward eager to palm the waxy, yellow orbs in their grimy fingers. I, who have always had an aversion to other people handling my food, hung back. Mrs. Hughes noticed my reluctance.

"Gerald." She held a fruit out to me. "Would you like a nice apple?"

I inched forward and accepted the gift from her hand. Coming from Washington State, where we picked apples fresh from the trees, I expected it to be like lifting the short skirt off the shapely thighs of a young maiden in the first flush of womanhood – the firm, warm flesh fragrant under delicate panties. Instead I nearly choked on sweaty, sagging cellulite shot through with a road map of varicose veins. Emboldened by Story Glück's example, I spat the sawdust into my hand.

"This apple tastes yucky!" I carried the repulsive mess to the trashcan and tossed it in.

Conversation ceased. Story Glück's face turned white with terror. Even April Mills, who'd been jabbering open-mouthed and spraying her neighbors with spit and bits of chewed cellulose, shut up. I returned to my place in the circle. My neighbors inched away from me, as if I were a dog that had rolled in organic fertilizer. Mrs. Hughes glared with the look of a hit man eying his target through a sniper scope.

"Let's get back to our lessons," she said.

The rest of the school day passed without incident. Thinking I'd escaped, I peddled my one-speed Schwinn bicycle home along Columbine after classes had ended. How foolish of me. As I panted and pumped my way up the hill in front of Lincoln's Hardware, I was too occupied to notice the white, produce van tailing me. Before I reached the crest, the driver gunned the motor, raced ahead, and pulled to the curb in front of me. I stood on the pedals and skidded to a stop. Two burly men in green aprons jumped out of the cab.

"Mr. Brasi wants to see you," the taller one said.

Something about the way he rested his hand on the box cutter attached to his belt told me I'd better not refuse. I rolled my bike toward the van's door that loomed before me like the entrance to Torquemada's studio apartment.

"Leave it!"

A chill wind from Lake Michigan cut through my jacket, but that wasn't the only reason I shivered. I abandoned my bike and got in. After driving in silence for twenty minutes we pulled into the parking lot of a large warehouse. Trucks marked with the logos of major supermarket chains mated with the loading dock in an orgy of commerce. I didn't realize it then, but this was the facility that stored apples for decades under ethylene gas for eventual distribution to grocery stores all over the country. The goons took me inside, hustled me up the stairs, and paused before a metal door smudged with black hand prints.

"Come in." The voice that responded to their knock sounded like burlap rubbed over a record needle.

The shorter goon grabbed me by the collar and hustled me inside.

"We brought the kid."

"Gerald, Gerald, I'm disappointed in you." The man behind the desk made a steeple with his fingers.

He was in his early fifties and wore tinted glasses even in the shadowy office. A smoldering cigar lay in the ashtray by the telephone. Despite the Sydney Greenstreet ceiling fan's slow rotation, the air was stagnant and oppressive.

"Do you know what friendship means, Gerald?"

I swallowed and shook my head.

"It means protecting what's important to the other person. Do you love your sister, Gerald?"

"Answer him!" The tall goon shoved me from behind and I stumbled forward.

"Yes." My voice came out scared and squeaky like that of a chipmunk in a leaf shredder.

"Imagine how it would feel if she got run over by a delivery truck, or if an accident at work exposed your father to a lethal dose of radiation." Mr. Brasi puffed his cigar and blew a plume of smoke at my eyes. "That's how I feel when someone says bad things about my produce."

"I'm sorry." I squeezed my legs together against the urgent need to urinate.

"You want us to make him disappear, boss?" the short goon asked.

"No, Sal. Gerald's our friend. You want to be friends. Don't you, Gerald?"

I nodded.

"Good. And when a friend gives a friend a gift, it would be impolite to refuse." Mr. Brasi reached into the drawer and withdrew one of the godforsaken apples. "Go ahead. Try it."

I'd have sooner eaten a handful of squirming maggots, but the vision of my sister seated in a wheelchair with a blanket over her shattered kneecaps while watching my father's lead-lined coffin being lowered into the grave haunted me. I closed my eyes and bit.

"How is it?" Mr. Brasi asked.

"Crisp." I swallowed a plug of revolting pulp. "And delicious."

He clapped me on the back. "Sal, I think we've got our new TV spokesman!"

That's how I began my career of mendacity. Perhaps you've seen me on the commercials. I told myself I had no choice, but in truth I was seduced by the money, the fame, the women. I thought I had it all, until all those lies my body stored sprang forth in the disease that will soon take my life. I can never repay the people I've deceived. I've forwarded a sworn confession including dates and names to the attorney general. I hope this last testament goes a small way toward making amends.

A Christmas Story

No matter the time of day, the boardroom of Specter Toys, a division of Specter Missile and Defense Systems, remained cloaked in shadows. The chief executive officer sat behind a desk on raised steel flooring and stroked his cat's long white fur. Both had a predator's pale blue eyes that pierced their victims' bowels with icicles of fear. A livid purple scar ran from the CEO's left eye socket to the top of his shaved skull. Perhaps the way he pinched his black cigarettes between thumb and index finger gave his subordinates some clue of his origin, but they referred to him only as Number Two.

A Japanese man stood before Number Two's desk. Although short in stature, his erect posture gave him the air of command. Liberal use of gel kept each of his gray hairs in place. Behind him a woman in a tweed suit and tortoiseshell glasses held a clipboard.

"The Yellowstone Nuclear Plant authorization is making its way through Congress. This time there will be no failures."

"Excellent, Number Three." Number Two formed a steeple with his fingers. "Now tell me about the Tina Anorexia doll."

"We launched the product last week, complete with miniature scale, exercise cycle, and case of diet cola."

"And the Junior Guantanamo prison kit?"

"Yes, sir, I'm told the interrogation rooms are quite realistic."

"How are the sales?"

Number Three swallowed. Despite years of practice in high stakes corporate negotiations, a tremor appeared on the corner of his mouth. "They're not buying, sir."

"What do you mean, they're not buying?"

"Times are tough. They've decided to spend their money elsewhere."

"I don't pay you to let them make up their minds." Number Two pressed a button on his armrest.

A trapdoor opened. Number Three fell into the pool under the steel platform. The water boiled with hundreds of piranhas, each biting a thimble of flesh from his body. Within seconds the skeleton sank to the bottom.

"Congratulations on your promotion, Number Four." Number Two stroked the cat and fingered the gold ring on his right hand. "Make sure merchants start playing recorded Christmas music the day before Thanksgiving, and keep it up until the shoppers' minds are numb. Have our corporate affiliates double their employees' unpaid overtime. Guilty parents spend more during the holidays. Aside from that, have our TV stations show Miracle on 34th Street over and over again. Encourages gullibility. What advertiser wouldn't love it? You may go."

The new Number Three scribbled notes on her clipboard and left to set Number Two's plans in motion.

"You know, Wotan." Number Two spooned caviar into the cat's crystal bowl. "This could be our best Christmas ever."

The Divine Parody

The Comedic Infernal

Midway through my life's journey, I went astray from the straight road and woke up alone in a forest of bad metaphors. Death would not have been more bitter than spending time in the midst of that rank prose. Fearing predators I huddled like a brush-tailed rat behind a rock all night. At sunrise I spied a golden hill in the distance and, figuring I might find some relief there, made my way through thickets of thorny comparisons and toxic adverbs. Before I had taken a dozen steps toward my goal, a three-headed beast blocked my path.

"Thank you for sharing your work with us. Although we find it imaginative and well-written, it does not meet our current needs. Best of luck with your writing career."

No matter how I twisted and dodged, the beast repeated its same reply. I turned away, hung my head in despair, and cried, "Oh won't someone help me?"

"Hi ho!"

I raised my head to find the spirit of Kurt Vonnegut standing beside me. With his wiry hair and brushy mustache he was not the older Vonnegut who'd mellowed with age but the younger, more sardonic author of Cat's Cradle and The Sirens of Titan.

"There is a way to reach your goal but to do so we must descend into the very bowels of despair. Are you willing?"

Pangs of doubt assailed me and I asked, "Am I worthy to embark on such a journey?"

"How can you think of failure when one who loves your work sent me to guide you?"

"Who else could it be," I asked, "but Aimee who signed my copy of The Girl in the Flammable Skirt at the LA Book Fair unless, of course, it was Allegra Goodman author of Intuition? Perhaps Sharon Olds?"

"Let's stop this discussion before it slows down the plot." Vonnegut lit a cigar.

I followed him through the bushes of cardboard characters and overused phrases until we entered a cave. When my eyes adjusted to the darkness, I found that we stood before a massive steel door. A bronze plaque hung beside the Diebold lock.

"Hope should be abandoned by those, that would here enter."

"What the hell is this place?" I asked.

"Exactly! It's the afterlife for those who've sinned against the English language." Vonnegut leaned close to the lock and spoke the magic words, "So it goes."

The door opened. Although I'd rather get a root canal with a masonry drill, I followed him inside. In the air e-mail messages flittered like bats made of ASCII characters.

"Dear Sir or Madam:

Please allow me to introduce myself. I am Barrister Augustine Bello of the Nigerian Gas and Petroleum Corporation and am contacting you regarding a proposition of mutual benefit. A few years ago…"

"Out of my way!" A man in a plaid sports jacket shoved me aside and dashed after the receding message. Nimble as he was, it always remained out of his reach.

"What is this place?" I asked.

"The antechamber where those who never cared about books spend eternity chasing get-rich schemes while bill collectors pursue them." Vonnegut turned. "Let's go."

Dodging the scam e-mails fluttering in the stagnant air, we walked downhill until we came to a river. Waterlogged copies of Angels and Demons floated like dead fish in its gray water. Thornton Wilder stood on the bank in front of a raft. When we got closer I noticed it was made of copies of Our Town that had been lashed together with mint dental floss.

"I can't take him across." Wilder pointed at me. "He doesn't belong here."

"The Muse sent him," Vonnegut said.

"Oh, he's following the Muse." Wilder sighed and lifted his pole. "In that case hop on board."

And so like countless students ferried to the tedium of adulthood by that play, we let Our Town take us into hell.

"I'm innocent. I tell you." Wilder leaned on the pole to propel the boat forward. "I never would have written that cursed play if I'd know it would spawn all those awful high school productions."

He complained so much that we jumped from the raft and waded to shore soaking our shoes and pant cuffs in the putrid water.

"Don't worry," Vonnegut said. "There's worse to come."

A huge screen was showing a Bruce Willis movie while hidden speakers blared Abba's greatest hits. I spotted a former teaching assistant of mine from college.

"Rajiv!" I called.

My friend replied to my greeting but I could no more understand his thick Bengali accent than I could understand his Calculus II lectures back at Ball State University. I wished him well and continued my journey.

"This is the land of virtuous illiterates," Vonnegut explained. "They include foreigners and tongue-tied engineers who couldn't put a sentence together if their lives depended on it. They are not punished but are banished from higher literature so they spend eternity playing video games and reading Maxim magazine."

We continued past ranch houses, condos, and shopping malls and then descended a set of concrete steps into a huge stadium. Instead of the normal seats the audience sat at wooden school desks, each with a huge coffee cup. Muscular demons in leather jerkins patrolled the aisles carrying stainless steel pitchers for refills.

On stage a man in a gray tunic stood at a lectern and recited, "Adams, Noel J. 316-642-2154. Adams, Noelle 316-815-4321..."

Vonnegut leaned close and whispered, "These are the boring poets who monopolized readings by going over their five-minute limit. Their punishment is to listen to the entire Wichita, Kansas phone book before they can use the bathroom."

"What about the ones over there being poked in their bladders with sticks?"

"They're special offenders whose introductions were longer than their poems."

I surveyed all the well-meaning faces. Pity moved me.

"Surely, that's too cruel. I mean, they don't know any better."

Vonnegut held up a hand to silence my protest. "If poetry dies, it won't be from persecution. It'll be because the good stuff gets drown out in a sea of mediocrity."

I thought back to all the hours I'd wasted listening to poems that rhymed capitalism with schism and racism. I admitted that he had a point. After a quick stop in an empty bathroom we descended to the third circle.

"L. O!" someone yelled.

Vonnegut grabbed my shoulder and pulled me out of the path of a runaway ice cream truck.

"What is this place?"

"The hell for those who overused acronyms."

I heard a scream and turned to see a man clutching his leg by a yellow, warning sign that said, "B.O.P.S."

"Beware of Poisonous Snake," Vonnegut said. "As their punishment the damned are condemned to a world containing only abbreviations."

We negotiated various hazards marked by signs such as W.M.L. (Warning Molten Lava), D.N.M. (Danger Nuclear Material), and C.T.Z. (Caution Terrorist Zone) before descending to the fourth circle where a group of people lay among gray stalagmites and sliced their own bellies open with rusty razor blades.

"Writers of bad instruction manuals." Vonnegut pointed to the document in one sufferer's hand. "For their crimes they're sentenced to perform do-it-yourself appendectomies using instructions similar to their own."

We departed the gruesome scene and paused by a man trapped under the wheels of the ice cream truck. Its bells played a macabre rendition of "Turkey in the Straw."

"Designer of a phone voice mail system." Vonnegut borrowed the victim's cell phone and let me listen.

"Thank you for dialing 9-1-1. Our operators will be with you in just a moment. After visiting the emergency room, why not stop at the Jolly Roger Restaurant? The Jolly Roger serves mouth-watering seafood with dinners starting at just $11.95..."

Vonnegut returned the phone and retrieved a blue-raspberry Popsicle from the truck. I was looking forward to cooling my parched throat but it was not to be. Before we descended to the fifth circle, the bear featured in numerous John Irving novels stopped us.

"Earl," it said.

Vonnegut tossed it the Popsicle and the bear consumed it wrapper and all.

"Earl." The bear brushed sweat from its forehead with a paw and stepped aside to let us by.

The next two circles passed faster than fifty pages of a Stephen King novel. In the fifth circle writers, who twisted syntax to make their work sound poetic, strutted around with their heads in place of their anuses. Blowhards, who used big words to appear smart, populated the sixth circle where every syllable they uttered made them smaller. A wall blocked the entrance to the seventh circle. I scored it with my thumbnail. It was paper mâché made from the novel Atlanta Nights by Travis Tea. Vonnegut and I circled until we found an opening.

"Halt!" demanded Jacques Derrida who stood blocking the gate.

"Let us enter!" Vonnegut said.

I scraped my shoes against a rock and left it smeared with Lilliputians.

"Shall we examine this statement?" Derrida lit his pipe. "On its face it appears simple enough but 'us' implies a privileged class, no doubt the industrial bourgeoisie. As Fournier said, 'Every request is a plea for justice,' so in fact you are asking to wait outside these walls until the great proletarian revolution ushers in an age of equality."

"Okay," Vonnegut said. "Don't let us enter."

"Very well, you may remain outside."

"Let me try." I approached Derrida and said, "The polhode rolls without slipping on the herpolhode lying in the invariable plane."

"That's good. That's very good." Derrida stood aside and knocked the ashes out of his pipe. "Have you considered publishing it in Social Text?"

"How did you guess that?" Vonnegut asked me.

"When you need something truly incomprehensible, nothing beats a physics textbook."

I expected flames and choking sulfur inside the walls but if not for huge tanks of liquid nitrogen coated with rime ice, I would have mistaken the seventh circle for an industrial park with clean, modern buildings and manicured lawns. We stopped before some kind of clinic. Horned nurses pushed patients in wheelchairs through its entrance.

"The seventh circle punishes coiners of political slogans that twist, I mean frame, meaning," Vonnegut said. "You know, phrases like death tax, terrorist surveillance program, judicial restraint, and family values."

A horrifying shriek came from inside the clinic and clawed at my eardrums.

"What's that?" I asked.

"Cool mint colon cleansing."

We walked on. After the cacophony of screams, the silence of the eighth circle was a relief.

"The land of censors," Vonnegut said. "They've had their tongues plucked out for denying speech to others."

He led me to an empty fire station, jumped on the pole, and slid to the deepest pit of hell yelling, "Whoopee!" I stared at the polished steel shaft. If I went down, there would be no climbing back, not that there ever was. I grabbed the metal with my sweaty palms, wrapped my legs around it, and let go.

When I landed in the ninth circle, the stench nearly made me retch. Demons in denim overalls were shoveling manure from huge, stinking piles into the open mouths of sinners buried to their necks. Many of the faces were familiar. I recognized Enron executives and a few former White House press secretaries.

"Tellers of official lies." Vonnegut held his cigar under his nose to mask the stink. "Seems fitting that they have to eat what they fed us for all those years. See that guy with the red hair? He wrote terms and conditions for credit cards that bilked the public out of billions."

I nodded and examined the sea of dreary faces. Then spotting my least favorite politician, I grabbed a shovel and ran screaming at the man. I would have bashed in his face if Vonnegut hadn't tackled me and sent the shovel flying.

"Let me go! He's a crook! He sold us out to the special interests!" I clawed at Vonnegut's mustache to get free.

Vonnegut's haymaker collided with my jaw and I saw flashes.

"Don't you see what I've been trying to show you, you idiot? Vonnegut banged my head against the ground with each word he spoke. "There's no Satan here!"

I sat up and looked around. All I saw were faces like my own. To some extent I had committed all the sins of the nine circles. Whoever would assign punishments here needed more wisdom and compassion than I had.

"So how do we get out of here?" I rubbed my sore jaw.

"That's easy. Just jump in any opening." Vonnegut dashed to the red-haired man, climbed into his mouth, and shimmied down his throat like a rabbit swallowed whole by a boa constrictor.

I dived in the politician's mouth, forcing myself past his jaws and down his esophagus. Fighting my way through his digestive tract, I realized the lies could be seen as sarcasm. I began to laugh. Then I cried for all the victims. Down became up. After climbing along the banks of a river whose name began with an L, I emerged into cool, night air and searched fruitlessly for my guide. Rocks rattled behind me.

"Kurt, is that you?" I turned.

One of the overall-clad demons, his skin glowing the Cerenkov blue of a swimming-pool reactor, stepped out of the shadows. I stumbled backwards, tripped, and searched the ground for a branch I could use as a weapon.

"Peace." The demon held up his palms. "When you showed me the way out, I decided to leave, too." He grabbed his right horn and pulled on it until his biceps bulged and the horn snapped off with a crack that startled a flock of sleeping birds out of the trees. "I quit!" He tossed his horn to the ground and yanked off the other one.

"Are any others following?" I asked.

"They'll come when they're ready. Where are we, anyway?"

"Judging by that lemur," I pointed to a face in a nearby baobab tree, "I'd say we're in Madagascar."

"Madagascar, huh?" The former demon offered me his hand and hauled me to my feet. "You think they have a drugstore nearby? I could sure use some aspirin."

Alone in the wilderness, I had little choice but to trust my new companion. He climbed a hill and spotted a road in the distance. After an hour hike through the grass we arrived there and chose a direction at random. It was little more than a dirt path but I was content to walk in silence beneath the stars.

The Comedic Purgatorial

We walked the dusty road in silence until dawn when the hot sun made the gastric juices my escape from hell left on my skin began to itch. My only consolation was that the stink repelled the malaria mosquitoes. I imagined my companion was as uncomfortable as I. Can a former demon get malaria? I didn't know.

After hours of traveling we still hadn't come across a drug store. No 7-Eleven. No KFC. Nothing! So when we happened on the Fianarantsoa Community College, we paused outside the concrete fence topped with broken bottles. At the gate a guard in khaki vest and shorts stopped us.

"You bwoys can't go in stinking like that." He tilted his eight-pointed cap back on his head. "You gots to take a shower first."

After much negotiation he hauled a garden hose to the gate, handed us a sliver of green soap, and draped a shabby towel the color of a concrete floor over the wall. My companion and I stripped off our filthy clothes and washed ourselves in the tepid trickle of water. I must say he was well endowed. I wasn't the only one to notice. A passing coed stopped in the courtyard and chewed her blonde braid while watching the former demon scrub our clothes in a galvanized-steel bucket. Fortunately the hot sun dried them quickly so he could dress before the poor woman missed too many classes.

"Hi, what's your name?" A beauty in an Afro approached my companion as soon as we walked through the gate. Her shorts revealed long, shapely, chocolate-colored legs.

"Er, Chad."

"Well Chad, you can call me Honey." She placed a hand on his massive bicep.

"Excuse me, ah, Honey," I said. "Is there some kind of student union building around here, someplace where we can get some aspirin?"

Without looking away from Chad's face she raised her finger in the vague direction of the sun. Working her other hand under his overalls she began fondling his nipple.

"Let's go, Chad." I tugged him from her grasp. "We have to get some aspirin for your headache. Remember?"

The convenience store in the student union building stocked aspirin as well as the bandages and disinfectant needed to dress the wounds left by removing the horns from Chad's head. I loaded up on cheese curls and Arizona Iced Tea too. The cashier, a red head in a prim blouse, giggled when we got to the register.

"You're going to need these." She took a large box of Magnum condoms from under the counter and added them to our purchase.

"Here you go, stud." After paying I handed Chad the thirty-six pack of extra large condoms.

The hallway outside the Andrianampoinimerina Conference Room was as good a place as any to clean Chad's wounds. For a demon from hell he sure was a pussy. As soon as I touched the divots on his head with the alcohol-soaked pad, he began to blubber. While I was cleaning out the dried blood, I thought I recognized a familiar voice coming from inside the conference room. I finished by taping two sterile dressings on Chad's head and hoped removing them wouldn't pull out too much of his curly hair.

"That should hold you until you get to a doctor, Chad."

"Doctor?" Chad's eyes widened. "No doctor!"

"Whatever." I realized then that I'd heard the voice from the conference room at the Idyllwild Summer Poetry Festival. "Mind if we step inside and listen?"

Inside poet Chris Abani read from Daphne's Lot while standing in the center of a circle of folding chairs. The audience consisted mostly of North Americans and Europeans in their mid-twenties.

"You're late!" a thin African man whispered. "Take your seats." He pointed to two empty chairs.

I was too busy listening to explain who we were. Nobel Prize winner Nadine Gordimer followed Chris. It would have been a good reading except for the sound of Chad rustling cellophane and chomping cheese curls. By the time Nadine finished, everyone in the room assumed my companion and I were enrolled in the Fianarantsoa Community College MFA program in creative writing.

After thanking the speakers the man, who'd spoken to us earlier, addressed the students.

"Welcome to the MFA program." He nodded to Chad and me. "I am your professor, Emmanuel Kwofi. You may be asking yourself how you can get an MFA from Fianarantsoa Community College in just seven weeks when other programs take up to two years. Simple. Instead of fighting human nature, we use it. By breaking your studies into seven modules of lust, gluttony, greed, sloth, wrath, envy, and pride we help our students obtain stupendous results." He flashed a brilliant smile. "So get a good night's sleep. I'll see you tomorrow at 8:00 AM when we begin with sex."

Next morning the writing students met in a rundown classroom. A weathered sheet of cardboard replaced the glass in one window frame and pale green paint peeled from the concrete walls. I sat kitty-corner from a woman in a sleeveless, gray T-shirt. Wire-rimmed glasses magnified her gray eyes and a few strands of hair frizzed out, like frayed insulation, from her dark braids.

After reading some examples from James Salter and Poppie Brite, Professor Kwofi told us to write the kinkiest thing we could possibly imagine. I fiddled with my pen. All I could think about was the woman in the T-shirt, the sweat stain between her breasts, the thin cloth revealing the shape of her nipples, body hair thick as felt under her arms, and how near my moment of climax she'd squeeze her legs together to grip my cock with her powerful pelvic muscles but I couldn't write that. It was too revealing. My sweaty shirt stuck to the uncomfortable, wooden chair as I struggled for hours to come up with something else, something more appropriate. I couldn't think of anything. A few minutes before 5:00 I scribbled my fantasy down in my blue composition book.

A read-and-critique session took place the following day.

"Who would like to go first?" Professor Kwofi looked around the room and pointed to a pale, Goth woman in black. "How about you, Eva?"

"Pass."

"Very well. Brett, would you like to share what you've written?"

A young man with blonde hair styled into three-inch dreadlocks sauntered to the front of the room with his masterpiece. The waistband of his jeans hung low enough to expose the elastic of his pale blue boxer shorts.

"Wazzup?" Brett leaned against Professor Kwofi's desk and began reading. "If my cock could talk, it would tell you you're fine. That it wants you to be mine. If you're into this, why not give me a little kiss. Yeah." He continued for what seemed thirty or forty minutes before raising a fist and ending with, "Peace, y'all."

"Any comments?" Professor Kwofi asked. "Yes, Tyler."

A woman in a pink dress put down her raised hand and asked, "Can he say that?"

"He just did." Professor Kwofi pointed to a white guy in Malcolm X glasses and a Che Guevara T-shirt. "Hampton."

"I think it's racist the way he appropriated black culture."

"I see." Professor Kwofi put an index finger to his chin. "Agnes."

"It's pronounced Og-Nay," said the woman I'd fantasized about. "I agree with Hampton. Brett can't write about the black experience unless he's lived it."

The read and critique continued. Hampton vowed celibacy until there was equality between the sexes, probably not much of a sacrifice in his case. Tyler described how her husband tied her spread eagle with silk scarves and dripped hot wax on her nipples. The class pronounced her work honest and daring as they did Og-Nay's historical piece about fisting Sappho. They labeled my work sexist and exploitative although Dieter, the German transvestite, seemed sympathetic. The only writer more scorned than me was Clancy, the guy in yellow-tinted aviator glasses who likened a woman's breast to an air launched cruise missile. By 4:00 I was ready to pack it in but we still had one more writer to hear.

Chad strolled to the front of the room and withdrew a sheet of paper from the front pocket of his overalls. While he unfolded it, Og-Nay, Tyler, Dieter, and Eva leaned forward like seals begging their trainer for a fish.

"It's simple, really," Chad read. "You want me and I want you so let's do away with all the small talk, go out in the woods, and hump like rabbits."

"That was wonderful!" Og-Nay said. "Your words are so honest, so direct." She batted her eyelids. "So penetrating."

Chad blushed.

"I like it too," Tyler added.

While clenching my jaws to keep from screaming, I looked around the room. Eva smiled like a Madonna. Dieter looked like he'd just eaten a fine meal. Even Clancy seemed pleased. I focused on Professor Kwofi who released his pursed lips and relaxed his wrinkled brow into an expression that said, "What the hell? I'm getting paid."

Classes dragged on. In the second week we wrote about food in the gluttony module. After that we tackled advertising copy (greed), haiku (sloth), and action/adventure (wrath). Although the Fianarantsoa Community College MFA program only lasted several weeks, my classmates made it seem like two years. Their criticism had little to do with the merits of the writing. Instead it reinforced the pecking order by ridiculing anyone expressing an original thought or an opinion at odds with the latest political trends. Two good things came from it. I began writing whatever I damn well pleased regardless of what they said, and I had plenty of motivation for the next module, envy.

"We're having a poetry slam, this Friday," Professor Kwofi announced at the start of the sixth week. "Judges chosen at random from an audience of students will score the original poems you recite. To motivate you to compete we're offering a trip to the heavens on the OmniDyne space plane as first prize."

I raised my hand. Having competed in poetry slams before, I had only one question. "Will the judges be able to understand English?"

I spent the whole week woodshedding a few poems I'd written years earlier. By Friday I felt confident I wouldn't stumble over my words or forget a line in the pressure of competition.

About a hundred students sat in rows facing a raised stage in the sweltering Andrianampoinimerina Conference Room. My classmates and I leaned against the wall while Professor Kwofi explained the rules. Five judges would score each participant's poem from one to ten and include decimal points to avoid ties. Of the eight competitors (Eva had chosen to pass) the three with the highest scores would advance to the second round and recite different poems. The one with the top score in that round would be the winner.

Clancy was first. Despite the heat he wore a leather bomber jacket with a hawk insignia embroidered on his chest.

"Ton Lok, Vietnam – While my buddies roast hot dogs over a C4 fire, Charlie hides in the jungle getting stronger. We drink beer. He eats cold rice and rat meat while plotting an audacious attack, an attack that will leave most of my company dead."

Being in his early twenties, Clancy could not have served in Vietnam. I suppose he was projecting a persona. He finished with a crisp salute and stood at attention while the judges delivered their scores.

"6.1"

"5.9"

"7.6"

"6.4"

"pi"

Adding these up gave Clancy a grand total of 29.14159635. Brett followed. The only thing more painful than listening to his talking-penis poem again was hearing the judges give it eights and nines. His score was 41.71828183. Tyler's erotic, Christian poem earned a respectable 39.414235 and Hampton's rant about US policy in Central American got 41.60217733.

Chad went next. He'd changed out of his overalls and into a pair of khaki slacks and a gauzy, white shirt that he'd unbuttoned to the waist. Rather than stand he sat on the edge of the stage to give the judges a better view of his golden, hairless chest and bulging pecs It didn't matter what he said. He was going to the next round.

I had the rotten luck of going next. After my introduction I climbed onto the stage and walked, footsteps sounding like drum beats on the hollow wood, to the microphone. I looked at the crowd. Chad's perfect score of 50 would outclass anything I did. I swallowed and began.

"In the library of unrecorded dreams
the blind scribe reaches for his quill.
Rolling the shaft between thumb and index finger
he gropes with the other hand for the naked parchment
yellowed as a jaundiced eye and thirsty for ink.
Mindful as a deer surrounded by wolves
he waits for a voice."

Okay, so it wasn't Dante but I got a score of 42.99792458, which put me in second place. I was feeling good until Professor Kwofi introduced the next poet and Dieter began bellowing from the audience before he got to the microphone.

"Tammy Faye Baker lies in a hospital room, her pillow smudged with mascara, an IV bottle dripping fluid the color of cotton candy into her veins."

Damn! He was using the old start-before-you-reach-the-stage trick. Why hadn't I thought of that? The judges awarded Dieter 44.6260755 points moving me into third place. With only one more contestant could I hold on and get into the second round?

As soon as Professor Kwofi introduced her, Og-Nay let the blue, terrycloth robe slip from her shoulders and climbed naked onto the stage. The crowd gasped as she began pulling an adding machine tape from her vagina and reading the words inked on the paper.

"The white, male power structure told me to write poems that were more universal. Universal? Hell! There's nothing universal about the poetry of privilege."

I was so engrossed in the primal image of her breasts, pubic hair, and thighs that I don't remember much about her performance except having a vague feeling that I would not be going out with her anytime soon. When the judges awarded her a 47.80665 putting me in fourth place, I sprang to my feet.

"No fair!" I yelled. "Using props is against the rules."

The judges conferred. After five minutes Professor Kwofi announced their ruling. Since Og-Nay's vagina was part of her body, it was not a prop. Her score would stand. I was out of the competition.

In a way it was a relief. I could relax and watch the final round. To no one's surprise Chad took first place. Professor Kwofi presented him with the ticket for the space plane ride and people crowded around to shake his hand. I decided to skip the party, not because I felt cheated but because I was ashamed of the petty emotions I let the slam arouse in me. I always wanted my writing to open people up and bring them together but I was on the verge of sinking into spite. The least I could do was congratulate the winner. Not long after I joined the line of well-wishers, Eva ambushed Chad with a long kiss and dragged him out of the room.

I felt certain we would write memoirs in the pride module but it was about literary criticism. Professor Kwofi explained that criticism had absolutely nothing to do with what the author wanted to say. Instead it was all about the critic. So, for example, writing about the relevance of quantum theory to Plato's Republic was okay even though quantum theory didn't exist until two thousand years after Plato died. I told myself that writing a criticism was just a game or a parody but I couldn't bring myself to do it. My previous scientific training wouldn't let me perpetrate that kind of crime against intellectual honesty. I became the only student in the history of the Fianarantsoa Community College MFA program in creative writing to enroll and not graduate.

On graduation day I stood in back of the Andrianampoinimerina Conference Room. The air conditioning was still broken and the temperature was over ninety degrees. My shirt reeked with the vegetable-soup smell I emit when I sweat. I applauded as each of my classmates received his or her degree. When the last one took her diploma from Professor Kwofi's hands, I slipped through the double doors, descended the stairs, and exited onto the dusty courtyard. The sun was hot on my face but the breeze dried my sticky shirt. I decided to hitchhike into town, take a bus to the capital, and see about a flight to San Diego. As I approached the gate, a voice called out.

"Jonté! Wait up!" Chad caught up with me and handed me the space-plane ticket. "I wanted to give you this."

"But you won it. It's yours."

"I never would have gotten here if you hadn't showed me the way out of hell." He wiped the sweat off his forehead. "Besides the Fianarantsoa Community College is hiring Eva as an assistant professor. I kind of thought I'd stick around."

The following day I took my seat on the crowded bus to Antanarivo. Baggage jammed the aisles and the air carried the meaty smell of sweating bodies. I didn't mind. While looking through the dirty window at the landscape of Africa, I daydreamed about my upcoming flight. Literary celebrities would probably be on board, maybe Maud Newton or Michiko Kakutani. Soon I'd be rocketing into space with the stars.

The Comedic Paridisical

The bus dropped me off at the Antanarivo Space Port where the security staff processed me with typical African efficiency. I was unsure whether I'd get lunch on the space plane so I bought a turkey sandwich and China Green Tips tea at the Starbucks. The space plane only held five passengers but the airport authorities simulated typical airline waiting areas by packing us into a cramped, janitor's closet. Needless to say I got quite close to my fellow astronauts. Sekou Mbutu, former president of the Central African Empire, sweated through his three-piece suit while sitting on an upended, steel bucket. A gold Rolex dangled from his wrist as he held a slim cell phone to his ear while conversing with his London brokers. The other passengers, his three wives, could have graced the cover of Vogue or Cosmopolitan. Sadly, uniformed agents of the International Criminal Court burst into the room and hauled the former president away before I could experience his famous sense of humor. Rather than continue on with the space flight, his wives left to work for their dear husband's release as well as the release of funds from his numerous Swiss bank accounts. Even though I was now the only passenger, I stood next to the mop until it was time to present my boarding pass and walk through the jet way onto the space plane.

I took my seat and set my green tea in the cup holder by the armrest without giving much thought to the mess the liquid could make in zero-g. Surely, they would have said something if this were a problem. While the flight attendant performed her mandatory safety demo, I savored the delicious emerald liquor. Ah, green tea. Green, the color of precious jade. Green of the mountains of China's Hebei Province where the Great Wall perches like the sinuous body of a dragon. Green as in, "All systems go."

The powerful engines spooled as the space plane took off like an ordinary jet liner and turned east toward the Indian Ocean. Moments later a voice came over the intercom.

"This is your captain, Dusty Weikoff. We're presently climbing to 65,000 feet where we'll shut down the air-breathing engines and fire up the rocket boosters. We're using a new oxidizer on this flight. I anticipate it'll boost our maximum altitude past the sixty-five miles we had been getting so sit back and enjoy your trip into outer space."

We cruised for another thirty minutes before the cabin went silent at shut down. Without the comforting, white noise of the jets I felt a moment of panic, but only a moment. Soon the space plane rattled with the rocket engines' roar. Inertia pressed me against the seat back as it accelerated. The sky outside my window grew black and I could see the horizon curve. The rockets cut out and I drifted weightless and silent. Spherical blobs of tea escaped through the opening in the cup's lid and floated like strange planets in the cabin.

Enthralled as I was in the scene outside my window, the last thing I expected was for my face to slam into the seat in front of me. I shook my head, blinked, and touched my sore nose to see if anything was broken. Oxygen masks dropped from the overhead compartments and dangled like grim, yellow, Christmas ornaments but there was no decompression in the cabin.

"Ladies and gentlemen, this is your captain, Dusty Weikoff. We seem to have collided with some kind of barrier. What the hell?"

Someone was knocking on the hatch. The flight attendant got out of her seat and looked through the window.

"Oh my God!" She put both hands to her mouth.

I went to look. An angel complete with halo, harp, and wings hovered outside.

"Guess we'd better let him in."

The flight attendant opened the hatch. Instead of a cold vacuum that would suck the air from our lungs and boil our blood, the atmosphere outside consisted of warm air that smelled of fresh hay and apple blossoms. The angel entered. He stood about seven feet tall, had golden hair, and wore a shining white tunic.

"Mr. Jonté, I'm here to escort you to heaven. This way, please."

He grabbed me around the waist and we flew out of the cabin. From outside it was clear what had happened. The space plane was stuck like a dart in cork to the inner surface of an enormous sphere. Not far away the Hubble Space Telescope hung from an overhead crane. A cluster of angels hovered around its opening with a slide projector that showed pictures of planets and stars. We flew on until we arrived at a platform that protruded from the upper surface.

"Just take those stairs." The angel pointed to some marble steps leading up from the platform. "You don't mind if I get going. Do you? I have a lot of consistency checks to perform for the Cosmic Background Explorer data. Have a pleasant stay." He flew off.

I climbed the stairs and ended up in a classroom where a man in a black cassock lectured on the geocentric theory and Catholic doctrine. With nothing else to do I sat in back but soon was squirming in the uncomfortable, wooden chair.

"Excuse me." A woman burst into the room. "I'm looking for Mr. Jonté."

"Right here." I stood and followed her out the door.

"Sorry I'm late." She spoke in a high-pitched, clipped tone. "I thought you'd be arriving at section 050 – Magazines, journals, and serials but your pilot changed course at the last minute." She wore a loose, 1920s dress with a long, pearl necklace. Her big eyes and dark eyebrows looked familiar like I'd seen her picture in an old, sepia photograph.

"What's with the classroom?" I asked.

"As you know, heaven means different things to different people. For some it means having their beliefs confirmed. Not for you, though. You want something more literary."

I recognized her then. She was Laura (Riding) Jackson who abandoned writing poetry in 1939 because it couldn't express the truth she wanted to tell. She led me through a narrow hallway and into a giant library where book stacks the length of freight trains stretched into the distance and dipped below the horizon.

"Heaven contains all the books that have been written. Sphere Zero is not terribly exciting unless you're doing research," she said. "It does hold the issues of the American Drivel Review that published some of your stories, though. I think you might like to browse religion in Sphere Two, science in Sphere Five, or literature in Sphere Eight."

"Wait a minute." I stopped walking. "You're telling me that heaven is organized by the Dewey Decimal System?"

"Well, we thought of adopting the Library of Congress classification but re-shelving all written knowledge would take too much effort."

"Do you have that lost Shakespeare play?"

"You mean Cardenio? It's in section 820."

Before I could reply we disappeared from Sphere Zero and rematerialized in Sphere Eight as if the Star Trek transporter beam had moved us. Riding brushed her hand along a row of books until her fingers came to rest on an ancient, leather-bound volume.

"Here it is." She handed it to me and waited while I read.

It was not one of Shakespeare's better works. The Aeschylus plays proved more interesting. Even though the latter were written in ancient Greek, I could understand them in heaven. I don't know how long I browsed in that library as time had no meaning there. The sections became blurred as Riding and I transported between spheres following my interests. Authors were there too. In the poetry section I found Kabir chanting at his loom and Mirabai singing of her longing for Krishna. Rumi recited while circling a stone pillar and Ryokan praised the moon of enlightenment. This provided an opportunity to discuss Riding's ideas on the limits of poetry.

"Surely, these mystics have expressed the truth through poetry," I said.

"Perhaps they've done better than most," Riding said, "but don't let the emotional effect of their words blind you. Truth is not to be found in sound and measure. If you examine what these mystics said, you'll find that they misdirected you and merely hinted at the truth."

"Some people have said poetry is religion without the trappings. Let's go to the religion section and try to find truth there."

Riding transported us to Sphere Two, where Mohammed recited the word of God while Matthew, Mark, Luke, and John compared versions of the gospels. I wasn't satisfied.

"What is this truth you were trying to express?" I asked Riding.

"The rightness of words used to express the mind of the communicator," she said.

"Can you give me an example?"

Rather than examine some text, we talked at length in perfect honesty as if our minds approached a marriage bed and shed their clothes. That intimacy fulfilled a need I'd tried imperfectly to satisfy with sex before. It was the need for connection, not physical pleasure. In the afterglow I asked about meaning.

"Are you aware of information theory? For example, the letter t is more common than q. Therefore, because of its rarity, q carries more information. I think the same thing holds in a story. Saying it's hot in the Sahara may be true but it doesn't convey much information. Saying that it's raining is more interesting. I judge the meaning of a story by how much information it contains."

"But then the amount of meaning in a story depends on the reader's background," Riding said.

"Exactly, just like the information carried by a letter depends on the language used."

We continued to browse the religion section. I found the writings of the Buddhist monk, Nagarjuna, but he was not there. Neither were several Sufis nor Theresa of Avila. A question nibbled at the edge of my awareness. It was as yet too unformed to put into words.

"You have something you want to ask me," Riding said. "Just say it."

"I need to check something first. Do you have a copy of Kurt Gödel's completeness theorem?"

"Of course, in section 510 – mathematics."

We located the book and I verified my understanding. The theorem states that there are statements, which cannot be proved or disproved by mathematics. I was onto something. At my request Riding summoned Kurt Gödel who materialized wearing a pair of round glasses and a bewildered look.

"Your completeness theorem," I said. "What do you think? Could you say language is constructed from a set of logical axioms? And if so, does your theorem prove a reality that can't be described by words?"

"It might." Gödel stroked his chin. "But it's quite a stretch to go from the formal logic of mathematics to the looseness of language."

We debated for hours. Although my brain lacked the horsepower to follow the details of his explanation, I grew convinced I was right.

"This heaven does not hold everything," I told Riding. "Take me to where words do not reach."

"Earth, hell, and these ten spheres contain all there is," she said.

Painful as it was, I knew what I had to do.

"I have to go back," I said.

"Are you crazy?" Riding raised her eyebrows. "You have everything here. Would you give that up?"

"There is more. I'm sure of it," I said. "That's why I couldn't find the Buddha or Nagarjuna. They live beyond words in the unconditioned."

She turned away from me as if my words were a dumpster filled with rotting corpses.

"Are you sure you want to go back?" she asked.

"No, but I have to try to express the unexpressed by writing the original story, the one true story."

"In that case, you'll need this." She handed me her pen

Though it was only a simple, silver ballpoint with a pushbutton tip, I hesitated. By accepting it, I allowed the possibility of abandoning the fellowship of poets and the joy of organizing my thoughts into stanzas. But the trappings of literature would be hollow without honest expression. As soon as I took the pen, I fell through the floor into the blackness and tumbled through space until I came to rest in my threadbare, office chair. A yellow, legal pad lay on the cluttered desk before me. My fall from heaven seemed prearranged and somehow necessary to working a greater purpose. For several hours I sat stunned. Eventually far from the stars, I lifted my pen and began to write. The heavens expanded.

Confessions of a Wallflower

What were my stepsister and her friends doing up there? Ever since the president began talking about invading Iraq, they'd spent their afternoons locked behind her bedroom door. One day after my last class I ran through the alley on Madison, so I could beat her home. I bounded up the stairs, dashed into her room, and stood next to her dresser with my back against the wall. It only took a few seconds for my body to disperse into the drywall. It's peaceful inside a wall. No one makes fun of my big ears, and if I keep quiet I can watch peoples' private moments from the safety of being unseen.

I first discovered my ability to disappear into walls in seventh grade when I was running from Ricky Green and his jerk-wad friends. I ducked into Wrigley's theater through the side door thinking I could exit the fire doors out back. Big mistake! The doors were chained shut. I hid in the shadows just praying that I wouldn't end up like Lenny Williams, whose parents had to eventually take him out of school. Then the house lights came on and Ricky's goons started walking down the aisles. Resting a two-by-four on his shoulder Ricky walked right toward me, but for some reason he passed by without seeing me. Since then I disappear into a wall whenever anyone gets threatening. Floors and ceilings don't work. Neither do lampposts and trees. The item I blend into has to be flat and at least as big as me. Maybe a giant Sequoia would be okay. I wonder what it would be like to be inside something alive.

But I'm getting off track. Most girls my stepsister's age would have posters of Avril Lavigne or Alanis Morissette plastered on their walls. Not Darla. She has Saddam Hussein. It's the younger, more confident Saddam from before the U.S. cleaned his clock in the 1991 Gulf War. Darla's room is filled with Saddam paraphernalia: Saddam coffee cups, Saddam videos, a mural featuring Scud missiles landing on Israel, translations of Saddam's novels, Saddam action figures, and even an autographed black beret. With all the run up to war you'd think my dad would be upset over Darla's fixation, especially since he's a parapsychologist working for the Company (you know, the CIA), but Dr. Richard Mackenzie, Jr. didn't seem to mind a bit.

The sounds of girl talk and footsteps thumping up the stairs came from the hallway. Darla and her two friends entered, dropped their pink

Hello Kitty backpacks, and locked the door behind them. All three had shirts tied around their waists and wore bandannas over their hair.

"It'll all work out, Darla." Libby McDonald sank to the carpet and rested her back against the bed.

"Yeah," Mattie McCoy said. "Saddam's gotten out of worse jams than this."

"That's easy for you to say." Darla tossed her head to get her long blonde hair out of her eyes. "I mean, the men you love aren't, like, facing an imminent attack. Ayatollah Khamenei's army hasn't been weakened by a decade of international sanctions, and Kim Jong-Il has all those rockets pointed at Seoul to protect him." Darla sat on her bed. "It's just so unfair!"

"If Saddam goes down, there are still other leaders," Mattie said. "How about Qaddafi? He's, like, really handsome."

"Don't even think it!" Darla narrowed her mascara-smudged eyelids and glared.

"I know!" Libby started bouncing like an unbalanced washing machine on the spin cycle. "Why don't you write Saddam a letter telling him how you feel? It would be so romantic. He could, like, carry it in his uniform while he defends Baghdad."

"What should I say?" Darla sat at her desk and took a sheet of flowery paper from the drawer.

"It can't be all boring and all," Libby said. "You need to, like, say something that will get his attention."

"How about this?" Darla recited as she wrote. "Dear Saddam, All Americans aren't as down on you as our president. I, for one, find you really hot. Especially that cute mustache and the way your uniform shows off those tight buns, when you review the troops…"

At the mention of buns I held my breath to keep from laughing, but a snort escaped my nostrils anyway.

"Patrick, you little brat!" Darla sprang to her feet. "You are so going to get it!" She pulled a tack from her crossed-sword-monument poster and stabbed the wall right where my stomach was.

"Ouch!" I rematerialized out of the wall. "That hurt!"

"Mom!" Darla threw open the door. "Patrick's spying on us again!"

"Patrick, leave your sister alone!" mom yelled from downstairs.

"She stuck me with a tack!"

"Well, she wouldn't have if you hadn't been hiding in the wall, would she?"

"Fine!" I went to my room and slammed the door. Who needed to listen to a bunch of stupid girls, anyway?

CIA employees must never ever bring secret documents home from work, but my father always had all kinds of interesting stuff in his battered briefcase. While others carried slick laptop computers, my dad continued to lug the brown leather briefcase he'd bought in the 1980s. As soon as he got home dad would lock it in the GSA safe by his desk. I guess he never realized my wall-blending ability could work on steel too.

On a typical Thursday night in February we assembled at the dinner table. Dad lit his pipe and stretched out his long legs so his size thirteen triple-D feet lurked like bear traps to snag the leg of anybody walking by. Mom served white corn, chicken breasts in cream sauce, and French bread. Our neighbor's sled dog Trixie, who always hung around at dinnertime, had Kibbles and Bits. Mom never ate, preferring instead to draw nourishment from topless sunbathing. To be social she sipped a glass of white wine with dad.

After dinner Darla retreated to her room to watch CNN, dad went to the garage to work on his 1/8 scale steam locomotive, mom stripped and jumped in the tanning booth, and Trixie's owner called her home for Iditarod practice. That left me with nothing to do, so I entered dad's office, pressed my chest against the safe, and blended into the massive block of steel. Inside I could only see a grainy, black-and-white view, hardly suitable for reading. Although it took a half hour of effort, I managed to spring the catch on the lock.

I rematerialized and sat at my father's desk to examine the briefcase's contents while rubbing my aching right arm. The black candles, dried-out corpse's hand, and Bill Clinton doll with a rusty needle in its chest didn't interest me. Instead I read the latest reports. Central Asia was proving a poor source of virgin's blood, the attempt to create a golem resembling Wolf Blitzer had failed when the creature washed down the sewer in a thunderstorm, and Karl Rove successfully summoned the demon A&! qz*rl at a séance in the Executive Office Building. None of this was out of the ordinary. I thumbed through a stack of documents stamped TOP SECRET in big red letters. There was a zombie spell and a medical report describing my stepsister's CCR-5 genetic defect. I jotted down the Latin phrases from the former. It could come in handy the next time Ricky Green hassled me. As usual I replaced dad's briefcase and locked the safe door.

In mid-March while the rest of us were watching the president give Saddam and his sons a 48-hour ultimatum on TV, the sound of a lightning bolt came from the second floor. Trixie, her fur standing up from static electricity, ran whining into the street. Dad and I rushed to my stepsister's room. We found Saddam pointing a nickel-plated automatic at Darla and jabbering like a phlegm ball the size of a canned ham was stuck in his throat. The air smelled of ozone and burning insulation. Darla cowered inside the pentagram chalked on the carpet with dad's open briefcase at her feet. I guess I must have left the safe unlatched on my foray that night. How else could Darla have gotten in? I recited the zombie spell and Saddam froze.

"Put down the gun!" I said.

Evidently, a zombie needed to understand commands to obey them. This posed a bit of a problem, since Saddam didn't speak English and I didn't speak Arabic. Dad removed the pistol from the dictator's grip, ejected the magazine, and cleared the bullet from the chamber.

"What are we going to do now?" Dad sat on my stepsister's bed, took off his plastic-rimmed glasses, and pinched the bridge of his nose. "If the Company finds out I took that summoning spell home, I'll lose my job for sure."

"Can't we just send him back?" I pulled Saddam's ear and poked him in the belly. He didn't respond.

"No!" Darla knelt at my father's feet and pressed her tear-soaked face to his knees. "Don't you see? If you send him back they'll kill him!"

"Doesn't matter anyway, Pumpkin. Congress never authorized the funds to develop the send-away spell." Dad shook his head. "I wish I'd never gotten involved in Operation Mary Mallon."

Although Saddam wouldn't obey spoken commands, he followed when I took his hand. I led him downstairs and stashed him in the tanning bed while the rest of us had a late dinner of carrot juice, duck in orange sauce, and pumpkin pie.

By morning the situation looked a whole lot brighter. All we needed to do was smuggle Saddam into dad's office. Then he could say he captured the dictator on his own initiative. A grateful Congress would boost the Occult Directorate's budget, and dad might even get a raise. There was one problem, though. Saddam would only follow me. Fortunately the CIA's take-your-child-to-work day was on the 25th. We'd only have to keep Saddam on ice for a week.

I hadn't been to the CIA's family day for a few years. Quite frankly, most of the stuff is for grade-school kids. But I'd sit through another day of rigging Paraguayan elections, imaging nudist colonies with KH-11 keyhole satellites, and lacing my stepsister's Doctor Pepper with hallucinogens to help my dad in an emergency. Those are my family values.

Dad figured we'd leave Saddam in the tanning bed in the interval. That's the nice thing about keeping zombies; they don't need to eat or go to the bathroom like the rest of us. Anyway, dad thought it would be a good idea to change Saddam's clothes, so he wouldn't be so conspicuous in case any of our neighbors got a glimpse of him.

"I'll do it!' Darla jumped to her feet and scanned the dictator's torso with her eyes. "He looks like he needs a bath too."

"That's okay, Pumpkin." Dad turned to me. "Patrick, do you mind?"

Even a bloodthirsty tyrant, who's murdered tens of thousands, deserves some privacy, so I won't describe what I found under Saddam's uniform. I dressed him in baggy corduroys and one of my dad's old SDSU sweatshirts.

Things seemed to be going fine, but dad hadn't counted on mom. She started feeling peaked in the overcast March weather and had me move Saddam to the broken freezer in the garage. The door had a hole in it, so he wouldn't smother or anything. I guess I could have paid more attention, but with Saddam safely stashed away he kind of slipped my mind in a couple of days. So when I saw a Goodwill truck leaving our block after I came home from skateboarding the half pipe at Calvin Coolidge Park on Saturday, I didn't realize we had a problem. Mom had taken Darla shopping at the army surplus store, and dad was watching Ted Koppel reporting from atop a Bradley Fighting Vehicle on TV. I was feeling pretty grungy, so I went to my room to change.

"Dad," I called, "where's my Ozzie T-shirt?"

"Gave it to the Goodwill," he said from the bottom of the stairs. "With your mom away it seemed like a perfect opportunity to get rid of some junk. You know what a pack rat she is. Finally unloaded that broken freezer too."

As I stared at the T-shirts in my drawer, I realized some granny would soon be having a stroke after finding the Butcher of Baghdad sleeping in the bargain she bought at the thrift store. "Uh, dad." I descended the stairs. "We've got a bit of a problem."

"What's that, son?"

"Saddam's in that freezer!"

Dad took the pipe from his mouth and held it pinched between his thumb and index finger, while the color drained from his face. His expression looked like Saddam's moments after I'd recited the zombie spell. Then dad's CIA training kicked it.

"To the car!" he said.

We combed the neighborhood in dad's 1972 Volvo 1800 E but didn't see the truck. Then I got the idea of meeting it back at the warehouse. The dispatcher directed us to the correct loading bay.

"Got it right back here." The driver opened the van's sliding door and raised the Tommy Lift level with the truck bed. "Found some old homeless guy sleeping inside. Seemed kind of harmless, but he must have been stoned or something. Let him out in front of the FOH shelter in Arlington. Hey! Where are you going? Don't you want your freezer?"

The Friends of the Homeless shelter was located in a colonial building next to a Popeye's Fried Chicken near the corner of 14th and Monroe. A half-dozen men in tattered clothing waited in the lobby by the pot-bellied stove. Oil lamps were attached to the walls instead of electric lights, and a woman in a calico dress and shawl carried linen into the back room. Dad and I had no choice but to join the line in order to talk with the attendant.

"Only room for one family left. You two!" The attendant who wore a powdered wig, long blue jacket, tan breeches, and a ruffled collar pointed at us.

Dad and I approached the desk, while the others grumbled and shuffled out the door.

"Curfew's at 7:30. We're heating water for the bath." The attendant fished a key out from the desk, dipped a feather in an ink pot, and made an entry in the ledger.

"You don't understand," dad said. "We're looking for Uncle Robert – dark hair, maroon SDSU sweatshirt."

"Haven't seen him."

"Does he have a thick mustache and a five o' clock shadow?" one of the homeless asked.

I nodded.

"Saw him with a toothless woman over by Quincy Park. Seemed like a harmless fellow. Kind of quiet, though."

Dad and I rushed to the park but found no trace of Saddam.

"I can't believe you lost Saddam!" Darla wailed when dad revealed the day's events over dinner. "Now I'll never have children!"

Dad dodged the plate she threw, and Darla stomped upstairs to her room. The stain her dinner of blueberries, blue corn tortillas, and blue cheese made on the wall looked like a pair of dolphins circling nose to tail.

"I think the best thing to do right now," dad knocked his pipe against the ashtray, "is to never say a word about any of this."

Dad had one last trick up his sleeve. Early Sunday morning we retrieved Saddam's Jockey shorts and drove to a kennel outside Williamsburg. Hounds jumped and bayed behind the wire fence, as we pulled to a stop in the gravel driveway. A man in a plaid shirt answered the door. His skin looked like leather cured in whiskey and coffee grounds.

"Hello, Dick. What can I do for you?"

"I was wondering if we might borrow Esperanza for a few hours," dad said.

"I suppose you can't tell me what it's for."

Dad shook his head. The man let the screen door slam. I was expecting him to fetch a bloodhound, but he returned carrying a Chihuahua wearing a denim vest with a Devils Disciples logo monogrammed on the back.

"If you don't mind me saying so, the boy seems a little young for this kind of work." He handed over the Chihuahua. Despite the vest Esperanza shivered in dad's arms.

"He's my son." Dad scratched Esperanza behind the ears. "Never too soon to learn the family business."

We got into the Volvo, I asked, "Shouldn't we use a bloodhound?"

"You watch too much TV." Dad turned the key. "Esperanza's the best tracking dog in the region. If she can't find Saddam, no one can."

Most dogs would have sucked scents from the car's open window with noses like powerful vacuum cleaners, but Esperanza only trembled on my lap and stared at the world with fearful, liquid eyes. When we arrived, dad had her sniff Saddam's underwear. Esperanza swept her nose over the sidewalk, trotted a block north, and then doubled back. Even at the early hour the traffic distracted her. After forty-five minutes Saddam's trail ended at a nearby Taco Bell with Esperanza barking at a fugitive bean burrito.

Darla declared she'd have nothing to do with the CIA take-your-child-to-work day, so despite the prospect of tedious presentations and hours watching the enemy agents lounge in their hotel rooms on closed-circuit TV I agreed to put in an appearance and make dad look good. We took the Metro orange line in to D.C. It was a ten-minute walk through the mall from the Smithsonian station to the Washington Monument, which housed the secret entrance to the CIA's Occult Directorate ever since they'd moved from the Sharper Image store in Tysons Corner. We bypassed the "Closed for Private Party" sign, took the elevator down to the underground complex, and went to dad's office. He set his battered briefcase next to his desk and logged into his computer.

"Says here the family members' program starts at 8:30 around the corner from the nuclear reactor. You know the way. Don't you, Patrick?"

Technically, I wasn't supposed to walk around unescorted, but everyone knew me. I took the elevator down a few stories and joined the others by the yellow and magenta radiation warning signs. I was marveling how the flashing red lights made the men and women in colorful ChemBio protection suits scramble like ants in a flood, when I heard a giggle that made my guts feel as if I was being prepped for bowel surgery.

"Hello, Patrick." It was Wendy Ostermann. She'd had a crush on me since she was four and I was eight. "I just got the new American Girl doll. Want to come over to my house and play?"

"Maybe later, Wendy." I inched away to avoid the faint odor of urine that always followed her around.

"Hello everyone and welcome to the CIA's family day!" A perky woman in a green park ranger's uniform clasped her hands to her chest revealing the veins in her massive forearms. "Now, who'd like to learn how to kill someone with a credit card?"

I pretended to need an urgent trip to the bathroom to ditch the presentation and then ducked into dad's office. Fortunately, he wasn't there. Rather than explain why I'd skipped the demo, I blended into the wall behind his desk. How relaxing it was to be hidden! When dad returned, he began visiting gossip sites on the Internet.

I was pondering whether my RX30 model rocket could send a capsule into orbit, when Number Two ducked his shaved head into the office. Dad pulled up a spreadsheet to cover up an on-line article on breast augmentations gone horribly wrong.

"Dick." Number Two pulled up a chair across from dad's desk. "You'll be glad to know we're pulling the plug on Operation Mary Mallon phase one."

Mary Mallon, I remember dad mentioning that name, when Saddam appeared in Darla's room. Just then I felt a cold, bony hand grab my shoulder. The dead fingers dug into my flesh, but I couldn't jump out of the wall with Number Two in the office.

"With 150,000 troops in Iraq I doubt we'll need to send an assassin to deal with Saddam." Number Two fingered the black spot on his forehead. Ever since angels had washed it from Mohammed's heart with snow, that black spot has been bouncing around the world causing mischief. Now it had come to rest on the man responsible for implementing the covert end of American foreign policy.

"That's a real load off my mind." Dad sighed.

I started shaking for real, when another skeletal hand began stroking my hair.

"Of course, we'll still pursue phases two and three." Number Two stood. "But I imagine you don't have as much of a personal stake in those."

As soon as Number Two left, I sprung out of the wall.

"Patrick!" Dad jumped out of his seat. "What's wrong? You look like you've seen a ghost."

"The hands." I pointed to the wall. "Someone grabbed me."

"It's just the dead Indian." Dad sat down.

"Dead Indian?"

"Sure," dad chuckled. "Every Federal building has a dead Indian in its foundation."

That news spoiled my dreams of eavesdropping on the movers and shakers in government. I suppose there are good walls in Europe or Asia, but I'd probably find dead Armenians or Cambodians there. Some knowledge can get you terminated, so by unspoken agreement dad and I never discussed Operation Mary Mallon. I searched for the name on the Internet, though. Mary Mallon was an Irish immigrant better known as Typhoid Mary. Factor in my stepsister's CCR-5 defect, which confers immunity to AIDS, and her infatuation with Saddam, and it wasn't hard to figure out the CIA wanted her and her friends to infect the leaders of the Axis of Evil. Even though Darla's adopted, that was a pretty cold thing for dad to do to her.

I only saw Saddam once more. Not long after the president declared victory in Iraq in front of cheering sailors on that aircraft carrier, our class took a field trip to the National Aerospace Museum. After spending the day looking at the Spirit of St. Louis, the Apollo 11 capsule, and other examples of American genius we piled onto the bus. On the way home I saw Saddam sitting on a street corner next to a woman in a stocking cap and torn denim jacket. I pushed my face closer to the window. Saddam's beard had grown out and his forehead was smudged with grit. The cardboard sign propped next to him said, "Need money for food. God Bless." It's funny. We sent soldiers halfway around the world to hunt for the enemy of democracy, but he was in the nation's capital all along. None of our leaders paid attention to the homeless. I guess the easiest place to hide is where no one wants to look.

I felt the crack of a soda can bouncing off my skull and heard Ricky Green's perverted laugh. My run in with the dead Indian had convinced me that hiding can sometimes be more dangerous than what you're hiding from, so I stood, rushed down the aisle, and planted a fist in Ricky's stupid face. The bus driver managed to break the fight up before I got killed. Since then Ricky's found other people to pick on.

In the end dad had nothing to do with Saddam's capture. As I heard it, the D.C. police busted Toothless Dorothy Decatur for breaking and entering in December. An officer noticed that her catatonic companion looked a lot like Saddam and called the CIA. The Feds flew Saddam back to Iraq and planted him in a rabbit hole for soldiers to find a few days later. In addition to a lot of silence the reward money bought Toothless Dorothy a new smile.

Dad offered to get me into the CIA's summer intern program. I haven't told him yet, but I want to do something else with my life, maybe something that uses my talent with walls and dead Indians like architecture or archaeology. Adulthood's a long way off. I still have time.

Menace II Your Arteries

I scribbled my signature on the form that absolved the LA Police Department of all responsibility should I be injured or killed and handed the clipboard to the public affairs officer.

"Just wait here and Officer Mencken will be with you shortly." She tore off the pink copy, handed it to me, and made off with the rest.

I imagined her taking it to the crime lab where big-brother types would extract my fingerprints and DNA profile and load the information into a massive database. I've always been suspicious of the police, but to understand the recent wave of gang violence I volunteered to ride along on a typical patrol of LA's worst neighborhood.

While waiting I fed a few quarters into a massive, gray vending machine that looked like it had squatted in the corner since the days of Dragnet. A paper cup dropped into the recessed opening and a dark liquid resembling runoff from a Jiffy Lube filled it. Fortunately, my escort sauntered into the room before I was tempted to drink.

"Officer Bud Mencken. Pleased to meet you."

I shook hands while trying not to stare at the massive pistol on his duty belt. With his crew cut and piercing, blue eyes Officer Mencken resembled George C. Scott, not the older George C. Scott who played Lieutenant Kinderman in The Exorcist III but the younger, more vital man who starred as General "Buck" Turgidson in Dr. Strangelove. I followed him out to a black-and-white Ford Crown Victoria in the parking lot. Once inside the squad car he donned a pair of wraparound sunglasses that had been resting on the barrel of the sawed-off shotgun that protruded from between the seats. Any reassurance his imposing physique inspired vanished when he removed a tiny, nickel-plated pistol from his sock and handed it to me.

"Know how to use this?" he asked.

"Of course." I'd never handled a gun in my life but confessing my ignorance would surely lower my standing in his eyes. I dismissed the possibility of an accidental discharge and stuffed it in my pants pocket that contained my change, Rolaids, and car keys.

"Let's roll." Officer Mencken reached for the shift lever on the steering column and we were off.

We headed west on Wilshire, took a left on Alverado, picked up the I-10, and drove east to the Alameda exit. From there we headed north to the 101 and looped past the Hollywood sign and the control tower at LAX. Soon the decay of South Central replaced the palm-tree-lined boulevards of Beverly Hills. After only five hours of driving we had arrived.

Something ominous was in the air. In this once vital community where entrepreneurs had sold cut-rate pharmaceuticals on every street corner, the residents now seemed dull and listless. Korean shop owners no longer chased African Americans out of their stores, and despite those chain nets the basketball courts were deserted. Mencken rolled down the window.

"Smell that?" His nostrils twitched.

"What is it?"

"Trans fat." He rolled up the window and put the air conditioner on recirculate in a futile attempt to clear the stench of deep frying from the squad car's interior.

"My God, I thought that was just in New York City."

"It's everywhere, my friend."

We rolled past a half dozen young men in hooded sweatshirts and triple-wide jeans. In their lipid-addled state they didn't have the sense to hide their French fries, chicken wings, and chimichangas when they saw a police car. One clutched his chest and fell dead from a coronary.

"Oh shit!" Officer Mencken ran a nervous hand over his brush cut.

"Should we call an ambulance?"

Instead of worrying about the dead man Officer Mencken pointed to the crown spray painted on the dirty, brick wall of an elementary school across the street.

"This is Mickey D's territory," he said. "Calorie abuse is out of control, but at least it hasn't been violent. Now it looks like BK is trying to muscle in. I don't have to tell you how many corpses will pile up if there's a turf war."

I looked around and noticed other signs of gang activity such as yellow spray-painted Ms, locals' hand signs (three fingers pointed down), and all those discarded cartons and wrappers. After a thoughtful pause Officer Mencken took action. He made a U turn and gunned the engine. After we traveled a half-mile we screeched to a stop in front of a one-story apartment complex.

"Five-O. Five-O," the lookouts yelled.

Mencken grabbed his nightstick and dashed into the courtyard. Dealers and users scattered, but due to their girth they were no match for the buff policeman. He singled out the slowest offender, grabbed him by the belt, and spun him into a stucco wall.

"Long time no see, Dough Boy."

"Oh man, what you bustin' my hump for?" The suspect bore a striking resemblance to Ice Cube, that is, if the rapper-turned-actor were to gain a hundred pounds.

"You know the drill." Officer Mencken kicked Dough Boy's feet apart and began patting him down. "You got any ketchup packets in your pockets?"

"I'm clean, man"

"Then what's this?" Officer Mencken held up a soggy, drooping fry. He cuffed the suspect's hands behind his back and marched him to the squad car. "You're a three-time loser, Dough Boy," Officer Mencken said once he got the suspect safely stowed in the back seat. "You know what that means. Mandatory sentence to a diet camp. For the next three years all you can look forward to is a salad with lemon juice after hours on the treadmill."

The suspect tried to play it cool, but I could tell he was rattled by the drops of sweat forming on his upper lip.

"But we're not interested in you," Mencken continued. "If you answer a few questions, the evidence just might disappear."

"What you want to know?"

"Tell me about BK moving on your turf."

"Oh man, they been spraying their tags around here all week."

"What does Ronald say?"

"That we got to move on them suckers by Saturday." The suspects eyes darted to the door as if he couldn't wait to fix.

Then Officer Mencken did something reckless. He suspended the French fry over his open mouth, dropped it in, and swallowed. My respect for this man grew. By this one brazen act he had earned grocery bags of street cred. Thugs would talk of him for generations.

We released the suspect at a deserted fruit stand and continued our investigation by scouting BK territory. As Officer Mencken had feared several yellow Ms had been sprayed on billboards and overpasses. One even covered a mural of the bearded king holding a paper cup and box of fries.

"I don't get it," I said. "Why would Mickey D's be moving on BK at the same time?"

"They're not," Officer Mencken said, "and BK isn't behind the graffiti on Mickey D's turf either. No." He stroked his chin. "We're looking at the work of a third party."

Of course, a third party could move in and pick up the pieces after a war between BK and Mickey D's. But who would be so ruthless?

Officer Mencken knew the answer. At this hour he thought it best to avoid the freeways, so we took Pico to Sunset Boulevard, followed that to Mulholland Drive, proceeded to Hollywood and Vine, got off on Sepulveda, and pulled to a stop in front of a large mansion on Rodeo Drive. It was of Chinese design with vermilion walls and a hipped-and-gabled, tile roof. The bronze lion dogs by the entrance stood in contrast to the nearby fashion shops and BMW dealers. While Officer Mencken tried to pick the lock on the front gate, a man in a three-piece suit approached me.

"Yo, I need money for some chicken nuggets." He held up a stained paper bag. "Want to buy some crack cocaine?"

"Get out of here!" I turned away to see what progress Officer Mencken was making.

He grew frustrated with the hairpin, drew his service revolver, and fired at the lock. The wrought-iron gate squeaked open on rusty hinges. I followed Officer Mencken into a spacious reception hall filled with scrolls of calligraphy, a giant portrait of Chairman Mao, and a woman screeching a song while strumming an out-of-tune stringed instrument. We exited to the back yard. If this was indeed the empire of a fat-food mogul, I couldn't tell by the half-dozen sleek beauties in bikinis sunning themselves by the pool.

"Ah, Officer Mencken! How kind of you to join us."

A man with a head shaped like a gigantic ping-pong ball stepped through the sliding door and onto the nonskid surface. He wore a floor-length, silk robe decorated with dragons and phoenixes. To his side stood a sumo wrestler, naked except for a steel-rimmed bowler and padded jockstrap.

"Hello, Jack." Mencken hooked his thumbs in his duty belt. "You've sure come up in the world since running that burrito stand in Costa Mesa."

"Me and the bitches are about to have some sushi and miso soup." Jack gestured to the dining room inside the sliding door. "Perhaps you'd care to join us for lunch."

"It hate to break it to you, Jack, but sushi's Japanese not Chinese."

One of the women rolled face down on her towel and loosened the strap on her top. When I looked back at the men, Jack's painted-on smile had changed to an O of displeasure.

"You know what we're here for, Jack," Mencken said.

"I can assure you, officer, there are no trans fats here. I can't speak for the other guys, but my chef serves only healthy, organic fare."

Officer Mencken's nostrils twitched. "Then why do I smell hydrogen?" He turned toward the utility room that would normally house pool-cleaning supplies in an ordinary home. "You wouldn't be bubbling it through cooking oil, would you?"

The sumo wrestler let out a blood-curdling kiai and charged. Officer Mencken drew his service revolver and emptied all seventeen rounds into the man's chest, but that only seemed to make the bodyguard mad. Something had to be done! I reached into my pocket for the pistol and withdrew the Rolaids instead. Distracted by the thought of a between-meal snack, the sumo wrestler changed course and headed straight for me. As the ton of fat and muscle barreled toward me, I feared I would suffer the same fate as Asafuji in the Kyushu Grand Tournament of 2006. Then I had a brainstorm. I waited until the last possible second before stepping aside. Momentum carried the Yokozuna into the pool, where his impact raised a massive tidal wave that swept the TEC-9 machine pistol from Jack's hands.

"Good work, kid," Officer Mencken said while cuffing the soggy mastermind of evil to the wrought-iron fence.

Officer Mencken and I stood by the gate while technicians in orange, hazmat suits loaded rusty, fifty-five-gallon drums of fat and several empty spray cans onto the flatbed truck for transportation to a level-four containment facility.

"What'll happen to them?" I pointed to the thirty-five illegal Chinese who'd run the trans-fat lab. Border Patrol agents herded them single file to waiting, green and white vans.

"They'll be repatriated and no doubt end up in a forced-labor camp, where they'll manufacture the low-cost clothing you and I love." Officer Mencken slapped me on the back. "Come on. I'll drive you back to the station."

We retraced our route. By the time we pulled into the parking lot it had grown dark.

"How about if I buy you a drink?" I asked.

"No, it's not over." Light from the dashboard illuminated his face. "I'm going back to the hood to negotiate a truce between the BKs and Mickey D's."

I said goodbye to that great, public servant and got out of the car. Imagine my surprise when I saw his picture in the obituaries a few days later. Dead of a heart attack at forty-two! It must have been that French fry. However long I live Officer Mencken's final words will echo in my mind.

"Wherever there's a fight so people don't overeat, I'll be there. Wherever there's a perp heating up some fries, I'll be there. I'll be in the way of bellies swelling with fat – I'll be in the way of kids laughing when they're hungry and know donuts are on the table. And when people are eating the stuff they braise, and going to the gym three times a week – I'll be there too."

Operators Are Standing By

It was around 8:00 when I pulled my battered Toyota Corolla into the driveway. There was no sign of my fifteen-year-old son. Jason hadn't called my cell phone or left a message on the answering machine. This wasn't like him. He never acted this way on the weekends I had custody. I phoned Melissa Sawyer's mother but she hadn't seen him. I poured a glass of Charles Shaw wine and sat down to worry. At 9:00 the phone rang.

"Mr. Cromwell?" asked a man with a deep voice.

"Yes."

"Mr. Brad Cromwell, father of Jason Ridgeway?"

"Yes. Is Jason all right? Is he hurt?"

"We're questioning your son at the Department of Homeland Security at 942 West Broadway. You can pick him up at 11:00."

"Wait! Does he need a lawyer?" I heard a laugh on the other end of the line, and the phone went dead.

What kind of trouble had Jason gotten himself into? I didn't wait until 10:30. Believe you me! I jumped in my Toyota, sped down the I-5, and paid ten dollars to park in a lot near the Federal Building. I rode the elevator up to the fourth floor, signed in with the receptionist, and took a pamphlet to one of the half dozen upholstered metal chairs in the waiting room. It resembled a doctor's office except for the huge, flat-panel TV mounted on the off-white wall. Tom and Katie were on Entertainment Tonight again. There was only one other person in the room, a middle-aged black woman with straightened hair. A tan overcoat draped like the weight of the world over her heavy frame. I looked at the pamphlet.

Frequently Asked Questions about DHS Interrogations

Why am I here?
As a friend or relative of someone being interviewed by DHS, you are here to take custody of the interviewee after questioning by federal agents on matters vital to the security of the United States.

Why must DHS release this person into my care?
While in most cases follow-up medical care is not required, many interviewees are disoriented after questioning and require transportation home and a quiet place to rest. After a few days in bed most can return to their normal daily activities. Bruises and minor lacerations usually heal after a week.

How do I treat electrical burns?
Keep the blisters clean and dry. You may wish to apply a topical antiseptic, such as Neosporin.

You mentioned follow-up medical care. Who pays if the interviewee needs to see a doctor?
DHS is not responsible for medical bills. Contact your private health insurer to see if your policy covers these expenses.

A muffled scream penetrated the soundproof walls. It was not unlike Jason's cries when he'd had his first cavity filled. The wall-mounted TV drew my attention like a hypnotist. Someone had changed the channel. A chubby man in a white chef's jacket was demonstrating the Fredco Home Rotisserie. A blonde, in a turquoise dress that revealed cleavage so deep a man could get lost in there for decades, stood by and watched the chef impale two raw chickens on a skewer and insert them into the device. Through time-lapse photography the chickens were browned, moist, and cooked to perfection forty-five minutes later. Cleanup was a snap, since the skewer and drip pan popped out for easy immersion in soapy water. I watched amazed. If I moved my microwave closer to the wall, I'd have room for the rotisserie in my kitchen. I took out a pen and scribbled the 800 number on the pamphlet.

A technician in a white lab coat escorted a limping black man into the waiting room. A wad of white, surgical tape held a bloody compress the size of a tennis ball over the suspects left eye. The black woman, hauled herself to her feet, took the suspects arm, and led him out. Another moan came from behind the door.

"So how much does the Fredco Home Rotisserie cost?" the blonde asked the chubby chef.

"Well Tina, if I were to say $200, would you consider that a good deal?"

"I bet I spend more than that eating out in just a few months." Tina opened her eyes in amazement.

"How about $150?"

"Definitely a bargain," Tina said.

"If I told you that you could get the Fredco Home Rotisserie for only $99.95, what would you say then?"

"Incredible!"

"Wait! There's more! If you order in the next twenty minutes, I'll throw in the food dehydrator and the steak knives absolutely free!"

I reached for my cell phone and dialed the number I'd written on the pamphlet. There were some tense moments that night. But when I heard the friendly voice on the other end of the line, I knew everything would be okay.

The Long, Bad Good Friday

It was late April and the owners of cluttered homes were too busy thinking of chocolate Easter bunnies to employ a professional organizer. Even the criminals seemed to take the month off preferring a walk in the flower fields to theft, extortion, or murder. All this left me with nothing to do. So after reorganizing my case files, I drove to the Container Store in Mission Valley to keep up to date with the latest advances in household storage.

For me combining my passions for fighting clutter and fighting crime seems natural. Like the old catalog, you can't bring yourself to throw away, the criminal takes up precious space, space better suited for the easy chair of economic prosperity or the throw pillows of art and culture. He needs to be stored where he belongs – jail or, better yet, the morgue.

I left the storage room of Adolfo's Mexican Bakery that housed my tiny office, drove down Roosevelt, and got on the I-5 at Carlsbad Village Drive. When my Volvo got up to 65 miles per hour, the steering wheel began shimmying like a topless dancer at a limbo contest so I slowed down and pulled into the right lane. Until I caught some cases and earned enough money for Al from Al's Auto Body and Copier Repair to fix the car's torn rotator cuff, I'd have to put up with the blaring horns and extended middle fingers from my fellow drivers. Ah spring! It brings out the best in people.

I took the Friars Road exit and parked in front of the Container Store. A boy dressed in the silk robe and dog-eared hat of a Taoist sage stood by the automatic doors.

"Lao Tzu said, 'A vessel is useful for what it is not.'"

Sheer poetry! For what did the Container Store sell if not emptiness? Still the lad's words would have seemed more profound had it not been for his blonde hair, blue eyes, and smattering of acne on his chin. I pegged him for a part timer, no doubt more interested in Radiohead than organizing and the Eternal Tao. For him putting everything in its place was not the spiritual experience it was for me. But I forgot these musings once I was inside. A 10 mg IV of Valium couldn't have calmed me more than wandering through the sparkling aisles stocked with the latest storage technology. Shelves, boxes, milk crates. The razor blades of daily frustration sheathed themselves. If only the whole world could be made this neat and tidy! Sadly, the plastic shortage, that had stemmed the tide of credit card offers and public hypocrisy, had also raised the price of food-storage jars beyond my budget. I needed a case soon.

I left the kitchen section, came upon a display of acrylic shoe boxes, lifted one from the stack, and turned it over in my hands. Ah, the simplicity of design. The perfection of geometry. If I went without ramen lunches for the next two weeks, I could take it home with me. Reluctantly I set it down. For now I could only dream. When I was in the office section, I got a call on my cell phone asking me to come to the Carlsbad Library, not the old extension on Carlsbad Village Drive but the main branch on Dove Lane by the La Costa 6 Theaters. I was to meet with the chief librarian, herself. Why had I been worried? City hall always needed someone to clean up their messes and I was their guy.

As I chugged up the 805 toward the merge, I reflected on what I knew about Maude Gallagher. A political appointee with little hands-on experience, she'd enraged the veteran librarians who'd been passed over for the leadership post. She had a reputation for getting tough jobs done with a take-no-prisoners attitude. When I arrived at the library, I approached a stooped man at the reference desk. A silver chain that looped over his neck kept his glasses from wandering away and his gray hair was cut like an ancient Roman's.

"Decker," I said. "Here to see Maude Gallagher."

He scowled at the mention of the chief librarian and ushered me into a mahogany-walled office located near the self-help section.

"Ah, Mr. Decker. So good of you to come." Maude stood from behind a cluttered, oak desk and took my hand in a firm grip. "Care for a scotch?" Without waiting for a reply she poured two tumblers from a crystal decanter and handed one to me. "Glenlivet. The mayor has it flown in from Edinburgh."

I took a sip. It was smooth, smooth as the skin on her face. She was a handsome woman with salt-and-pepper hair and an athletic body that had me believing she could crush beer cans in her vagina. If this weren't a professional visit, I'd have cleared the papers off her oak desk and made love to her right there. But why would a rich and powerful woman like her be interested in a guy like me, a guy who when he goes looking for love comes away with a Swiffer mop and a package of vacuum cleaner bags?

"Mr. Decker, I need your help."

"Of course! I'd start with the papers on your desk. Divide them into three piles: those you have to work on, those that are optional and less than two weeks old, and the optional ones that have been around longer. Then every two weeks throw away the third pile."

"No, Mr. Decker. It's about books. In spite of Miss Ridley's reservations about how you handled the Kite Runner affair, I've decided to give you another chance."

"Cut the crap, Babe! We both know I'm not here for some run-of-the-mill overdue book case." The secret of dealing with the powerful is to show them they don't intimidate you. I could tell my strategy was working by the way she squeezed her lips together.

"Not for one overdue book, no." She turned her computer display so I could see. "Look at this."

It was a list of over a hundred overdue books featuring Entropy by Design checked out by Pat McGroin, a Law and Order – Victimless Crime Unit DVD checked out by Seymour Butts, and Chicken Soup for the Sociopathic Soul checked out by Mike Rotch. Other offenders had used aliases like Sarah Bellum and C.F. Icare.

"Somebody's forging library cards."

"Exactly! I want you to find out who and terminate their library privileges." She handed me an envelope packed with one-dollar bills. "Terminate them with extreme prejudice."

"Don't worry, Babe. Once I get my teeth into a case, I'm like a terrier with a vacuum cleaner nozzle." I withdrew my .50-caliber Desert Eagle from my shoulder holster and jacked a round into the chamber. The special ammo could drop a charging rhino, just the sort of stopping power the forces of righteousness needed to keep the elephants out of the atrium. "I'll need the addresses and phone numbers from the bogus application forms."

"Already done. See Brad on your way out." When I was halfway through the door, she added, "I trust I can count on your discretion. I don't need to tell you the panic that would occur if news of this got out."

"Of course." On my way out I stopped at the reference desk.

"Her highness wanted me to give you these." The male librarian lisped dragging his s's out like a Spaniard from Barthelona. He handed me a stack of photocopied library card applications.

"I take it you're not too fond of her."

"For God's sake! She thought The Life of Pi deserved the Nobel Prize in Literature. Please!" He turned his attention to the teenage girl with magenta hair who was standing behind me who asked, "Does ear wax melt like other wax and can you use it in soup?"

I left Brad to his duties and stopped for meat and cookies at the F Street Café before returning to the office and examining the applications. From the different handwritings I concluded I was dealing with a conspiracy not a lone, deranged reader. I dialed one of the phone numbers and got a recorded message saying it was out of order. A man with a gravelly voice answered when I dialed the second.

"Committee to Reelect Duke Cunningham."

"Yes, is Euripides Pants there?"

He hung up. More calls would get me nowhere so I drove to some of the addresses listed on the applications. The first took me to the cable company. I didn't go in. Those guys wouldn't know a book if it crawled out of their sphincter. The second address was an empty lot on Hemlock. The third was a warehouse in an industrial park off Palomar Airport Road.

I scouted its perimeter, noticed two workers putting old computers in the back of an unmarked step van at the loading dock, circled to the front, and entered the lobby. A plastic plant with leaves in need of dusting stood by the door. I began neatening the magazines on the coffee table. Without some Silver Mesh Magazine Files it was the best I could do. When I turned over a copy of Field and Stream, I came upon a sight that chilled my heart into a twenty-pound frozen turkey. It was how I remembered it from that fateful day – the yellow border and glossy photo of Africa on the cover. I set down the copy of National Geographic faster than I'd drop a Gila monster with halitosis, and turned to the receptionist.

"So what is this place?" I asked.

"It's a charity. We send old PCs to Nigeria to help struggling entrepreneurs start businesses."

"Have any luck?"

"Some." She pointed to a photo of a man, balancing a loaf of bread on his head, displayed in a simple, acrylic box frame. "That's Barrister Mbiko. He started an e-mail business soliciting partners to free money from abandoned bank accounts. He pulls in more than three million a year.

"Do you have an employee named," I looked at the application in my hand, "Hugh G. Rection?"

They should have hired a receptionist who was more polite to the general public. Her reaction told me I wouldn't find any answers there. There was only one thing to do, return to the library. On my way I stopped at the office and checked the mail. I had a letter from the library saying I owed a $70,000 fine for an overdue book, The Ruins of Machu Pikachoo, a book I'd never seen before. Clearly someone was trying to scare me off. But who?

When I got to the library, a woman I hadn't seen before was standing behind the reference desk. Breasts, shoulders, and hips - everything about her was filed in the right place. She had hair the color of birch Elfa Shelving, eyes as blue as a Polo Desk Chair, and a body as ergonomic as a Good Grip Grout Brush.

"Decker." I handed her the photocopies of the forged library card applications. "I need a list of all the books loaned to these patrons. It's for the chief librarian's special project."

"Of course, Mr. Decker. I'll just be a minute."

While she was getting the list, I reflected on the state of relations between the sexes. I realized I'd cut off my own uvula with a pair of rusty scissors for a woman like her. But what was the chance she'd fall for a down-on-his-luck private eye/professional organizer with a bad credit rating and one un-descended testicle? She returned a few minutes later, set a stack of papers on the desk, and leaned forward giving me a view down her shirt.

"Here you go."

"Thanks." I thumbed through the documents.

"I'm Fiona, by the way." She fanned her cleavage with a withdrawal slip. "It sure is hot in here. I could take these clothes right off." She yawned and stretched. "This heat makes me sleepy. I feel like going back to my place and crawling into bed. What about you, Decker? You feel like taking a nap?"

"No, I have work to do."

I bid Fiona goodbye and headed out. What a beauty! It was a pity she'd never go for a forty-eight-year-old guy like me, a guy with a prolapsed colon who lived in a crummy studio apartment with his mother and whose bank account balance rarely got above the double digits.

I hit the used bookstores on Carlsbad Village Drive to see if the missing library books had made it into their inventory. The Christian bookstore was a wash. But when I entered the Black Octopus, my psychic antenna received a trouble signal reading ten over seven. Maybe it was how the books were askew on the cluttered sale table or maybe it was the owner's tiny, pig-like eyes. Either way I was on my guard when I approached the counter.

"I'm looking for Eulogy for a Dead Plant. You have it?"

"Nope." The owner crossed his beefy forearms over his chest.

"How about The Great Capybara Rebellion of 1911?"

"Sorry."

"Mind if I look around?"

"It's a free country."

I wandered the stacks until a suspicious book in the cooking section caught my eye. I double-checked the printout. Indeed, The Feminist Collective Placenta Cookbook was on the list of overdue books. As I bent to retrieve it from the bottom shelf, I heard the rack of a pump-action shotgun. Milliseconds later its blast shredded copies of Julia Child and The Joy of Cooking just inches over my head. I rolled, drew my .50 caliber Desert Eagle, and sighted at the fleeing bookstore owner. I got off two wild shots but he was already out the door.

I ran after him down Roosevelt, past a skateboarder clutching a gunshot wound to his arm, and into the crowded farmers' market. A finger poke to the throat and two quick elbows to the face cleared the Cub Scout leader and his troop from my path. Overturning baby strollers and shoving grandmothers in wheelchairs out of the way, I pursued the bookstore owner past Yummy Fudge and the 911 Tamale Stand but couldn't get a clear shot. He took cover behind a pyramid of Granny Smith apples, raised his shotgun, and click.

"Game's up!" I inched forward my pistol aimed at his head. "Put down the shotgun and come out with your hands in the air."

The bookstore owner stared at the defective weapon that had betrayed him. As he bent to set it down, a shot rang out and he collapsed. Shoppers screamed and threw themselves to the ground, their artisan breads and organic tomatoes making an Abstract Expressionist collage of terror on the pavement that would have done Jackson Pollock proud. Frantically, I looked in doorways and open windows searching for anything that would give the assassin's location away. I heard the whine of a dirt bike's engine and fired two rounds at the receding, leather-clad rider with a TEC-9 slung over his shoulder. My shots went wide shattering the Washington Mutual Bank's plate glass window and setting off the car alarm of a late-model Audi in the parking lot.

In the aftermath of the shooting I sat on the curb while police radios squawked from squad cars and officers took witnesses' statements. In his off hours Detective Kobo Dashiki split his time between African dance and studying for the Shingon Buddhist priesthood. I sensed trouble at the first sight of his rumpled suit jacket.

"You know, Detective. With some closet organizers your clothes wouldn't get so wrinkled."

"You've gone too far, Decker. This time your karma's gonna catch up with you. This time I'm yanking your PI license."

"I don't think so. I got juice with city hall." With my thumb and index finger I inched my cell phone out of my jacket pocket, dialed the chief librarian, and handed it to Dashiki.

"Is a PI named Decker working for you?" Dashiki's smile sagged like a stalk of celery kept outside a Curver Food Storage Container. "Yes, Ma'am. I understand." He returned my cell phone. "I guess you're free to go." Then a manic gleam came to his eyes. "But I'll need to keep your pistol for evidence."

I handed it over. There was no other way. True, I still had the "Baby" Glock I wore on my ankle. Its hollow-point bullets could leave an exit wound the size of a 7 ½" x 6 ½" x 3 ½" clear storage box, but without my .50 caliber Desert Eagle I was vulnerable. I had to solve this case before the assassin took advantage of my weakness. Clearly, the killer had murdered the bookstore owner to keep him from talking but there had to be something I was missing, some pattern I wasn't seeing. On a hunch I dialed the chief librarian.

"Maude? Decker. I'll be in your office in half an hour. Make sure Fiona and Brad are there."

They were all assembled when I got there, Maude digging through the stack of papers on her desk that could benefit from some file organizers, Fiona reclining in an office chair with her legs parted to reveal a glimpse of panties, and Brad standing by the doorway and shifting his weight from one foot to the other.

"Thank you for meeting me here." I set my printouts on Maude's desk. "You may have heard the owner of the Black Octopus Bookstore was murdered just an hour ago. With his death all my leads have vanished."

Fiona closed her legs, Brad stopped fidgeting, and Maude continued rustling papers.

"Then I asked myself, who would benefit from embarrassing the chief librarian?" I spun on my heels until I was looking into Brad's eyes. "The veteran librarians. That's who!"

The reading glasses slipped off Brad's nose. "If you're insinuating…"

I pulled my Glock from its ankle holster and aimed it at his Mont Blanc distinguished service pen.

"As I was saying, veteran librarians would have the most to gain if Maude were to lose her job. But which librarians?" I pointed to the printouts. "I cross checked the Library of Congress numbers of the missing books with their location in the stacks. They all lie between this office and the reference desk!"

"All right. I did it…" Brad glanced at Fiona. "Jesus, Fiona! Wear a bra! Your nipples are showing!"

And indeed they were. I wanted to fondle them right there in the chief librarian's office. But why would a woman like Fiona let a guy like me touch her, a guy with an overdue student loan from 1976 and a prostate the size of a canned ham? Taking advantage of the distraction, Brad ran out. I raised my pistol and aimed.

"Stop!" Maude said. "You can't fire a gun in here. It's a library. You have to be quiet."

I pulled the throwing star from my pocket and flung it at the receding law breaker. A scream came from near the health and wellness section.

"Sorry, Mrs. Lundesborg!"

It seemed I'd have to apprehend Brad the hard way, unarmed. I drew the bolo knife from my sleeve and ran after him. Nothing motivates a man like fear. Brad ran faster than an Olympic sprinter on steroids. I caught up with him briefly by the magazine display and cut a nick out of his shoulder with my bolo knife but he toppled the magazine rack in my path tripping me up with two-month old copies of Newsweek and Sports Illustrated. Lungs burning and bunions aching, I chased him through history, current events, and fiction until I cornered him in the reference section. He held me off throwing volumes of the Encyclopedia Britannica. When he ran out of ammunition with V through Z, his eyes darted back and forth for something to save him. He fixed on the Unabridged Oxford English Dictionary, hoisted it over his head, and turned to face me.

"Don't do anything rash, Brad." I lowered my knife to appear less threatening. "Put the book down and we'll talk."

He put it down, all right, right on my head. I went out like the power in the 2003 Northeast blackout. When I came to, I was sprawled on the carpet with Brad garroting me with microfilm of the San Diego Union Tribune from 1995 to 1998. I scrambled for my bolo knife but it lay just a fraction of an inch out of reach. If only I could extend my arm…

The room began to spin as lack of oxygen made me woozy. Suddenly, I imagined myself in Donna's Rancho Santa Fe mansion seven years earlier.

"So where should we go for our honeymoon?" She raised her body on her elbow so the sheet fell away. Her breast peeked out of the gap like a one-eyed sea cucumber looking out of its cave, a very lovely sea cucumber indeed. "I know, the Maldives. There was an article some time last year."

Before I could object, she sprang from the bed and pranced into the study.

"No!" I ran after her but arrived too late.

Like a yellow Niagara Falls of death, thousands of National Geographics tumbled from the overstuffed bookshelf onto her vulnerable body and crushed her into the parquet floor. With the only woman I ever loved gone, I had nothing to live for. I took the Maldives issues from her twitching hand and prepared to bludgeon myself to death.

Then I thought of all the innocents victimized by clutter. I could not let what happened to me happen to them. From now on I would dedicate my life to fighting disorder.

Hah! I grabbed the knife, severed the microfilm, and buried the blade in Brad's windpipe. He made a gurgling sound like a garbage disposal chewing on a stainless steel teaspoon. Then he collapsed. I returned, bruised and winded but otherwise in fine spirits, to the chief librarians office with news of my success.

"Well, if you don't need me anymore," Fiona moved toward the door, "I'll get back to shelving the returns."

"Not so fast, Fiona." I intercepted her before she could get away. "When I said all the missing books came from near the reference desk, I left one out, The Feminist Collective Placenta Cookbook, the same Feminist Collective Placenta Cookbook that contains a recipe for Mediterranean Placenta Salad by a Ms. Fiona Blackwell. Brad's little scheme to embarrass Maude wasn't enough for you so you sold the missing books to the Black Octopus Bookstore. And when you thought the owner would talk, you killed him."

"Please, Decker." Fiona got down on her knees. "I had to do it. I needed the money to pay my health insurance premiums. You've got to let me go."

"No way, Fiona. You're going down."

"Okay." Her tongue traced an arc on her carmine-red lips. "Sounds like fun. You want me to do it here or in the AV room?"

I could have helped her if only she'd offered me a sign of contrition. But why would a woman like her offer sexual favors to a guy like me, a guy who suffers from both erectile dysfunction and premature ejaculation?

"I gotta hand it to you, Decker." Detective Dashiki returned my handgun. "You sure work a crazy investigation. Let's head down to the Terminal Bar for some brewskies."

"I'll meet you in a few hours, Kobo. I have some things to finish up here."

"What could possibly be left?" Maude asked after Detective Dashiki hauled Fiona away and the coroner removed Brad's body.

"We still have an hour until closing time, enough to start organizing that desk."

"All right, Decker." Maude moved close enough for me to smell her perfume, perfume as intoxicating as a hit of cocaine on a brisk, Peruvian morning. "But I must tell you that I took your advice. I put all my clothes in three piles and decided I didn't need any underwear."

As she swept the papers from her desk and lay back like a flesh-tone desk pad with non-stick backing, I wondered what her game was and more importantly whether I could still bill the city for the hour.

Radiator Dog Saves the Day

1

On a hot August morning the black lab stretched out on the concrete driveway in front of Walt's Radiator Repair. Rex was an intelligent dog, who was not easily amused. Most dogs would be content to spend a lazy summer day sleeping in the shade of an old gnarled pine tree but Rex got bored and lonely because Walt was busy working on a tan Nissan Sentra.

Rex ambled down Roosevelt to see that nice collie, who smelled of propylene glycol, but she wasn't home. Rather than head back to the shop, Rex continued his stroll. Hell, Walt would be busy until noon. Those Japanese cars always took longer to repair than the American models. It felt good to be out walking. His rear leg, made stiff by the steel pin, began to loosen as exercise warmed his muscles.

What should he do today? An image of someone he hadn't seen in months formed in Rex's mind. He remembered a man, who used to stop by the garage and rub Rex's ears. Rex had sensed the worry that burdened his friend. Acting on his concern, Rex took a right on Tamarack, until he smelled fresh ocean air. He followed the Coast Highway, turned left, and trotted down Palomar Airport Road, until he arrived at the entrance of a large modern office building.

Rex sat on his haunches in front of the glass doors. A blonde woman in a neat turquoise blouse and black skirt came out. When Rex saw her, he wagged his tail.

The woman asked, "Do you miss your master, boy?" and patted Rex on the head. She held the door open, and Rex trotted inside. He passed the gleaming silver bank of elevators, took a right down the hallway, and stopped in front of a door labeled "Electrical."

Rex inserted his nose in the gap between the frame and the door, pried the door open, and forced his way in. Once inside he stood on his hind legs, front paws resting against the wall. He furrowed his brow and cocked his head, while he studied the circuit breakers in the gray steel panel. Rex began scratching at the wiring. Blue sparks jumped from the cables and filled the air with the smell of ozone.

2

My day deteriorated after only an hour at work. Someone had found a critical flaw in the software. Now the release would be delayed for months. Pittsburgh wanted answers. Every time I tried to work on my report to Marchetti, I got side-tracked with another crisis. The latest had taken place fifteen minutes ago, when Helen informed me she was quitting in order to open a marmot farm in North Dakota.

I could have handled the stress, if I'd been able to sleep. But for the past week I'd spent nights curled into a ball of tension, gazing at shadows on the wall through bloodshot eyes. The only reprieve from my personal hell came from my friends the animals, like Thumper Cat, the neighbor's Manx, who greeted me whenever I got home.

Wondering how to phrase things, so we could all keep our jobs, I turned back to my report. When I reached for the keyboard, the screen went black. I went to the hallway and found all the fluorescent lights out.

"Server's down," said Helen.

"How do they expect us to get any work done?" I replied.

"Someone smelled smoke. We'll have to evacuate," Francine announced moments later.

I grabbed a flashlight and shepherded employees down the dark stairwell and out the front door. We stood blinking in the sunlight, while firemen checked the building. Francine called the power company.

"SDG&E says it'll take four to five hours. You might as well go home," she told us.

During the drive home, I decided to visit my old pal, the radiator dog. I parked at my place and walked over to Walt's Radiator Repair.

The radiator dog lay on the driveway, his chin resting on one paw. As I walked toward him, he raised his golden eyes to look at me and thumped his tail against the concrete.

"Hey buddy, how are you doing?"

He got slowly to his feet, stretched out his front paws lowering his head, and ambled over to me. He leaned against my knees, while I stroked the glossy black fur on his wide head.

"You look tired. Been sleeping all day?"

He found an old tennis ball and dropped it at my feet. I picked up the ball, soggy with dog drool, and tossed it into the field beside the garage. He ran after it, his floppy ears swept back by the wind, his mouth open in a big doggy smile. He moved pretty well, even with that pin in his leg. It hardly bothered him at all.

Sundaes Will Never Be the Same

I did it all for Kelly. Who wouldn't? I remember when I first saw her and how her thick, blonde braid bounced between her tanned shoulder blades and the vertical fabric of her running bra. Even from several feet away the scent of her skin whispered that here was someone solid, not just a fantasy. I even loved her imperfections, the tiny breasts, the dark spot on her eye, her awkward nose. I wanted to rest my head on her strong shoulder. I had to have her and I did but keeping her was another matter altogether.

The night I learned of the threat to my bliss started out well. We'd just made love and I lay enfolded in the marvelous warmth of her.

"I'm thinking of enrolling in this teaching program in Chicago." She sat up leaning on an elbow. "My friend Stuart went there last year. You can earn money teaching at a target school while you get your teaching certificate."

"Sounds cold!" I tugged her toward me. "Besides," I whispered, "those inner-city schools are hell."

"I've got to do something, Jimmy." She pulled away. "Look at me." She stared at her naked body. "I'm thirty-four and I can't go on earning minimum wage as an editorial assistant."

"But Chicago?"

"There aren't any jobs for me here. Maybe if I was an engineer like you but I was never good at math."

"Why don't you write text books like Natalie?"

"Jesus, Jimmy!" Kelly got out of bed, stepped into her panties, pulled up her jeans, and stomped, breasts jiggling around the bedroom. "Natalie only gets by because her father bought her that condo. Where's my fucking bra?" She searched under the bed without any luck and pulled her blouse over her head in defeat. "I'm tired. I'll call you, tomorrow."

Alone at midnight, I did what I always do when I can't sleep. I made ice cream. I heated a carton of cream in a sauce pan and added fresh thyme, stripping the tiny leaves off the stems with my fingernails. Then I turned on PBS. Once the liquid cooled, I put it in the blender with some white peaches I'd bought at Whole Foods. A pinch of salt and a half cup of sugar were all it needed before I transferred the mixture to the ice cream maker I'd bought for two dollars at a garage sale. By the time Charlie

Rose had finished interviewing Carly Fiorina, I was dipping my spoon into a bowl of frozen perfection. The herbs made it special. I put the remainder in the freezer and went to bed.

I brought the rest to Curtis and Jean's pot luck that weekend where the hosts strong-armed guests into choosing my concoction from among the cake and store-bought cookies on the kitchen counter.

"You ought to sell this shit." Curtis dropped the plastic spoon into the paper cup he'd been eating from.

"Thanks." I let his compliment roll off my back. Curtis was one of those supportive people who were great for your ego but didn't help much in the reality department.

"No, I mean it." He grabbed my arm. "You really ought to sell this shit!"

I have a theory that the road to ruin is paved with sugar. I imagine George W. Bush munching brownies while ordering troops into Iraq, Napoleon planning the Battle of Waterloo with a tummy full of peach Melba, and Bill Gates giving Windows Vista the go ahead while sipping a Frappuccino. Whether or not historians confirm my suspicions, I know my downfall began with the desserts at Curtis and Jean's party.

"I've found a local job with lots of growth opportunity for you." I refilled Kelly's wine glass. "It's an executive position at an aggressive start up."

"What is it?"

I went to the kitchen and returned with a 32-ounce plastic container I'd decorated with the equations of quantum chromodynamics.

"Vice President for Sales and Marketing of Quark Ice Cream!"

"Quark Ice Cream?"

"You know how everyone's been after me to sell my homemade ice cream? Well, I'm finally going to do it. Strictly wholesale, of course. Supply restaurants and gourmet shops. Bert over at the Ragin' Cajun said he'd take some and Ramon at Chez Monique wants some too. Your job would be to round up more customers. Since I'll be making small batches, we have to concentrate on the high-end market, people who'll pay top dollar for quality and style. I can't pay you much to start so I'll give you forty-percent ownership in the company. What do you say?"

"Jimmy, you don't have to do this."

"I know, sweetheart. I want to. I've had this dream for a long time. It would be a shame not to pursue it. So how about it? Are you on board?"

"Okay." She laughed, tossed the container into the air, and caught it. "But where did you come up with Quark?"

"A unified field theory of taste!"

I spent $2000 for a commercial freezer and another $500 for plastic containers with the Quark logo.

"Mind if I take an hour to run a few errands?" I asked Sharon, my boss at Digitronics on Monday morning.

"Go ahead." She barely looked away from her computer monitor.

It took a half hour to drive to my destination in to El Cajon. Henkelmeyer's Ice Cream had been in the same one-story, concrete building since the 1960s. I entered and waited while a woman in a candy-striped blouse packed scoops of chocolate and peppermint to a precarious height on a sugar cone for a Latina girl.

"I'm here to see Mr. Henkelmeyer," I said.

"Harry!" the clerk yelled. "Somebody's here to see you!"

A gnomish man emerged from the inky shadows. With his curly hair and mustache he could easily have been mistaken for former Israeli Prime Minister Yitzhak Shamir.

"Help you?" He wiped his hands on his apron.

"I'm Jimmy Sandoval. We talked about you making some ice cream, twelve 2.5-gallon containers." I unfolded the paper I'd taken from my pocket and handed it to him. "Here's the recipe. I scaled the quantities up from two quarts."

"Peaches, thyme," Henkelmeyer said after putting on his reading glasses. "$1200!"

I swallowed. "That's a bit out of my price range. Can you do anything cheaper?"

"The peaches got to be fresh?"

"I guess not."

"Okay, I'll use canned. Save $200 on the ingredients and labor."

"I don't know about canned. What if we reconstituted dried ones in hot water?"

"Fine. My cousin makes salad dressing for Henkel's Own. He can get all the tarragon we want. Cheap! Save you another $100."

I nodded. "Do a good job and I'll probably give you a dozen orders a week." You have to say these kind of things in business.

"That'll be $900 for twelve containers of peach-tarragon." He made some notes on the recipe. "Will that be cash or credit card?"

Wearing a black gown that revealed the honey-toned skin of her back and shoulders, Kelly was waiting for me when I got home from work.

"Put a jacket and tie on." She wrapped her arms around me and grabbed my ass. "I'm taking you to dinner."

"What's this a…"

"Just do it." She shoved me toward the bedroom.

After a chaotic ride in her Volvo, we arrived at a candlelit table for two arrayed with enough cutlery to service a dozen diners at Sizzler. The food was exquisite, flavored foams, frozen spheres of gazpacho in cones of Spanish ham, and Chilean sea bass cooked sous vide and topped with gold leaf. Kelly waited until dessert, tamarind sorbet sprinkled with chili powder, to make her announcement.

"I got us Honey Bees. I know you wanted strictly high-end but they'll buy an order a week for each of their nine San Diego locations." She took a sip of wine. "Am I good or am I good?"

"You're fantastic!"

"That's why I quit my other job so I can work for you full time."

"Here's to the American dream, baby!" I touched my glass to hers.

On Wednesday I arrived at work at 8:30 and tried to concentrate on signal processing algorithms but my mind drifted from Nyquist's Theorem to Kelly. Had she picked up the order from Henkelmeyer? Who would she deliver to first? All morning images of my smiling customers fought for attention with C++ programming. Around 12:30 I grabbed a turkey sandwich from the cafeteria and ate at my desk so I'd be ready for the 1:00 design review. As I was crumpling the wrapping paper, my cell phone rang. It was Bert.

"Jimmy, I thought you promised me something special! If I'd have wanted pumpkin, I could have gotten it at half the price and I would have waited for Thanksgiving!"

"What are you talking about? It's peach-herb."

"Have you tasted it?"

Just then Sharon stuck her head into my cubicle. "You ready?"

"Look Bert, I've got to go. I'll sort it out. Okay?" I hung up. "Just give me a sec, Sharon."

I dialed Kelly. After five rings her phone transferred me to voice mail.

"The party you're trying to reach… Kelly Martin… is not available. Please leave a message after the tone."

"Come on, damn it." I drummed my fingers on the desk waiting for the beep. "Kelly, it's Jimmy. Something's wrong! Don't deliver any more ice cream. I'll explain later."

I set my cell phone to vibrate and dashed to the conference room. If this had been any other day, I would have blown the meeting off but the engineering vice president was there. I couldn't get out of it. I don't recall how the meeting started. I only remember sitting through Anderson's dreary Power Point slides while my cell phone vibrated like a rattlesnake.

"As you can see the BPSK gives better performance at low signal to noise than QPSK."

I stared at the graphs of bit error rate versus signal to noise ratio while my plans went down in flames. Kelly better have gotten my message or else we could kiss Honey Bees goodbye.

"Of course, we get better throughput with QAM," Anderson droned.

I looked at my watch. When would this damn thing end? I should have seen it. Henkelmeyer screwed me so I wouldn't become competition. I swore to God. If that bastard didn't refund my money, I'd burn down his store.

"Jimmy," Sharon said.

"What?"

"How's the filtering going?"

All the faces were looking at me.

"Oh, uh, we're right on track."

"But we've never used QAM before," the vice president said. "How do you expect to balance performance with sampling rate?"

I did what I do best under pressure. I improvised.

"I don't know if you're familiar with the Lobachevsky method. A group at UC Berkeley applied it to QAM and got a fourfold reduction in bit error rate. I won't bore you with the details. It has to do with eigenvectors in signal space. I could have spent time going over the same old methods but considering that kind of improvement I thought it better to do a little research."

The VP frowned and scribbled in his notebook. The meeting went on for another hour. As soon as it ended, I called Kelly and chanted, "Please God. Please God," while her phone rang.

"Hello."

"Kelly, please tell me you didn't deliver the rest of the ice cream!"

"As soon as I got your call, I stopped but I'd already dropped off half the orders."

"Honey Bee's?"

"No."

"Thank God. I'll see you later."

I hung up and phoned the ice cream parlor.

"Henkelmeyer, you son of a bitch! You don't mess with Jimmy Sandoval and get away with it. You're dead. Understand? Dead!"

Anderson chose that moment to walk past.

"Sorry Fred." I covered the phone's mouthpiece. "Contractors."

I spent the rest of the afternoon searching the web for commercial ice cream machines and settled on the Fiorenza 2000. It was beautiful, brushed chrome steel and curves like those on a Dallas cheerleader. I could just see it in the living room next to the commercial freezer. Sure it cost $5000 but I'd have to spend the money eventually. I placed the order and added an extra ten percent for rush delivery.

I stayed home Friday to accept delivery. I'd planned to go to work after the Fiorenza 2000 arrived but how could I resist making one batch? I'd reconstituted the dried peaches and stocked the refrigerator with cream the previous night so all I had to do was blend with sugar and tarragon before feeding the mixture into the machine. It was beautiful. The Fiorenza's hum sounded like the Hallelujah chorus to my ears and all without the need to add ice. Twenty minutes later I filled half a container and tasted the result. Ambrosia! It was peachy! It was tarragony! It was not pumpkiny!

I checked my watch. There was still time to make another batch. That's how the wasted afternoon began. For me making ice cream is like smoking crack. Once I start, it's impossible to quit. I kept the ice cream maker's freezing cylinder spinning like an Iranian uranium enrichment centrifuge. By mid afternoon I'd filled twelve containers. Instead of going to work for a few hours I phoned Kelly. We would deliver the orders together.

As our reward for a job well done we spent the night drinking plum wine and making love. The phone woke me the next morning. It was Bert.

"Jimmy, what's with you? You gave me the stinking pumpkin again."

I walked naked to the kitchen and tasted some of the leftover ice cream. Overnight it had undergone a strange, alchemical transformation. The good news was that in the event of a pumpkin shortage, I had a substitute, one that cost three times as much.

Bert met me at the loading dock in back of the Ragin' Cajun. He was a big man, six feet tall and almost as wide. He stood with his arms crossed over his chest and the container of afflicted ice cream at his feet.

"Sorry Bert." I gave him the wrinkled one-hundred-dollar bill that had already changed hands three times.

"I'll give you just one more chance, Jimmy." He stuffed the bill in the pocket of his white, chef's jacket.

"Thanks, man. You won't regret it."

"Just one thing." He lifted the ice cream container. "No more peaches and no more herbs."

"You got it." Technically, that was two things but who was I to argue.

Relieved that the confrontation hadn't gotten violent, I hauled the container to my car. I could have taken Kelly with me but I was the owner. Apologizing was my responsibility, not hers. Besides, someone had to buy supplies for the next batch while I was busy groveling. A stray dog was nosing around the dumpster by my car. He had a wiry coat and Porky-Pig tail, a terrier-Akita mix no doubt. He was thin. No doubt he hadn't eaten in a while.

"How you doing, boy? Hungry?" I set the ice cream down by him and pulled off the lid.

The stray approached the ice cream as if it were a ticking bomb, sniffed, and turned away.

When I got home, Kelly met me at the door.

"Good news!" She held up a bottle of wine. "You know how you always say we have to use the best ingredients? Well, instead of buying three-bill swill I bought two cases of this wonderful Shiraz for your wine ice cream. It costs a little more but I wouldn't work for a company that sells junk." She poured me a glass.

It was good until I looked at the price. Even at $100, I'd be losing $10 on each container of ice cream I sold. Still it might smooth things over with the angry customers. Kelly and I fired up the Fiorenza. While we were loading it with wine and cream, the doorbell rang. It was a sheriff's deputy.

"James Sandoval?" He looked at the assembly line in the living room and raised his eyebrows.

"Yes."

He handed me a restraining order that said I was to keep away from Murray Henkelmeyer, his store, and his employees.

"I was meaning to apologize," I said. "It was a misunderstanding."

"I just deliver the paperwork." He handed me a clipboard. "Sign here."

"Jimmy, it was fantastic, a work of culinary genius! If you keep this up, I'll have to triple my order."

"Thanks, Bert. Glad you liked it. I'll have another batch for you Thursday." I hung up and turned my attention to the computer in my office cubicle.

With the ice cream crisis solved I could finally concentrate on my real job. I set up a simple Monte Carlo routine to model the receiver output, fed this into a filter function, and sent the output to a demodulator. When I began the simulation, a bunch of hexadecimal garbage filled the monitor.

"Shit!" I pressed control-alt-delete to reboot the computer.

In my confusion I hadn't noticed Sharon standing in the entryway.

"We need to talk," she said.

I followed her to her office where the engineering VP was standing by the window and looking through the Venetian blinds.

"You've been distracted lately." Sharon slid into her chair and opened the folder on her desk.

"We haven't been happy with your performance." The VP let the blinds drop and turned away from the window.

"Sorry, some problems at home," my voice squeaked. "Everything's under control now."

Sharon's eyes softened with a hint of sympathy.

"I'm afraid that's not good enough." The VP sat down. "Hexagon's crucial to this company's future and I can't have anyone on my team who isn't totally committed."

"I understand, sir. I sorted all my problems out and am ready to devote one hundred ten percent."

"Here's a check for your outstanding wages along with your unused vacation time." Sharon slid the folder toward me. "This also explains how to continue your health insurance under COBRA."

"You're firing me? I can't believe you're firing me after all the weekends I worked on the NSD project!"

"Jimmy, please," Sharon said.

"Nobody can rest on their laurels in today's business environment." The VP's eyes narrowed. "If you don't pull your weight, you're out of here. It's that simple."

I went back to my desk and began loading my things in a box, pens, pencils, the coffee cup that saw me through so many long nights, and the Dr. Evil action figure the signal processing manager had given me after I led the encryption team. Maybe it was for the best. Maybe the universe was telling me to give up the distractions and commit myself wholeheartedly to the ice cream business. In a year I'd be laughing at Sharon and that idiot VP.

I carried the box filled with my former career to the parking lot. It was surprisingly light. As I circled my Toyota Camry, I was already formulating my plan B. If my orders tripled and I made $50 on each tub of ice cream, I could clear $60,000 a year after paying Kelly. It wasn't outstanding but I could live on it. I rested the box on the bumper while opening the trunk. I'd probably have to buy a bigger vehicle to handle all the deliveries.

A middle-aged woman in a gray pantsuit was waiting at the door when I got home.

"Is this the," she looked at her clipboard, "Quark Ice Cream Company?"

"That's right." I set the box down and unlocked the door.

"I'm Gail Wexler from the Liquor Control Board." She followed me inside. "We've had a complaint that you've been selling alcohol to minors."

"Me? Selling alcohol? Ridiculous!"

She held up an empty container of Quarks' wine flavor.

"Oh! Well, I sold Shiraz ice cream to restaurants. If it's anybody's fault, it's theirs."

"You make ice cream here?" She looked at the Fiorenza 2000 and freezer in my living room.

I nodded.

"All right," she said. "Thanks for your time."

"I'm citing you for running a food business without a public health license." The county health inspector tore the yellow copy off a form and handed it to me.

"Look." I held up my hands. "I'm new at this. Okay?"

"You really have a mess here. Your ingredients are improperly stored and your cleaning of utensils is spotty at best. Have you even taken a food safety course?"

I sighed. "What do I have to do to make this good?"

"Look, you can't do this here." The inspector dropped his arms to his sides. "Pay the fine and move your operation to a proper facility and I won't shut you down."

I didn't feel like going out but I'd already promised to take Kelly to see the director's cut of "An Unmarried Woman" at an art house theater in Kensington. When I arrived at her apartment, she was on the phone.

"That's great!" She motioned for me to sit and closed the door. "I always believed in you, Stuart. Yeah, love you too. Bye." She hung up and spoke to me while she changed her blouse in the bedroom. "Things are really going well in Chicago. Stuart completed his probation period. He really loves his kids."

"Good for him."

I had to do something. When Kelly emerged putting in an earring, I spoke.

"Kelly, you've done a kick-ass job." I handed her two hundred-dollar bills leaving my wallet more or less empty. "In fact, things are going so well that we're expanding into a new facility." Some may call my failing to mention the health inspector a lie of omission. I call it creative spin. "So why don't you line up some out of town customers? Try North County or even Irvine."

"Wonderful." She wrapped her arms around me.

I was pretty sure Kelly was satisfied but I had to solve the next problem, money. I needed a commercial space but I'd already blown through my savings and no bank would give me a loan. Fortunately, Bert knew someone who could help.

On Saturday afternoon I met Mrs. Li in a deserted Chinese restaurant on Convoy. It was one of those upscale places with a fish tank loaded with those goldfish that had heads that looked like penises. As I approached her table, the bodyguard, a man with a shaved head who was the size of a sumo wrestler, stood and moved out of earshot. As with most Asians, Mrs. Li's skin was smooth so I couldn't really tell her age.

"You must be Jimmy. Do you like Pu Erh tea? It's good for the digestions." She poured me a cup without waiting for my response.

The tea had a musty flavor I didn't care for at all but the deep-fried rice cakes filled with sweet bean paste were much better.

"Thanks for seeing me. I…"

Mrs. Li held up her hand for quiet. She said nothing, merely drank her tea and stared at me with eyes that were hard as obsidian. Sitting in the uncomfortable silence I felt my armpits itch with the first drops of sweat. Maybe this was a mistake. Maybe I should get out of there. As I was about to leave, she spoke.

"Twenty thousand dollars." She placed an envelope on the table. "You will repay me twenty-four in three months. If not, you will get to know Mr. Wong."

The bodyguard cracked his knuckles and smiled revealing a gold tooth.

It took a month to rent a space, furnish it with a kitchen, and get it past inspection. During that time I paid Kelly with the loan shark's money. I even gave her a raise to keep her from getting any more ideas about

Chicago. When I was finally ready to resume production, Mr. Wong paid a visit to my new space.

"Mrs. Li sends her greetings." He smiled showing the gold tooth and walked inside uninvited. "Very impressive but will you be able to repay the loan on time?"

"Are you kidding? I have so many customers lined up it'll be a snap. See that?" I pointed to the ice cream machine. "That might as well be a machine for printing money."

Later that day I called Bert to see how much wine ice cream he wanted.

"Jimmy, that flavor is so last season. Even Henkelmeyer is making it, and at half the price you charge."

Henkelmeyer! The bastard had to have planted an informant somewhere. If I could deliver a different flavor to each customer, I could find the rat by seeing which flavor Henkelmeyer copied. Or maybe I could make a flavor so awful that he'd lose business if he copied it. Bacon, yeah bacon would screw him. What was I thinking? I had to earn money fast. To do that I needed a flavor he couldn't make money copying and I knew what it was.

Saffron, the most expensive spice in the world! It's made from the stigma of crocus flowers. Workers pick 75,000 blossoms by hand just to get a pound of the stuff. If you wanted to buy it, it would cost over a thousand bucks. I needed a cheap supply, something that would undercut Henkelmeyer, and I knew just where to look, the Axis of Evil.

The black burqa covered the woman from head to foot except for the tiny opening for her eyes, a rectangle that reminded me of something savage and medieval like the window of a prison cell. When I saw her leaving the Al Hamod Market on El Cajon Boulevard, I almost turned away but I had no choice. If I didn't earn enough money to repay the loan shark, I'd be dead or wish I was.

I entered and wandered the deserted aisles looking at dried fava beans and cans decorated with flowing Arabic script. There were desiccated lemons, bottles of pomegranate juice, dried white berries, and flat breads but no saffron. I approached the man behind the cash register. He was obviously a graduate of the Mahmoud Ahmadinejad school of fashion wearing a suit jacket over his open-collared shirt.

"Do you have any saffron?" I asked.

He reached under the counter and produced a few orange threads in a clear container not much larger than a thimble.

"I was thinking of buying in bulk." I leaned closer and lowered my voice. "Maybe you've got some product from Iran. If you can arrange delivery, I'll pay cash."

"You want to do business with Iran?" The cashier fingered his scraggly beard.

"Yes."

"And you want to buy in quantity?"

I nodded.

"I'm sorry," he said. "I didn't hear you."

"Yes."

"And you will distribute this powder how?"

"I'm going to put it in ice cream."

"FBI! On the ground, motherfucker!"

The door to the back room burst open and a dozen men with pistols flooded the room. Somehow I went from staring open-mouthed at the cashier to face down on the concrete with a knee on my neck and my hands cinched behind my back. Nose aching I was hauled to my feet and frog-marched outside past a group of burqa-clad gawkers and into a black SUV with tinted windows.

They drove me to an unmarked, government building and hustled me into a tiny room, where I waited alone for over an hour. Eventually a man in his mid forties entered and took a seat.

"We know about the anthrax," he said. "If you tell us about the plot, things will go easier for you."

I stared at my interrogator across the gray, steel table. How could this be happening?

"I only wanted to make ice cream," I said.

In prison you have to be in a gang to survive. It's a fact of life. Black, Aryan, Mexican or the gang I was placed in by default, Muslim terrorist. Needless to say, the latter was not popular with most of the prison population. It started as soon as I arrived and walked the dreary corridor toward my cell.

"Hey Osama, I'm gonna cut your balls off!"

"You're dead, camel fucker!"

The hoots and catcalls continued long after the guard locked me in my cell. The accommodations were a definite step down in my quality of life, a thin mattress, gray concrete walls, and a steel toilet with no seat. Then again, you have to stay alive to have a quality of life. On the bright side I had the place to myself since any cell mate would most likely kill me.

Meals brought back all the insecurities of high school. After receiving a block of hamburger, peanut butter, and oats fried into something resembling (and tasting like) a brick, I carried my tray into the dining hall and looked for a table. In high school the worst that could happen if you sat at the wrong table would be getting ridiculed by the jocks. Here I could get a knife in my kidney. As I wandered among the denim shirts, tattoos, and testosterone, I heard hostile whispers.

"Keep moving, asshole!"

"Not here, Osama!"

I sat at the only table available, the one where the guys with long beards had saved me a place. We ate in silence, me sawing at my so-called lunch with the flimsy plastic knife and my companions looking at me out the corners of their eyes. All had dark facial hair and olive skin. One had a long scar on his cheek and wore some kind of skullcap. Though he had a slight build, the others deferred to him by setting down their forks when he paused and only picking them up when he resumed eating. His eyes had a fanatical intensity, bright blue irises floating in yellowed sclera. When he finished eating, he turned to me and spoke with the voice of the desert wind on sandpaper.

"You should grow your beard."

What choice did I have? Despite having beards that had grown out red and patchy in the past, I quit shaving and suffered the maddening itch on my face. Meals continued in silence until a week later.

"You will come to prayers on Friday," the leader told me. "Tell the guards. They will not interfere with your 'religious freedom.'"

On Friday night a guard escorted me into a classroom. The chairs had been moved against the walls and a half dozen men from the lunch table were prostrating while the man with the skullcap sang in Arabic. I joined them and then while kneeling listened to a sermon in a language I didn't understand. When the guard got bored and left, the man in the skullcap turned toward me as did the others, all dark eyes and scowls. How long would it take the guard to come save me if I screamed? The man in the skullcap took a step toward me, and then another.

"Brother!" He wrapped his arms around me and pulled me to my feet.

Someone turned on a tape of Middle Eastern music and I was surrounded with hugs and slaps on the back.

"You are a hero!" A man pumped my hand. "My name is Rashid Talibani. You may call me RT."

"I lost three fingers making a bomb to blow up the Zionists but in my wildest dreams I would never have tried what you attempted!"

"I am Hassan." The man with the skullcap put his arm around my shoulder. "Come. We will eat."

One of the men broke out a pack of Fig Newtons and passed it around.

"I am sorry, my friend. This is all I can offer. Some day you will come to my village and we will have a real feast." Hassan sat and motioned me to do the same. "So tell me. What is your theory of jihad?"

"Jihad?" The cookie caught in my throat. "Jihad, well I think the idea behind jihad is to attack your enemy."

"Exactly! So simple yet so profound. Tell me. How did you come up with your plan?"

"It was nothing. Really."

"You're too modest." Hassan embraced me while addressing the others. "See? It's like I always told you. A real jihadi must be humble."

I guess the popularity went to my head. There's nothing that boosts the ego like hardened enemy combatants pointing to you in the hall and asking, "Hey, my friend! How are you doing?"

They wanted my advice too.

"Do you think nerve gas or plastic explosives are more effective in our struggle?"

Intoxicated with my newfound fame, I ignored my companions' shortcomings, the hangings, the beheadings of foreign journalists, and all that tedious talk about enriching uranium. I began playing the terrorist role model with more gusto, lecturing my new friends on the need to give our lives at a moment's notice to show our commitment to the cause. What harm could it do? We were locked in prison. There was absolutely no chance I'd ever be called on to back up my reckless words. Hassan praised me at our Friday meetings.

"Ah Jimmy, with a hundred men like you at my side, we could bring back the caliphate."

One Tuesday morning a guard told me someone had come to see me. I followed him to a room where reinforced glass separated prisoners from their visitors. I scanned for an empty booth until the guard tapped me on the shoulder and pointed. There she was! My Kelly! I rushed to the booth and picked up the phone.

"Kelly! Thank God!"

She'd dressed modestly in slacks and a loose blouse that hid her magnificent figure but I'd never seen her more beautiful.

"Jimmy, I've been worried sick." She winced as if I'd run over her hamster or something.

I realized she'd seen me stroking my fundamentalist beard.

"They…" She sobbed. "They said you were planning to do horrible things."

"It's not true, Kelly. You know me. I would never hurt anyone."

"Are you all right?"

"I'm fine."

We talked about her questioning by the FBI and how much we missed each other.

"We're trying to get you out," she said. "So don't worry, darling. I'm running our business. Mr. Henkelmeyer has been very helpful."

"Henkelmeyer!" I slammed my fist on the table. "I'll kill that bastard!"

Kelly flinched and covered her ears while I pounded the phone on the glass. Within seconds three big guards came and hauled me away.

"My friend," Hassan said. "Is it true that a jihadi must act immediately when an opportunity presents itself?"

"Of course," I said.

We were outside in the exercise yard. On the opposite side a bunch of skinheads were working out with free weights. Hassan had told the guards it was a special holiday that required outdoor worship so the whole terrorist crew was with us.

The armed guards in the towers took little notice when Hassan began chanting and walking toward the other side of the yard. The others followed repeating every fifth or sixth syllable. I did the same feeling a little foolish. We kept walking and I began to worry about getting into a fight with the skinheads. When he saw us coming, the biggest one sat up from doing bench presses. He must have weighed two hundred eighty pounds and he had a physique fit for violence. I looked back and forth between the terrorist and the skinheads. How far would I go with this? If these guys pulled knives, Hassan could just forget it. The confrontation never happened. Instead the big guy merely dried himself with his shirt and left with his friends.

Suddenly a hurried conversation in Arabic broke out. Hassan dived for a backpack hidden among the weights and tore it open. Eager hands reached for the grenades he passed out. RT threw one into a guard tower. It exploded sending the men inside careening through the air. Gunfire broke out. The scene was a confusion of smoke and bearded terrorists with grenade pins in their teeth. The man beside me fell to the ground grasping his belly. I felt something heavy placed in my hand.

"Pull the pin, Jimmy! Pull the pin!"

I threw the thing as hard as I could to get it away from me. An explosion knocked me off my feet. Hooded gunmen firing Kalashnikovs entered through the hole in the prison wall.

"We're free, brothers! We're free!"

A white pickup truck stops. A dozen turbaned men get out of the bed and enter my store. They stand around fingering their beards and fiddling with their assault rifles until the leader speaks.

"I would like two scoops of tutti frutti in a cone."

Since escaping from prison two years ago, I've turned my store, Infidel's Ice Cream, into the largest ice cream parlor in Pakistan's Federally Administered Tribal Areas. I'm safe here. The Pashtuns have given me refuge. It hasn't been a bad life exactly. I can get all the saffron I want along with other flavors like dried lemon, sumac, and even opium.

If you're reading this, I ask you not to believe the rumors that I was a sleeper agent or that I killed seven guards in my escape. I'm a peaceful guy who loves making ice cream. That's all. And if you can get word to Chicago, tell Kelly I miss her.

I dip my scoop into the tub of multicolored ice cream. If there's one thing I've learned from my misadventures, it's this. Just add enough fat and sugar and you can make anything taste good.

Missionary Position

"You want something, Mr. Terry?" The bra-less Indian girl moved closer to the table so the corner lifted the already short hemline of her tattered, silver dress even higher.

"A line for me and my amigo." Terry Elgan placed a few ten-thousand-peso notes on the table and slid them toward the girl's smooth thighs.

"Thanks, Rev." The other man at the table, an Aussie named Gilroy, raised his bottle of Aguila beer in salute. Gilroy was a squat, muscular man with shoulder-length blonde hair whose khaki, gringo vest marked him as a tourist. Nobody who'd been in Colombia for more than a few weeks would be caught dead in one of those.

Minutes later the girl returned with a mirror complete with two lines of cocaine on its surface. Within seconds after she set it down, the first line had already disappeared up Gilroy's nose.

"Ah, this is the life." Terry bent forward and snorted the second line with the same rolled up bill that Gilroy had used. "All this and wholesale prices too." He leaned back as the jolt of excitement slammed his nervous system.

"So." Gilroy rubbed his nose. "I'm taking those two German girls clubbing, tonight. Want to come?"

"Why Gilroy, I'm surprised at you! Asking a man of the cloth to go out whoring with you!" Terry's laughter broke out into a series of coughs. "Not tonight, mate. I have to write my monthly report to the home office." He motioned to the serving girl. "Juanita, I need a little physical therapy."

She led him by the hand up the rickety stairs to the bedrooms that were rented by the hour.

Dear Mrs. McNulty,

Sorry not to have written earlier but I've been a little under the weather. Fortunately, the chloroquine seems to have the malaria on the run and I should be back on my feet in a few days. Ramon has been like a mother hen. I know I should be grateful but it's hard to sit on my hands after making so much progress converting the FARC guerrillas. You remember Subcomandante Marcos? Well, he agreed to let me preach a sermon to the camp next time I visit. That is if I can stop Ramon's fretting about my return to the jungle bringing on a relapse.

Sadly, things have been difficult in San Cristobal. The police arrested Maria's son on some trumped up charge and I had to bribe them with the church renovation money to free him. This delayed needed repairs but Id' gladly put up with leaky pipes and peeling paint to know that a member of my flock is safe. Although, if you could see fit to send a little extra in next month's remittance, we could sure put it to use.

Yours in Christ,
Terry

He clicked the send button and a swarm of electrons raced away carrying his e-mail from San Cristobal, Colombia to the Pan American Gospel Fellowship in Raleigh, North Carolina. The words had come easily to Terry that night. No doubt they'd been fueled by the afternoon's pharmacological stimulation. He left the cyber café and hurried down sidewalks jammed with peddlers' wares on the cement. Hopefully, he'd make it to the Papagayo Hotel before Gilroy and the German girls left for the night.

━━━━━━━━━━━━━━━━━━━━━━━━━━━━━━━━━━━━━━━

He was alone on a dark, deserted street, his footsteps echoing off the walls of brick buildings. Something didn't feel right. He stopped but the footsteps didn't. He turned. A dodo bird in a leather jacket, Tasmanian tiger, giant passenger pigeon with a baseball bat, and some kind of zebra with stripes on only half its body were tailing him. When he crossed the street, the animals followed. When he quickened his pace, they matched his stride. He reached into his pocket for his Glock pistol and realized he'd left it in his car. He ran.

"Can't you go any faster than that?" The zebra laughed while galloping beside him.

He was so surprised to hear the animal talk that he almost didn't notice the passenger pigeon swinging the bat from above. He ducked in the nick of time and the Louisville Slugger whooshed over his head.

Heart hammering and breath ragged he came to the top of a crest. The parking lot was on the other side of the river. He could see his Hummer in aisle G. Muscles burning he made for the bridge. As he set foot on the metal, he heard a growl behind him and felt the Tasmanian tiger's teeth puncture his ankle. Stumbling, pain stabbing with each step, he forced himself to keep going, the thought of the Glock in his hands drawing him onward. He knew that if he looked back he was a goner.

The passenger pigeon landed in front of him and held the baseball bat tapping it against its palm. Terry skidded to a halt and turned to see the others approaching.

"What do you want from me?"

"Payback," the Tasmanian tiger growled.

"But I never did anything to you."

"You made us extinct." The dodo bird flicked open a butterfly knife.

"Yeah, happy Urf Day, motherfucker," the zebra said.

Terry looked back and forth. There was only one way out. He climbed onto the rail and jumped.

Green light woke him. It was everywhere. Like a drowning man Terry thrashed until he clawed the sheet off his face. His head hurt. He'd never mix cocaine and barbiturates again. The naked woman next to him was sitting up with her skinny, tattooed arms crossed over her D-cup breasts.

"Who are you?" he asked.

She answered in German, not the harsh German of World War II movies but the sexy German of Marlene Dietrich and fishnet stockings. Terry understood none of it but he liked its tone. He also liked the decaying elegance of the woman's bruised thighs and her dyed hair's black roots. After learning several new words for a woman's body parts he searched the threadbare hotel room for his pants and found them soaking in the bathtub. He took a soggy walk to his own hotel, changed, and returned to the cyber café to check on his remittance.

My Dear Reverend Elgan,

Barbara has been forwarding your monthly reports to me and I'm impressed with your selfless dedication to the Lord's work. Each year the trustees award the ten-thousand-dollar Herman K. Walters Grant to the missionary who best represents the Fellowship's work. I'm proud to announce that you are this year's winner. The funds will be in your next remittance.

Yours truly,
Bishop Alvin Townsend

Ten thousand dollars! Terry clapped his hands and spun his chair in a circle. With that much money guaranteed he could put a long-delayed plan into practice. An hour later he was standing in front of the iron gate outside the largest mansion in San Cristobal.

"I'd like to see El Gordo," he said into the intercom.

A remote-controlled motor swung the gate open. Terry entered and followed the driveway past Mercedes and BMWs to the front door where a bodyguard, whose suit jacket was too small for his massive upper body, frisked him. Once satisfied Terry carried no concealed weapons the man showed him into a wood-paneled study where the drug lord was watching soccer on a flat-panel TV that covered an entire wall.

"Sir," Terry said, "I'd like to offer a business proposition that could benefit us both."

Despite his nickname El Gordo was surprisingly thin. He wore a scarlet smoking jacket and sat in a La-Z-Boy recliner.

"Go on." El Gordo set down his cognac.

"You might say I'm an expert on tourism. The local attraction that draws the most visitors from all over the world is your fine product but the problem is distribution. That's where I come in. If you could advance me a kilo, I'll repay you once I've sold it." Terry folded his arms satisfied that even if he didn't sell anything, he could still repay the drug lord with his award money.

"A kilo? You want me to sell you a kilo?" El Gordo's laughter could be heard all the way in Medellin. "My friend, I only deal in quantity." He looked Terry up and down while holding his cigar between his knuckles like an extended middle finger. "What the hell! You amuse me. I'll front you a kilo but beware of Colombians with chainsaws, my friend. You saw the movie 'Scarface?' Well, if you don't repay me, the same will happen to you."

The bodyguard ushered Terry out and after a bit of a delay produced a bag of white powder, which Terry hid in an Adidas shopping bag but not before trying a little sample. Once outside the mansion the flowers were a deeper red and the peoples' smiles glowed as if they'd used radioactive toothpaste. What was so bad about radioactive toothpaste, anyway? Terry's pulse sounded like hail on a corrugated tin roof and he practically skipped back to the hotel. He was so absorbed in his plans that he didn't notice the unmarked car tailing him. The next thing he knew, two guys in sunglasses and leather jackets had shoved his face against a wall and handcuffed his wrists behind his back. The larger of the two spun him around.

"Hey man, what the f…"

"I'm Captain Benitez of the San Cristobal Police." The smaller cop fished the passport out of Terry's pocket. "You're under arrest for narcotics possession."

They hustled Terry into the back seat and drove off turning left on Calle Libertador away from the city center and police station. Out of a haze he began to recognize this for what it was.

"All those lawyers and courts are so inconvenient. Don't you agree?" Terry twisted to take the weight off his handcuffed wrists. "Perhaps I could pay you the fine."

"Fine?" Captain Benitez said. "I could lock you up for twenty years."

Terry began bargaining. The big cop took a meandering drive while they negotiated the bribe and after a tour of beautiful, downtown San Cristobal they settled on three thousand dollars. That and the price of the confiscated cocaine would use up Terry's award money. It was a painful lesson but at least it was one he could walk away from in one piece.

"Just one thing," Terry added. "It'll take me a few days to put together the money."

"Three thousand five hundred," Captain Benitez said as he stored Terry's passport in the glove compartment.

When the car stopped in front of Terry's hotel, the big cop unlocked the handcuffs and released him.

Terry was already coming down from the cocaine when he returned to the cyber café and found another e-mail from the bishop.

My Dear Reverend Elgan,

There's been a change of plans. Your messages of hope have so inspired me that I want to see your ministry with my own eyes. Therefore, I'm coming to Colombia to award your check personally. I'm really looking forward to it. It'll do this old preacher's heart good to get out in the field again. I arrive on the 15th.

Yours truly,
Bishop Alvin Townsend
PS – Sadly, since most of my outreach was spent in Africa, my Spanish is not up to snuff. If you could have someone pick me up at the airport, I would greatly appreciate it.

Terry stared at the monitor. Each blink of the cursor brought him closer to destruction. If the bishop found out he had no church, it would all be over. Everything began to irritate him, cigarette smoke, the woman talking in the telephone booth, and the cashier who needed a shave. Then Terry had an inspiration and reached for the keyboard, his fingers composing a symphony of deception.

Dear Bishop Townsend,
It is with great disappointment that I beg you not to come here. It's not safe. There have been several disturbing incidents that I have omitted from my reports so as not to alarm Mrs. McNulty. Most involve kidnappings. As you may have heard, the kidnappers often send the victims' body parts to their families to ensure payment. And even when the ransom is paid, the victims often turn up castrated or dead.
In addition to civil war and narcotics trafficking we've had an increase in street violence. Two local gangs, the Quinidos and the Santa Fes, have been battling it out for turf. The innocent get caught in the crossfire too often for comfort.
Sir, I'd love to hear of the lessons learned from your service to Our Lord but I'm afraid it will have to be through e-mail. San Cristobal, at least at present, is just too dangerous.

Respectfully,
Terry Elgan

The reply came almost immediately.

Arugula

Terry,

Thank you for your concern but I've learned you can't do the Lord's work unless you're willing to take risks. In my ministry I've faced down Mau Maus and angry Hutus and God has always protected me. And at 80-years-old I don't have that much to lose anymore. If God wants to take me, then I'd rather it be while I'm doing His service.
See you on the fifteenth.

Alvin

It had to be him. The bald man in a Hawaiian shirt stepped through the sliding glass doors into the airport lobby and searched the faces of waiting tour guides and limo drivers. He had a wiry build and carried a worn, leather travel bag that looked like it had been dragged on the pavement all the way from North Carolina. Terry considered abandoning the bishop to the crowd and unfamiliar language but that wouldn't get him his award money so he held up a cardboard sign with the bishop's name in magic marker. The bishop nodded, smiled, and approached.

"Bishop Townsend, nice to finally meet you in person."

"Please call me Alvin." The bishop had a surprisingly strong handshake for someone in his eighties.

"Let me carry your luggage." Terry took the heavy bag and nearly dislocated his shoulder. "I have you staying in the Hotel Dorado. We can catch a cab outside." Terry lugged the suitcase toward the exit. If his scheme worked, the bishop would be on the very next flight back.

As planned Gilroy and a Russian coke head named Sergei, who was once the number two Elvis impersonator in Vladivostok, were waiting outside in front of a 1978 Buick Regal. Both had dyed their hair black to appear more Colombian but the coloring had left stains of their foreheads. On a nod from Terry, Gilroy approached.

"Quando la perro va pepe." He pulled a toy pistol from his pocket and motioned toward the car's back seat. "Quando la perro va pepe!"

"We better do as he says." Terry feigned a look of panic but it was hard given Gilroy's pathetic Spanish. How long had the Aussie been in this country, anyway? "If we cooperate, he'll probably just drive us to a bank machine and make us withdraw the daily limit. If not..." Terry swallowed.

He turned and reached for the car door but a commotion made him look back. Somehow the old man had gotten hold of Gilroy's gun hand. He delivered a devastating punch to the ribs and flipped the Aussie head over heels so he landed on the sidewalk like a piano dropped from a twelve-story building. The toy pistol went flying. Spectators applauded. From the driver's seat Sergei panicked and stomped on the accelerator. Tires squealed as he steered around taxis and pedestrians. A startled grandmother hopped to the curb as her walker disappeared under the Buick's tires. Sergei lost control, plowed into the side of a green and white city bus, and fled the scene chased by the bus driver and several angry passengers.

Meanwhile the bishop was stomping Gilroy's ribs. Terry winced each time a New Balance walking shoe struck flesh. After a dozen or so kicks he realized he ought to step in and save his pal.

"Look!" He touched the bishop's shoulder and pointed. "There's our cab."

When they got in the back seat, the bishop asked, "Should we call the police?"

"No, they were probably in on it."

"Strange sounding Spanish, the guy was speaking," the bishop said.

"It's Quechua, the local Indian language."

"Quechua, right." The bishop pointed at the cab driver. "Ask him if he's accepted Jesus as his personal savior."

Terry translated.

"Si," the driver said. "Soy Católico."

The failure of the bogus kidnapping meant that Terry had to create a church from scratch. Problem was he hadn't gotten out much. In fact, the only person he knew with a suitable space was Lorena, the madam of the brothel where he spent the Fellowship's money on women and blow. Fortunately, he was a good customer and she agreed to lend the downstairs to him for a modest fee.

While the bishop rested from his long flight, Terry got to work, taking down the liquor posters and moving tables into the storage room. He arranged the chairs in rows and tacked crosses on the walls. There wasn't much he could do about the bar except hide it behind some paint-splattered plastic sheeting.

For a rest he took a seat in the office and ransacked Lorena's desk for some blow. All he found was a pair of pink, crotchless panties, which he examined while trying to refine his plan. Now that he had a church, he had to figure out what a pastor actually did so he could fake it. His past experience at the Haynes Non-Denominational Bible Church was little help. All he'd done there was repeat sermons he'd copied off the Internet until the trustees fired him for an inappropriate relationship with a minor, Hell, that girl didn't look a day younger than sixteen!

Sermons! He still had the CDs from Dr. T. Jefferson Passnauer's Hour of Praise. Once translated into Spanish, the bishop would never know the difference. What else could he do? Terry spun the panties around his index finger. The sick! Terry stuffed the panties in his pocket and rose from the chair. He had an idea.

━━

"What is this place?" the bishop asked as he followed Terry up the steps to a turquoise, concrete building.

"Drug treatment. I try to help Colombia's cocaine problem however I can."

On seeing their bibles and clerical collars the sleepy guard removed a set of keys from his pocket and unlocked the front door. There didn't seem to be any organization in the lobby, just unshaven patients in bathrobes and a bored nurse painting her nails carmine red behind the reception desk.

"Terry, qué pasa?" A thin man with haunted eyes and a prominent Adam's apple rushed over.

"Hola, Miguel." Terry shook hands and asked in Spanish, "What are you doing here?"

"The wife threatened to leave unless I quit the cocaine so I came here for a week until she calms down. It sucks. You can't even get beer." Miguel pointed to the bishop. "Who's he?"

"Someone from headquarters checking up on me." Terry nodded to the bishop who smiled uncomprehending the Spanish. "I have to pretend to be a priest so they'll keep sending money."

Miguel nodded. Such scams were common practice among addicts everywhere, many of whom were Terry's friends and were in this very facility. Soon Jorge, Fidel, Carlos, Esteban, Roberto, Pablo, Porfie, Juan, and Guillermo gathered swapping stories and complaints.

"Hey, do me a favor, guys," Terry said. "Pretend we're praying so I can impress the bishop."

They got on their knees while Terry recited a few "Nuestro Padres." As Terry and the bishop rose to leave, Miguel asked, "You got any stuff?"

"My friend, a priest's job is to bring comfort to the sick." Terry handled him a bible. "You'll find all you seek in here."

Miguel's eyes grew bright when he opened it and found the bag of powder hidden in the cavity Terry had hollowed out of its pages.

Next morning with the bishop by his side Terry stood in front of his congregation of coke heads and prostitutes. He'd snorted a couple lines to give him inspiration for the service and the room was expanding and contracting like a whale's lung. Giselda, the transvestite, was looking good in the front row with her beehive hairdo and leopard-print miniskirt. Juanita and the rest of Madam Lorena's girls, at least the ones not working upstairs, had dressed more modestly. Gilroy was there too. Now blonde again, he sat in the back row wearing shades to disguise his facial bruises. He'd even brought the two Germans. Terry smiled at the one he'd slept with and tried to see down her shirt. What was her name anyway?

"If you'd like to say a few words, I'll translate." The floor seemed to give like a trampoline as Terry stepped away to yield the podium to the bishop.

"Thank you. Thank you, Reverend Elgan for allowing me to speak, today." He turned to the congregation. "And thank you for worshiping with us this fine Sunday morning. When I first began my ministry almost fifty years ago..."

Giselda batted her heavily made-up eyelids at the bishop as Terry translated. It wasn't a good translation. When he didn't know a word, he simply recounted the plot of a movie he'd seen. In this case it was "A Few Good Men" with Jack Nicholson and Tom Cruise. Ten minutes into the talk a man in mechanic's overalls entered and looked puzzled until he spotted Juanita in the third row. Then he jostled through the crowd and tried to pull her from her chair. She slapped his hand. A series of shushes silenced their heated whispers and the mechanic trudged upstairs alone.

Strangely, the bishop didn't appear to notice. After translating the thirty-nine-minute introduction, Terry began his cribbed sermon in Spanish. Even though they understood little, the cocaine tourists sat politely, all except Sergei who mumbled and scratched the imaginary insects swarming his neck. All that squirming made Terry's skin crawl but he fought the urge to tear off his shirt and run for the showers. Gilroy bent forward to hide behind someone's shoulder while he snorted a line. Giselda winked and licked her lips.

"Poshyol ty'!" Sergei stood and jerked like an epileptic.

"Hallelujah!" Terry shouted. "They shall speak in new tongues!"

He continued his sermon but when he reached the part about the Apostle Paul saying, "You can't handle the truth," the sound of a prostitute's fake orgasm came from upstairs.

"Qué amigo nos en Cristo!" Terry sang to cover the noise.

The prostitutes joined in but Giselda opened her legs revealing that he/she wore no panties. Terry shoved his hymnal in the bishop's face to block the view and motioned to Gilroy to get her out of there.

"What's going on here?"

The singing stopped. All eyes turned to Captain Benitez at the entrance.

"We're having a Sunday service with our distinguished guest, Bishop Alvin Townsend of the Pan American Gospel Fellowship." Terry reached for the plastic bowl on the table. "Friends, it's time to pass the collection plate. Please give generously so we can pay the license fee for our new renovations."

"Excellent!" Benitez smiled. "Please continue."

The service concluded with a few more hymns. After Terry gave Benitez the collection money and shook hands with his congregation, the bishop spoke.

"That woman, the one with the spotted skirt."

"Yes?" Terry held the railing as if an earthquake would begin any minute.

"She genuflected when she entered. We don't do that in our church. Speak to her about it. Won't you?"

A few days later Terry, the bishop, and Sergei (a.k.a. Ramon) were in a battered Toyota on the road to Hayacampo. It was better to brave leeches and yellow fever than risk another fiasco at "church." The car hit a bump.

"Chyort voz'mi!" exclaimed Sergei, a.k.a. Ramon, from behind the steering wheel.

"Quechua?" the bishop asked.

Terry nodded and closed his eyes. The longer they spent driving through the jungle in search of the non-existent Subcomandante Marcos and his band of Christian FARC guerrillas, the better. Terry had chosen a safe region to travel through, no guerrillas, paramilitaries, or illicit cocaine labs. In about a week they'd return empty-handed to San Cristobal just in time to put the bishop on his plane home.

The car's bouncing lulled Terry to sleep. He dreamed of Juanita unbuttoning her shirt to reveal her brown-tipped breasts and how her hand reached for his zipper. The German girl was there too, naked except for a spiked, Prussian helmet. Sergei slammed on the brakes jolting Terry awake.

"Chto za huy!" the Russian said.

A dozen men in camouflage fatigues blocked the road. All carried Kalashnikovs and hid their faces behind bandannas.

"Looks like we found your friends." The bishop smiled and got out.

The guerrillas yanked the others from the car and shoved them down a muddy path that led into the jungle. When Terry reached for the cocaine in his shirt pocket, a guerrilla shoved him so he went sprawling face first in the dirt. His reward for not scrambling to his feet fast enough was a rifle butt in the kidney. Even worse, he lost the cocaine. After a few minutes they arrived at a clearing. The guerrillas positioned their captives on one side and then crossed to the other.

Games will be games but when the FARC guerrillas chambered rounds into their assault rifles and aimed, Terry realized the fun was almost over. Sergei babbled in Russian. They say your life passes before your eyes in these situations but all Terry could think about was the cocaine he'd lost only a few hundred feet away.

"For God's sake," Bishop Townsend bellowed. "If Subcomandante Marcos learns that you've killed us, he'll have your asses!"

When they heard that name, the guerrillas lowered their weapons. What Terry hadn't realized was that the FARC actually had a subcomandante named Marcos. Having long lived in the shadow of the Zapatista leader with the same name, the FARC's Marcos had chosen to take the guerrillas on a raid deep into government territory. Many of his men would die but at least the TV reporters would finally be talking about him instead of that other guy.

After a long, mosquito-bitten slog through the jungle they arrived at the FARC camp, a ramshackle assortment of dingy tents, bearded guys shaving with rusty machetes, and busty leftist women in tight olive-drab T-shirts. Terry had no time to admire the ladies. He and his friends were shoved into the subcomandante's tent.

The man sitting behind the walnut desk looked familiar but Terry couldn't place him. Then he remembered. Subcomandante Marcos bore a striking resemblance to Norm from the TV show "Cheers," that is, if Norm held a Colt .45 pistol and spoke only Spanish. To Terry finding Norm in the middle of the Colombian jungle seemed unlikely but no more unlikely than finding a two-hundred-pound desk in his tent.

The bishop poked Terry in the ribs. "Ask him if he's accepted Jesus as his personal savior."

With nothing better to try Terry did so. The subcomandante's laughter could be heard all the way in Chiapas, for like all good Marxists he believed religion was the opiate of the masses.

"I believe religion is the opiate of the masses," he said. "And you know what happens to drug pushers in Colombia?"

"They buy mansions and fast cars and have lots of women?"

"True." Subcomandante Marcos inserted the magazine into his pistol, chambered a round, and aimed at the tent pole. "But we still shoot priests. Nothing personal, mind you. It's just that reporters love a good priest shooting." He lowered his weapon. "Of course, they love the story of a guerrilla showing mercy to a worthy adversary even more. I'll give you a sporting chance. Preach a sermon on Sunday. If you can convince me there's something to this faith of yours, I'll let you go. If not..."

The millipede crawled out from under the dirty bowl. Brown, segmented it moved each tiny leg deliberately as a Tai Ji master. Terry took off his shoe, smashed it into a splotch of yellow goo, and went back to reading his bible. Neither Sergei nor the bishop had understood the conversation so Terry told them they were to be the subcomandante's guests until the Sunday service. There was no need to worry them. He'd explained that the guards were there to protect them and that they had to remain inside their mildewed tent due to an impending AUC paramilitary attack. Each day they woke early. The bishop led them in prayer until the guards came with a meager breakfast of tepid water, rice, and banana. The menu repeated for lunch and dinner with the addition of some gristly meat.

The heat and humidity came long before midday. They sat shirtless and unwashed listening to the whine of mosquitoes and the guards' laughter. Terry flipped through his bible trying to remember the sermons of Reverend Doctor Passnauer but all he could recall were a few fragments. If only he hadn't lost his coke.

"It's no good." Terry closed his bible. "How do I preach to a bunch of atheists and killers?"

"You've got to scare them." The bishop leaned forward. "Let them know what's in store for them after they die. Nothing brings a sinner around like a good hellfire-and-brimstone sermon."

Terry nodded and looked at Sergei. The Russian would be looking a lot worse if he were going through withdrawal. He had to have some coke. The next time the bishop left for the bathroom, Terry confronted him.

"You holding?"

"No, no have."

"Come on man, don't bullshit me. You'd be freaking now if you didn't have any coke."

"No have!" Sergei held up his hands.

"Just give me one line. I'll pay you a hundred bucks when we get back. A hundred bucks, man!"

"Am I interrupting something?" The bishop entered and went to his cot.

"No!" Terry glared at Sergei. "Nothing!"

Terry went back to his bible but the King James English seemed opaque. Soon he was fantasizing about a FARC woman, her frizzy hair under her fatigue cap. In his mind he wrestled her cargo pants over her hips. Then she slit his throat. He closed the bible and turned to the bishop.

"What made you become a missionary?"

"I suppose God did."

"Come on, Alvin. That's not an answer. Why did you choose to risk your life in countries where they didn't even listen to you? You could have done any number of other things."

"It's where I can do the most good." The bishop took a breath and let it out. "A doctor can heal the body for a lifetime but a minister heals the soul for eternity."

"I'm not getting anywhere. Maybe you should give the sermon, Sunday."

"And steal your moment of glory? No way!" The bishop put a hand on Terry's shoulder. "Everybody has doubts, son, but going ahead anyway, that's faith. Open yourself up to God. Let Him speak through you and you'll do fine."

The days passed until it was Sunday morning and Terry found himself with bowels loose standing in front of the assembled guerrillas. He hadn't had any blow for over four days. How was he supposed to function? The bishop stood by him and took his hands.

"Lord." He bowed his head. "You've given us the chance to preach Your word to ears that sorely need to hear it. Let us accomplish Your will. Amen." He squeezed Terry's hands and sat down.

Terry looked at the faces, the sneers, the looks of boredom, and the subcomandante's jagged metal grin. Each of the fighters held an assault rifle. Terry had no idea what to say.

"Let me tell you about my church," he said in Spanish. "It's located beneath a whorehouse. Most of my congregation are addicts except for the putas. I don't think they use. We have a transvestite named Giselda who's so good at makeup that she fooled the good bishop here."

The guerrillas laughed.

"You may ask why I don't have a better church, one with upstanding members like mayors and businessmen. Maybe it's because I'm not upstanding or maybe it's because my church is what a church is supposed to be, a place we can practice acceptance and forgiveness. If God made both scorpions and lambs doesn't He love the scorpions too? And doesn't it take a scorpion to preach to the scorpions?

"That's about all I have to say to you. You may want to shoot me now and that's okay. I just ask that you let my friends go. This so-called ministry of mine isn't their fault. It's mine."

Terry stumbled out of bed around noon. Bleary-eyed and head aching he made it to the bodega a block from his hotel for coffee and a newspaper. It had been three weeks since the incident in the jungle. To his surprise the guerrillas had released them and after awarding Terry the ten thousand dollars the bishop had flown back to North Carolina with a glowing report about the work he was doing in Colombia. Terry had paid off Captain Benitez and El Gordo with the money leaving him pretty much where he'd started.

He found a table near the entrance, opened the paper, and found a picture of Subcomandante Marcos. Government soldiers had killed him and his FARC fighters near Hayacampa. Even in death this Marcos had been relegated to page two.

Terry reached for his cup. There was a reflection of Jesus on the coffee's surface. He stared at the long-suffering eyes and tired expression like that of an exasperated mother of a troublesome child. Terry shook his head. He really needed to cut back on the blow. He placed a few coins on the table and walked away leaving his coffee untouched.

Fox Slapping

Cliff Nardo followed the Asian woman into the limousine. The subtle perfume she'd applied to her cleavage seemed to evaporate from her soft skin as soon as the driver closed the door behind them. Her shimmering dress left plenty of cleavage visible, too. Cliff would have found it more pleasant resting his head there than attending the premier of his new movie, Total Effect 3 at the Cannes festival. The studio had entered it out of competition. They'd said it was unfair forcing independent films to compete with this Hollywood blockbuster but everyone knew the movie was a dog. At least they'd hired this beauty to be his escort for the night. He'd have to get her name.

When the limo stopped in front of the Grand Palais, Cliff donned a pair of sunglasses to hide his bloodshot eyes and took the escort's arm. Paparazzi lined the red carpet much like the Vikings in his first film, Tears of the Falcon. God, those were better days. Cliff forced a smile and prepared for the questions that were sure to come but the photographers rushed past to a bald man behind him.

"Vin Diesel! Can we have a few pictures? What are you working on now?"

The escort squeezed Cliff's hand in sympathy. They entered the theater and took their reserved seats. After some opening remarks by someone speaking French, the lights dimmed and the movie began. It was even worse than he'd remembered. The plot was contrived, the characters two-dimensional, and his performance had all the sizzle of overcooked broccoli. The crowd booed. They'd never booed when he was starring in Head Tripping on TV. The only comfort came from his escort who put her arm around his shoulders, leaned close pressing her breasts against his side, and whispered, "They don't know the real you. You are a great actor who will show them how great you are once you get a good part."

It got better. She rested a hand next to his groin when they kissed. Her mouth was hot as if she wanted to swallow him right there in the theater.

"Let's get out of here," she said.

They snuck out a side exit and took a cab to her hotel near the dock. In the elevator he slipped a hand inside her dress and held her breast feeling the nipple come alive under his thumb. They found the door to her room. While she searched for her key, he kissed her neck inhaling the scent of her. The door opened. She tossed her handbag on the bed and pressed her body against his.

"I have to take care of some lady things." She ran a hand over his belly before walking to the bathroom. "Why don't you have a drink? I'll just be a minute."

Cliff poured himself a glass from the bottle of Korean soju vodka on the counter, kicked off his shoes, and sat on the bed. The room was nothing special, just a place for a bed and TV. He looked in the woman's purse and found tampons, wallet, and a Taiwanese passport. Li Mingxia. So that was her name. Passport photo looked terrible, though. He took a drink. Should he take off his clothes? No, better to wait. It would be more stimulating when she undressed him.

He took another drink. The alcohol warmed his throat. The day hadn't turned out that badly after all. Maybe he still had a chance to revive his career. He'd call his agent first thing in the morning and tell him to stop accepting crappy roles, no matter what they wanted to pay him. Yeah, from now on only serious parts. Where was that woman, anyway? He was too drowsy to get up. Even holding the glass took too much effort. It slipped from his fingers spilling Korean vodka on the carpet.

An Asian man in an olive drab uniform trimmed with red was leaning over him when Cliff came to.

"Where am I?" He grabbed the officer's lapels. "I demand you release me at once!"

A half dozen uniformed men burst into the room. Cliff struggled to free his arms from their grasp. Something stabbed his bicep and he fell asleep once more.

"Are you feeling calmer?" the officer asked.

Cliff tried to speak but a rag had been tied over his mouth. He was lying on a bed in some kind of hospital room.

"I hope you realize how fortunate you are. Few men have been honored like you. Now you must prepare yourself." The officer removed Cliff's gag. "The Dear Leader wishes to meet with you."

Cliff showered, shaved, and put on a loosely fitting blue suit. After a ride down Pyongyang's wide, lonely boulevards, his limousine stopped in front of a structure that looked more like a mausoleum than a government building. The officer ushered him inside into the presence of Kim Jong-il. The Dear Leader sat at the head of a conference table on which bottled soft drinks had been arranged. He wore his customary pressed field jacket and over-sized glasses but appeared thinner than in news photos. After shaking the dictator's offered hand, Cliff sat next to him and opposite a woman translator.

"The Dear Leader asks how your journey was."

"You can't hold me here," Cliff said. "I'm an American citizen. There are laws."

Kim Jong-il toyed with his pen while listening to the translation, which took significantly longer than Cliff's statement.

"The Dear Leader wishes to assure you that his intelligence agents are very thorough. He has seen their reports. They state that you drank the drugged soju in Miss Park's hotel room willingly. You chose, Mr. Nardo, perhaps not consciously but somehow you must have known that by swallowing the liquor you were accepting the greatest role of your career." The translator listened while Kim Jong-il spoke and then continued. "Mr. Nardo, the Korean people are starving. With enemies all around, I must buy weapons. I cannot give my people rice but I can offer them hope. That's why I want you to revive your role as Peter in a socialist version of the TV series Head Tripping. We'll call it." The translator paused and wrinkled her forehead. "Fox Slapping. I believe you've already met your costar."

The woman who'd tricked him entered the room, this time wearing fatigues and thick-rimmed glasses instead of a gown.

"Miss Park will play Park Mun-hee who takes over an organ of state security after her father, the beloved colonel, dies. Instead of a marijuana-smoking hippie, you will be a soju-guzzling Czechoslovakian wild and crazy guy who fled here after that country fell to the Yankee imperialists. Together you will infiltrate rings of spies and saboteurs to see that they're brought to justice."

"Speaking of soju." Cliff examined the bottles in front of him. "I could use a drink"

"So sorry, Mr. Nardo. You'll need all your clarity to serve the Korean people." Kim Jong-il motioned to the officer. "Major Lee will show you your new quarters. If you have any difficulties, inform him. He reports directly to me."

Alone except for a portrait of Kim Il-sung and two armed guards, Cliff waited in the hall while the major finished his business with the dictator. Both guards were over six feet tall and had massive bulges under their cheap suits where a pistol would be. Clearly Cliff's only option was to play along for the time being.

The heavy oak door opened and Miss Park stepped out of the conference room. After her betrayal Cliff expected her to rush past eyes averted but she stopped to chat.

"What did you think of our Dear Leader?"

"Given the choice between him and the Cote d'Azur." Cliff looked her up and down. "I'd choose France."

"Just what I would expect from a spoiled westerner." Her face grew red. "I gave you a chance to serve the Korean people but you'd rather waste your life on drinks, whores, and degenerate entertainment."

Cliff watched her stomp away. Even in fatigues her figure was stupendous. Her ass was tight and round like a pair of firm peaches. Must have been all that marching and Tae Kwon Do training.

"Are you ready?" Major Lee gestured toward the stairs. Once they were in the limo, he opened his briefcase. "You know, I'm quite a fan of yours. Would you mind autographing a few photos?"

"I suppose not."

"Thank you." The major offered a pen and removed a stack of computer-printed photos most likely downloaded from one of Cliff's fan sites.

"I see you're going to make me work for a living." Cliff took the photos. He wasn't sure what an autograph would sell for on the black market but it must be worth something. "All this effort is going to make me thirsty. I'll need…"

"Soju?"

"Exactly."

"I'll see that it's arranged." The major tipped his head in a curt nod.

With the help of the soju Cliff repeated his performance in the TV show that was almost a scene-by-scene remake of Head Tripping, never bothering to learn the names of the staff. If he called them Mr. or Miss Park, he had a seventy-percent chance of being right so why make the extra effort? The cast spoke Korean but Cliff delivered his lines in English to be dubbed in post production. He suspected it didn't matter what he said and later proved it when shooting a night scene in a darkened "missile-testing laboratory."

"You never apologized for kidnapping me but if you go out dancing with me, I'll forgive you." Cliff rested a hand on Miss Park's shoulder. They were both hiding under a desk while the villain's flashlight scanned the room.

"I could never date a man who wasn't a party member." Miss Park brushed Cliff's hand off. "Now, can we get back to the script, please?"

Cliff never heard a reprimand or any feedback whatsoever. One day after eight weeks of filming, Major Lee asked him into his office.

"Mr. Nardo, how are you getting along? Do you like your apartment?"

"It's satisfactory."

"And the food? Have you developed a taste for kimchi?"

"It's all right."

"Good. Good." Major Lee offered a cigarette and when Cliff refused lit one for himself. "There's something I was hoping you'd explain to me. What's the meaning of the phrase, breaking the fourth wall?"

"Oh, in the theater the fourth wall is the imaginary wall between the audience and the stage so breaking it means letting the audience become part of the story or having the story somehow infiltrate the audience."

"Infiltrate. Yes, that's what I thought." The major leaned back and blew smoke at the ceiling. "Television is so backward in this country." He sat forward. "The Dear Leader wants to show we can make something as avant garde as in the west. How could we break the fourth wall on Fox Slapping?"

"Set a mystery at the TV studio?"

"I like it." Major Lee scribbled notes. "How about filming a documentary on the making of Fox Slapping at the same time?"

"Now you're getting the idea."

"But I fear doing dialog in Korean wastes your considerable improvisation talent." The major slapped the table. "We'll shoot in English and translate later. Let me talk to the producers."

"Miss Park, how do you respond to rumors of counterrevolutionaries on the Fox Slapping writing staff?" the reporter asked.

"In this time of peril for our nation no one remains more patriotic than the staff of Fox Slapping. All have dedicated themselves fervently to the Juche Idea and the Songan Revolution. Following the benevolent guidance of our Dear Leader we will rain nuclear fire on our treacherous enemies and usher in a glorious workers' paradise."

"Well said." The reporter turned to Cliff. "Mr. Nardo, how do you like Korea. Have you tried kimchi?"

The theme song played over a montage of missile tests and marching soldiers.

Spies walk by night
MiGs fly by day
Dear Leader guides us
Set and sure on the way
Fox-slapping strangers
who met on the way

The scene opened in a crowded office

"Are spies subverting the masses, waging war on working classes? Are saboteurs making your five-year plan late? Then call a security organ of the state. You accuse. We retaliate." Chung Ae-cha cupped her hand over the phone's mouthpiece to speak to the man, in plaid pants and an open polyester shirt who had just entered the office. "Mr. Kratochvil, Miss Park wants to see you in her office." She lowered her voice. "She's with a suspect."

Petr Kratochvil shimmied over to Park Mun-hee's office and yanked open the door. The conversation inside stopped as Mun-hee and the old man seated across from her turned.

"Ah Petr, this is Mr. Kim, an old friend of my father's. He's with DPRK Television." Mun-hee looked at the clock. "Since you were late, we started without you."

"Those foxes kept me at the disco all night." Petr slumped in a chair, his legs spread wide. "I know I should get to bed early I can't refuse a girl with PERKY KOREAN BREASTS."

At the mention of PERKY KOREAN BREASTS Mr. Kim buried his face in a handkerchief and broke into tears.

"You've got to help me, Mun-hee! If you don't, they'll send me to reeducation through labor!"

"It's all right, Mr. Kim." She circled the desk and patted his shoulder. Then kneeling beside him she asked, "Why don't you tell us what your problem is?"

"Spies have been using this new TV show to send coded messages about our nuclear secrets to the enemy. I'm the censor so the authorities will hold me responsible. I'm so ashamed. I was afraid to look foolish so I let them broadcast dialog that I didn't understand." Mr. Kim sobbed. "I failed my duty to the Dear Leader!"

"Don't worry, Mr. Kim. We'll find out who's responsible. Now why don't you take your wife to the Juche Tower and take your mind off your troubles?"

"Thanks you, Mun-hee. I don't know how I'll ever repay you." After a great deal of bowing, Mr. Kim dried his eyes and left.

"Are you crazy, Mun-hee? The Nuclear Directorate has its own police force. If you go digging dirt in their sandbox, you might as well measure yourself for a prison uniform. And gray isn't your color."

"Maybe a mere Marxist-Leninist would leave it for the authorities to investigate." Mun-hee rose, circled her desk, and stood nose to nose with Petr. "But as a follower of the Great Leader's Juche Idea of self reliance, I'm not going to let the man who saved my father's life go to jail. I'll investigate it myself."

"Fine."

"Fine!"

"Good."

"Good!"

"I'm going."

"Go!!!"

At the sound of Mun-hee's door slamming, Ri Ho-bang jumped off Ae-cha's desk and scrambled after Petr.

"New case, boss?"

Petr brushed past, entered his own office, and slammed the door in Ho-bang's face. Ho-bang turned to look at Ae-cha. With his mussed up hair, sparse beard, and loose tie he resembled a puppy that just learned it was on its way to the dinner table.

In his office Petr sat with his feet on his desk and slurred the words to a song.

"Spies walk by night. MiGs fly by day…" He drank soju from the bottle.

Someone knocked.

"Excuse me, Mr. Kratochvil." Ae-cha shuffled inside and stared google-eyed at her supervisor. "I'm worried about Miss Park. She ran out forgetting all about the 9:30 Juche-study group."

"Forgot the study group?" Petr jumped to his feet and dashed out the door leaving the soju behind.

The GAZ-69 jeep screeched to a halt in front of the DPRK TV building. Petr jumped out, tossed the keys to a startled guard, and ran inside. Moments later he returned, handed the guard some money, and rushed back in. He found Mun-hee in the studio.

"Oh." She touched his shoulder. "You were worried about me."

"Worried?" He stood straighter. "About you? No, the station is close to a good restaurant that serves the plentiful food grown under the scientific direction of our Dear Leader Kim Jong-il. After we wrap up the case, I thought we'd stop by for a little kimchi, a little bulgogi, maybe a little sexual intercourse." Petr ducked the roundhouse kick Mun-hee launched at his face. "What's the matter, Mun-hee? The Great Leader said Korean women should bear lots of sons to make the nation strong. Why, with my Slavic genes you can breed an army of workers to man mining, agriculture, and heavy industry."

"Not with someone who isn't a party member." Mun-hee slapped a stack of paper against Petr's stomach. "Take a look at the script. If it contains the coded message, we'll have to question the writers."

They sat down. Mun-hee unwrapped a candy bar while Petr read aloud.

"Petr Kratochvil shimmied over to Park Mun-hee's office and yanked open the door." Petr moved his index finger down the page. He skipped ahead. "Here it is in the stage directions. It says, 'Mun-hee and Petr interview Writer Choi.' Let's go."

When Writer Choi saw them approach, he darted out of the room and ran through a news studio setting the anchor's toupee askew as he fled. The news man, ever the professional, continued reading his story about rice production quotas as Petr and Mun-hee raced past. Petr returned, readjusted the newsman's toupee, and sped off again.

Meanwhile on sound stage three, two 1950-vintage North Korean soldiers huddled in a foxhole on top of a snowy ridge.

"Our food's running out. We should return to headquarters for more supplies."

"The major ordered us to hold this position until relieved. Marching out with our comrades or being carried as a corpse are the only ways I'll leave this mountain."

"Fool! Why should we sacrifice our lives for nothing? No one will ever come here." The soldier dropped his meager rice ration to gawk at the woman who dropped a half-eaten candy bar on his plate as she ran by.

Writer Choi headed for a set that resembled a steel mill, where two dozen dancers in denims, hard hats, and heavy boots kicked in unison.

"One thrilling innovation
every ingot he makes
One worker's motivation
eliminates costly mistakes..."

Choi burst through the chorus line sending several dancers sprawling. He ran toward the exit but a Bessemer converter blocked his path.

"Give it up, Writer Choi." Mun-hee approached, her hands balled into fists. "We know you put the secret message in the script."

Choi grabbed a metal bar to defend himself but didn't see Petr sneaking up behind him. As Choi raised his weapon, Petr pulled the lever dumping the ladle's load of fake steel on the fugitive. It was all over or was it?

"It's true. I sent the message." Writer Choi said in interrogation. "But I was only trying to help a woman I met in an underground karaoke club. I swear on the Great Leader's grave."

"Go on," Mun-hee said.

"She told me her father was dying and that I was sending his final greetings to his brother in the south."

Petr and Mun-hee stopped inside the entrance to the karaoke club to let their eyes adjust to the dark. He wore an Elvis outfit but the only disguise she could find in the costume department was Pulgasari, a Korean Godzilla.

"Roofies?" A bearded man showed a plastic bag filled with red pills that were shaped like stars.

Petr shook his head. A woman was singing the Internationale on stage while the audience waved hammer-and-sickle glow sticks. According to plan Petr and Mun-hee split up. He would attract the spy's attention and Mun-hee would follow her back to her lair. The quickest way to do the former was by singing so after a short wait Petr inserted a tape into the eight-track player and took the mic.

"Hello, I'm Petr Kratochvil with DPRK TV. I'd like to sing a song I wrote just last week.

You ain't nothing but a running dog
crying all the time..."

The music was what the audience had been waiting for all their lives. They went wild with a spontaneous display of rhythm, moving their feet to all the latest dances such as the twist, the mashed potato, and the Lindy hop. The secret police appeared nervous. If this riot of emotion remained unchecked, saddle shoes and plaid skirts would soon replace AK-47s and Mao Jackets.

"They said you was working class
that was just a lie
You ain't never caught a revisionist
and you ain't no friend of mine.
Thank you. Thank you very much."

After handing out several sweaty scarves to eager women Petr retired to the bar where he soon heard a voice that quickened his pulse.

"Mind if I buy you a drink, comrade?"

She was everything a Communist could want with breasts like SS-19 missiles and legs that could distract even the most dedicated nuclear inspector. From the bar stool beside him she began her sob story.

"My dying father needs to get a message to his brother in the south." Her fingernails stroked Petr's forearm. "If you could help, I'd be most grateful."

"Ah, ah." One glance at the short skirt riding up her thighs and Petr forgot the plan.

When he finally remembered, the spy had already strolled off leaving only the coded message behind. Petr scanned the crowd and found Mun-hee leaving the ladies room.

"She's getting away!" He pointed. "There!"

Petr's yelling alerted the spy who ran, broke a heel, threw her shoes at her pursuers, and took off again.

"Pardon me. Excuse me. Pardon me." Petr and Mun-hee made their way through the crowded nightclub.

Meanwhile a man pushing a fruit cart paused to mop his brow. The spy crashed through the rolling produce stand showering the crowd with tomatoes and bananas. Petr and Mun-hee skidded around the corner after the spy as a pair of workmen carried a sheet of plate glass into the corridor. Noting the approaching spy they turned the glass parallel to her path and let her pass. Relieved they turned the glass once again and Petr crashed through shattering it into a million pieces.

The spy burst out the fire door and ran down the steps knocking a baby carriage from its mother's hands. It bounced down the stairs toward the street as a truck filled with beams produced by the dedicated workers of the Wonsan steel mill approached. The driver laid on his horn and stepped on the brakes but these failed. Petr jumped and grabbed the carriage in a flying tackle that sent the baby soaring in an arc that ended in a spectacular catch by Mun-hee. The two investigators returned the child to its mother and after several deep bows all around resumed chasing the spy along Mansudae Street.

They gained on her but hadn't realized the date. The spy crossed Changgwang Street seconds before the May Day parade cut off pursuit. She stopped and waved while the soldiers, T-72 tanks, and mobile artillery that separated her from Petr and Mun-hee rolled by. All the investigators could do was admire North Korea's military might as the spy got away.

That night Petr and Mun-hee sat in a van on embassy row with a cadre of secret police.

"That one." Mun-hee put down the night-vision scope as the officers went to arrest the man outside the Swedish Embassy.

"How did you know?" Petr asked.

"The size 12 DDD high heel was too big for a woman's foot so I knew the spy was a transvestite. Since there is no sexual deviance in North Korea, he had to be a foreigner, most likely attached to an embassy. That man's wearing eye shadow. Unless he's Green Day's lead singer, he has to be our spy."

"Mr. Nardo, how can you act in this surprise ending when you haven't seen a script?" The reporter held the microphone up to Cliff's mouth.

"I'll stay in character and improvise."

"Does it worry you that the ending is being broadcast live?"

"No, it gives it an edge that makes it exciting."

"Good luck." The reporter motioned to shut down the camera and the crew packed up leaving Cliff and Miss Park alone backstage.

The on-air light turned red. Miss Park squeezed Cliff's hand and they walked onto the set.

"Admit it," Petr said. "With all those women hanging all over me after my song, weren't you a little bit jealous?"

"Why should I be jealous?"

"Because we belong together, Mun-hee, like Marx and Engels, like rice and kimchi." Petr opened the door.

They entered Mun-hee's office and stopped.

"Who are you?" they asked in unison.

A bald man in a cheap blue suit was sitting behind Mun-hee's desk flanked by Ae-cha and Ho-bang.

"Petr Kratochvil, your friends have told me about your problem and I'm here to help. Due to your excellent service to the state I'm prepared to overlook your past and induct you into the Communist Party."

"That way you can marry Miss Park." Ae-cha dabbed her eyes. "I just love a romantic ending."

"Are you ready to take the oath?"

Cliff stared at the red star on the bureaucrat's lapel. Bastard! Because of the documentary Petr joining the Communist Party would look like Cliff joining the Communist Party. He'd be damned if he'd give the North Koreans that kind of propaganda victory. There was only one way out and it wouldn't be pretty.

"Before I do, there's something I need to confess."

The bureaucrat nodded as Cliff moved closer.

"Ho-bang, ever since you started working here, I've felt a deep friendship for you. All my talk about women was a lie. It's you that I love!" Cliff kissed the junior detective full on the mouth. "Let's run away to Massachusetts and get married!"

Miss Park's mouth fell open. The bureaucrat started yelling. Something heavy collided with the back of Cliff's head and everything went black.

The car stopped by the banks of the frozen Yalu River. On the Korean side was nothing but barren ground and leafless trees that reached for the wan sun like skeleton arms clawing their way from some mass grave. Across the bridge was China and a representative from the American embassy. When a guard opened the door, Cliff struggled out of the back seat. The exertion made his injured ribs feel like his lungs were filled with broken glass. Once outside he stood shivering. The cheap, cotton jacket they'd given him in prison did little to protect him from the cold. Major Lee circled the car and gave the order to remove the handcuffs.

"You're lucky the Dear Leader found your stunt artistic." The major blew on his hands to warm them. "As for me, I wish we'd kidnapped Robin Williams."

Middle Class Man

No one knew what the meeting was about, not the employees sitting on folding chairs ten columns wide by twelve deep nor Donna from HR who'd set the chairs out. Despite her colorful scarf, the scene in the warehouse was drab - concrete floor, cinder block walls, and a lonely podium made of the same gray metal as the doors.

Punctual as always, CEO Derek "Chainsaw" McIntyre started the meeting precisely at 8:30. He had red hair, pockmarked skin that always seemed sunburned, and a neatly groomed mustache. His body was trim and fit as only those of people who spend hours at the gym are although anyone who knew him would doubt he enjoyed the exercise.

"I won't beat around the bush." The microphone squealed with feedback and McIntyre turned it slightly. "Is that better? As you know, business hasn't been good for several years. Back at corporate we've examined the numbers and we just can't keep going this way. We've decided to close the plant."

The audience erupted with murmurs.

"Hold on." McIntyre held up a hand for silence. "In recognition of your loyalty the board is going to provide each of you one week's pay for every year you've worked as severance."

A crash came from overhead and broken glass clattered on the floor. Heads rose to see a man with a chin the size of a bulldozer rappel from the broken skylight. Despite his flashy entrance he dressed in business casual, khakis and a polo shirt monogrammed with an M. Seconds after touchdown, he released the nylon climbing rope, dashed to the microphone, and grabbed the CEO in a headlock.

"I'm Middle-Class Man here to single-handedly battle the systemic problems contributing the economic decline of the American middle class. You'd better hire all these workers back or you're going to get it."

"Going to get what?" McIntyre asked.

"I'm going to give you noogies so severe that you'll need a bigger hat size." Middle-Class Man moved his giant fist toward McIntyre's scalp.

"It's…" McIntyre struggled in Middle-Class Man's grip. "It's all the federal regulations that are killing us. I can't hire them back unless you get OHSA and the EPA off my back."

"EPA huh?" Middle-Class Man let McIntyre go. "Very well, I'll take care of it."

Flanked by aids lugging briefcases and laptop computers, EPA Administrator Katie Barstaff exited the House Rayburn Office Building onto Independence Avenue to wait for her limo. After a frustrating meeting with the congressman from West Virginia, all she wanted was to return to her office, take off her heels, and pour herself a big glass of the Kentucky bourbon she kept in the bottom drawer of her desk.

A lavender SUV cut across two lanes of traffic and screeched to a halt in front of her. Shocked by the driver's recklessness Administrator Barstaff didn't realize the danger until it was too late. Before she knew it, a man in a polo shirt got out, knocked down her aids, and grabbed her in a headlock. Within seconds she was prisoner in the backseat of the SUV as it sped away. Stranger still a gorilla was driving.

"Who are you?"

"I'm Middle-Class Man here to single-handedly battle the systemic problems contributing the economic decline of the American middle class."

"All right, who's the monkey?"

"That's Numb Chumsky. I liberated him from the Yerkes Primate Research Center after some psychologists taught him to speak using American Sign Language."

As if on cue Chumsky grunted and gestured.

"What's he saying?"

"He says the I-95 is backed up and that he wants a banana but I didn't bring you here to talk about language acquisition in primates." Middle-Class Man held up his fist. "If you don't eliminate your job-killing regulations, I'm going to give you such a powerful set of noogies that you'll regret it!"

Derek "Chainsaw" McIntyre was late. Middle-Class Man stood outside the corporate headquarters looking at a parking lot that was empty except for a BMW and a green-skinned man digging holes in the asphalt with a jackhammer. Middle-Class Man checked his watch. It was 6:30. With nothing better to do he watched the man work. After completing each hole, the green man planted a sapling, added potting soil, and sprinkled it with water. Then he began digging another hole in a seemingly random spot.

Around 7:00 McIntyre emerged from the office.

"Mr. McIntyre, sir!" Middle-Class Man took a deep breath. "Just smell that sulfur dioxide! As you can tell, I took care of the EPA. Now how about reopening the factory and hiring back those laid-off workers?"

"Wish I could help but I can't compete with all that cheap labor in China." McIntyre took out his keys and walked to his BMW.

"China, huh? I'll take care of it." As he was leaving, Middle-Class Man asked the green man, "Who are you?"

"I'm Global-Warming Man here to single-handedly put an end to climate change."

Security at the Chinese Communist Party's compound at Zhongnanhai was among the best in the world. Guards chosen from the People's Liberation Army's elite October First Division patrolled the perimeter and no expense was spared equipping the facility with advanced electronic surveillance. However, all this manpower and technology was no match for a man armed with American know-how and a pair of Craftsman wire cutters from Sears.

After his kidnapping Chinese leader Hu Jintao woke to find his wrists secured to the metal chair he sat in. He screamed for help.

"Yell all you want to, Hu Jintao." Middle-Class Man stepped out of the shadows. "No one can hear you."

"Who are you?" Hu Jintao rotated his head and rolled his shoulders to loosen the muscles in his sore neck.

"I'm Middle-Class Man here to single-handedly battle the systemic problems contributing the economic decline of the American middle class."

"What do you want from me?"

"What do I want?" Middle-Class Man stepped behind the Chinese leader, wrapped a forearm around his neck, and vigorously rubbed his scalp with the knuckles of his free hand. "Don't play games with me, Hu Jintao! Stop keeping your currency artificially low, raise your wages and environmental standards to U.S. levels, and start enforcing copyright protections or else you'll be sorry!"

"You're... you're asking me to commit economic suicide. If I did that all our jobs would go to Vietnam or Burma."

"Burma, huh? I'll take care of it."

For anyone who's penetrated security at Zhongnanhai, breaking into a Russian missile silo is a snap as two officers of the Strategic Rocket Forces found on returning to the control room after their morning vodka and caviar break. Both were quickly subdued with powerful headlocks and then handcuffed by a man in a polo shirt and a silver-back gorilla.

"Let's see." Middle-Class Man examined the control panel and began turning dials. "Here we go. Sixteen degrees forty-eight minutes north, ninety degrees nine minutes east."

"Who's the monkey?" a Russian asked.

"That's Numb Chumsky. He speaks sign language."

The gorilla grunted and gestured.

"What's he saying?"

"He's asking whether it's pronounced Rangoon or Yangon and he wants a banana."

Chumsky made more gestures.

"Now he says ten, nine, eight, seven, six, five, four, three, two, one, liftoff!" Middle-Class Man punched a red button and the control room shook as the ICBM went on its way.

On his second visit to Zhongnanhai Middle-Class Man found Hu Jintao peeking out of the turret hatch of a T-99 battle tank. Instead of the usual suit and tie the Chinese leader was wearing a leather helmet and olive-drab fatigues.

"Hey Hu Jintao, I took care of Burma. Now how about raising those Chinese wages?"

"Screw you Yankee Middle-Class Man! We like our economy the way it is!"

Motors whirred as the turret turned and the tank's 125mm cannon lowered to point directly at Middle-Class Man.

"Fire!" yelled Hu Jintao.

Fortunately for Middle-Class Man his Eddie Bauer Kevlar polo shirt protected him from the blast. After the debacle at Zhongnanhai he retreated to his secret lair in Muncie, Indiana to plan a new economic strategy.

"We need to find something we can sell to the Chinese." Middle-Class Man set a bowl of microwave popcorn on the table in front of Numb Chumski.

Chumski stood up, pointed at the world map, and gestured.

"What's that, Chumski? Sell them opium. That's a splendid idea! I wonder why no one has ever thought of that before."

In a greenhouse, the size of a football field, workers in polo shirts scurried about examining poppies for signs of insects and disease, checking mineral levels in hydroponic fluid, and repairing electronic equipment.

"Quite an impressive operation you have here," Global-Warming Man said.

"And we're well on our way to becoming carbon neutral." Middle-Class Man pointed to the roof. "During the day solar cells power the pumps and charge the batteries they run off at night."

"What are you growing, anyway?"

"We're growing opium to sell to China." Middle-Class Man crossed his arms over his chest in satisfaction.

"But that's illegal!"

"It can't be illegal! It's all natural!"

"If the DEA catches me again, they'll put me away for thirty years." Global-Warming Man dashed toward the exit.

"Damn government bureaucrats!" Middle-Class Man raised his arms over his head and waved. "Attention everyone. Gather round." The workers formed a circle. "I'm sorry I'm going to have to lay you off."

The workers dropped their tools and started toward the door.

"And I'm going to need your polo shirts back," Middle-Class Man added.

Chumsky the gorilla stood from the computer control station and rested a hand on his mentor's shoulder.

"I'm afraid that means you too, Chumsky."

The gorilla hung his head.

"Try to think of the bright side," Middle-Class Man said. "It's the creative destruction that's the engine of American competitiveness."

Chumsky gestured.

"Of course you can use me as a reference."

The gorilla began removing his shirt.

"Aw, what the hell. You can keep the shirt."

With nothing better to do Middle-Class Man went to the park and watched a pickup basketball game. As always his sympathy was with the underdog so instead of concentrating on the dribbles, dunks, and fast breaks, he paid attention to a man in a yellow jersey sitting on the sidelines.

"Why aren't you playing?" Middle-Class Man asked.

"Bad knee. Doctor says I need surgery but I don't have health insurance."

"Knee surgery, huh?" Middle-Class Man grabbed the injured man in a headlock and using the pressure of his forearm against the carotid artery quickly rendered him unconscious.

Seeing the scuffle the basketball players surrounded them.

"What are you waiting for? Can't you see he needs knee surgery? You!" Middle-Class Man pointed at a bald man wearing a headband. "Bring me some rubbing alcohol and a kitchen knife."

Postmodern Adventures of the Scribe

"Robbery at First Union Bank on Second Avenue. Hostages taken," the dispatcher's voice said over the police radio.

"Here we go again." The Scribe slipped his tablet computer into the utility belt and put on his mask before taking the stairs from his second-story condo to the parking garage.

As superheroes went he wasn't much to look at. Though not unhandsome or out of shape, he lacked the musculature of The Human Mole or the agility and sheer animal presence of The Lemur. He could not shoot fire from his eyebrows or outrun a lightning bolt. His powers were subtler but more far reaching. By using a pen, a tablet computer, or simply composing his thoughts, the Scribe could alter reality. Bending the laws of physics and creating wild coincidences were nothing to him. The only limitation to his powers was that the new reality had to conform to a classic three-act plot structure – setup, conflict, and resolution.

The Scribe drove his 1982 Volvo to the scene, parked in a nearby Wal-Mart, and walked toward the flashing lights until a policeman stopped him at the barricade.

"Sorry, sir. You need to stay behind the police line."

The Scribe studied the policeman's face, the crinkles around the eyes and tired but patient expression. Clearly, he was not displaying enough attitude. The Scribe wrote on his tablet.

"Hey, Looney Tunes!" the policeman said. "If you want to dress up for Halloween, that's your business but keep your ass behind the barricade!"

That was better. The Scribe slipped his stylus back into the tablet and stowed it away.

"That's okay, Bret. He's with us." A middle-aged detective in a tan overcoat brushed the policeman aside.

"Sure thing, Detective Mukasey." The policeman glared at the Scribe as he let him pass.

"So what do we got, Ted?" the Scribe asked.

"Three perps tried to hold up a bank just as a squad car happened by." Detective Mukasey sipped coffee from a paper cup and winced. "They're holed up in there with a dozen hostages. The negotiator's on the way.

Let's not do it like last time. I want to end this thing without a lot of bloodshed and property damage."

"How about something more character-driven?" the Scribe began scribbling. "Suppose the negotiator is black and the hostage takers are racist skinheads?"

"That just might work."

An unmarked car pulled up. A man resembling Forrest Whittaker got out and marched over to the SWAT team commander.

"Here's how things are going to work. Nothing happens without my say so. Even if you have all three perps dead in your sights, you don't shoot unless I tell you to. Hell, you don't even take a bite of your sandwich unless I tell you to." The negotiator put on his headset and called the hostage takers. "Gentlemen, it's a hell of a situation we've got here. Talk to me."

Things went mostly as expected. A few hours into the drama the Scribe sensed sagging interest so he made one of the hostages a diabetic who needed her insulin. In the end all the hostages escaped unharmed except for the embezzling bank manager who'd orchestrated the robbery to cover up his crime.

When the Scribe got home, he stripped off his yellow leotards and put some Coltrane on the stereo. Sitting on the couch in his underwear he tried to relax. TV was out of the question. He created drama all day and didn't need more during his time off. He looked at the entertainment section of the newspaper before crumpling it up and throwing it away. All the mumblecore movies were at the downtown art houses. There was nothing close except multiplexes and Hollywood blockbusters. He could pick up some woman in a bar but he already knew how that story would end.

The Scribe went into the bedroom, stared at the nightstand with the red telephone on top, and paused wondering if he should open the drawer. Sure, he'd been overdoing it lately and he'd promised to confine his pharmaceutical recreation to the weekend but it had been a rough night. Didn't he deserve a little relief?

The Scribe opened the drawer and took out his kit. Inside the false leather case he found a chunk of glowing, green metal about the size of a marble. Using a rat-tale file he sanded off about a teaspoon of filings onto a hand-held mirror. Then he snorted the powder through a rolled twenty-dollar bill.

"Shit yeah!"

The Kryptonite rush hit him immediately and he fell back onto the bed. The initial chill in his sinuses was soon replaced by warmth. For the time being he could be an ordinary man without the need for every event to further some master plot. There were no endings that had to tie up every question. Most of all, he didn't have to think about people and their problems.

With his mind stilled the Scribe stared at the ceiling and the simple, unchanging pattern of pebbling on its white surface. It was like one of those visits to his grandparents' house in the country when he was little. No TV, no video games, just the sun, tall grass, and the neighbor's homely dog.

He must have fallen asleep because the phone woke him. His scrabbled toward the nightstand and knocked it off. It fell to the floor with a bang. He dived and picked it up.

"Hello." The Scribe picked at the crusted blood on his nostril.

"Scribe, it's General McAllister at the Joint Chiefs. We got a little situation out here in Rocky Flats. Some terrorists got a hold of a nuke and they're threatening to blow it up unless we release Scarfazulla Amin, their leader. With the elections coming up in November, the President wants to end this thing in a way that displays competence and plays well with the voters. A helicopter will pick you up in seven minutes."

Two helicopter flights and a supersonic ride in the backseat of an F-15 E Strike Eagle got the Scribe to Rocky Flats in a little under two hours. The scene at the nuclear weapons facility was all spotlights, armed guards, and anxious generals in uniforms weighed down with gold braids.

"Glad you could make it, Scribe." General McAllister dismissed his special operations escort and led the superhero into the administration building that had been setup as a temporary command post.

Inside Army and Air Force officers relayed commands to the troops, encircling the facility, and planes flying overhead. A large video display showed a map of the continental US and the likely path radioactive fallout would take. The patch of red around Colorado changed to a swath of dark pink engulfing Kansas City, St. Louis, and most of the Midwest.

"The terrorists are holed up in one of the assembly buildings. We designed them with six-inch walls of reinforced concrete, not that it matters much. If they set off that nuke, the fireball will reach all the way to Denver."

The Scribe followed General McAllister into an empty office.

"You like scotch?" Without waiting for a reply the general filled two tumblers from a bottle on the desk, slid one forward, and sat in the Herman Miller chair. "So how are we going to handle this?"

"What if one of the workers got left behind only the terrorists don't know it?" The Scribe sipped his drink. "Smooth!" He put down the glass and leaned forward with his elbows on his knees. "Anyway, then the worker could relay the terrorists' positions over his cell phone."

"Be good if the worker was a minority," General McAllister said.

"Black? Latino? Arab-American?"

"An Arab-American single mother whose husband lost his life serving in Afghanistan."

"Then she could disable the alarms allowing the special forces to sneak in and overwhelm the terrorists." The Scribe began writing on his tablet.

When he finished, he looked at the door expecting the general's aide to rush into the room with good news. Nothing happened. He squirmed and tapped the tablet with his stylus. As a diagnostic he wrote a description of the general's bushy eyebrows. General McAllister's brows remained bare as a porn star's bikini line.

The poison jellyfish of panic wrapped its stinging tentacles around the Scribe's heart. It had to be the Kryptonite. Its lingering effects had robbed him of his powers. He began to sweat. It was all he could do not to scream.

"General, I need to get some new batteries for this thing." The Scribe gestured toward his tablet and dashed out the door.

In the bathroom he splashed cold water on his face and stared at the reflection of his bloodshot eyes in the mirror. What was he going to do? He tore several paper towels from the dispenser. The general's aide burst in.

"Sir, the general wants to know how much longer you'll be."

"It'll take as long as it takes! You think it's easy arriving at an ending that's both unexpected and inevitable?" The Scribe blotted his face dry, wadded the paper towels, and threw them in the trash. "I thought you were supposed to get me some batteries. Six AAs and make them lithium not those crappy rechargeables. Excuse me. I'm going someplace where I'm not interrupted every fifteen seconds."

The Scribe stomped out and eventually found a seat on the stairs outside the building's entrance. Other than giving him a few strange looks the soldiers in battle gear who went in and out left him alone. He wrote on his tablet.

Major Dirk McCullen rolled up to the Rocky Flats perimeter on his Harley Davidson.

No one showed up. The Scribe tried again.

As an owl flew over the electric fence, Lieutenant Able Fujimori wished he could overcome the barriers of race and sexual orientation as easily.

There was no owl, not even a sparrow. Maybe the problem was that he was being too timid. Something bold might kick start his superpowers. The Scribe picked up his stylus. This time he'd pull out all the stops.

Seconds after the Scribe set down his stylus, an orange and green flying saucer appeared over the compound. The roar of jet engines rattled windows as the F-22 Raptors that were flying air cover made their attack approach on the intruder. The Scribe stabbed the tablet with his stylus in a frantic editing session designed to correct his mistake but it was no good. The flying saucer fired a death ray that swatted the F-22s from the sky. The fireball lit up the night and filled the air with the smell of burning jet fuel.

When the flying saucer landed inside the perimeter the troops began shooting with mortars, machine guns, and M-16s. Within seconds the M119 howitzers opened up, peppering the UFO with shells every few seconds. Explosions and tracer rounds made it seem like the orgasm at the end of a Fourth of July fireworks show. Despite the flash and noise the bullets and shells simply bounced off the flying saucer's skin. A hatch opened.

"Cease fire!" yelled an officer.

The Scribe held his breath as he scanned the soldiers' tense faces. Despite the near certainty of death the brave men and women held their positions determined to face whatever horror emerged. Then a Welsh corgi trotted out of the spaceship and paused at the bottom of the ramp.

"What a cute little puppy!" said a two-hundred-pound master sergeant.

The corgi opened his mouth in a doggy grin and projected a heat beam from his forehead that melted all the soldiers' weapons into slag.

While the troops were swearing and shaking their burned hands, a thin man in a silver spacesuit emerged from the spaceship and descended the ramp to stand by the little dog. His shiny hair had been combed back and held in place by some greasy, alien pomade.

"Heard you boys was in need of a little assistance." The alien took out a pack of Lucky Strikes, struck a wooden match on his sole, and lit up. "Klaatu barada nikto."

"Woof!" The corgi fired a disintegrator ray from his forehead that vaporized the assembly building and the terrorists inside so all that remained was an eight-foot deep crater. The soldiers, all battle hardened veterans, looked back and forth from dog to the destruction he'd caused.

"Guess that about does it." The alien crushed the cigarette under his heel. "Cuddles will stay behind to make sure you don't get in any more trouble."

Leaving the firemen to deal with the crashes and the medics to treat the soldiers' burns, the alien went back inside and closed the hatch behind him. The corgi sat on his haunches to watch the flying saucer rise and hover about twenty feet above the ground while it began to rotate. Colored lights spelling LSMFT appeared on its surface. Then within a fraction of a millisecond the flying saucer shot out of the atmosphere, left Earth's orbit, and was three quarters of the way out of the solar system before anyone could say, "What does that abbreviation stand for, anyway?"

Alien Dog Destroys Russian Bombers
Lemur Assists Police in High-Speed Chase

"What bullshit!" The Scribe threw the newspaper in the trash and got his hypodermic needle. There was less reward money after the Rocky Flats fiasco so he was economizing by injecting instead of snorting. No matter. Soon he'd be on top again. He'd just tied off his arm with a belt while holding the needle in his teeth when he heard an emergency on the police radio. There was an armed standoff on Mulberry Street.

When he got to the scene, he spotted a familiar car parked by the ambulance. The giant drill bit on its grill could mean only one thing. He looked around and sure enough the Human Mole was standing next to Detective Mukasey.

"Ted!" The Scribe waved and hurried over. "What's going on? How's it going, Mole?"

"Hey Scribe. Tough business at Rocky Flats." The Mole flexed his claws as if he couldn't wait to start digging.

"Nothing you need to worry about, Scribe," the detective said. "We've got it under control."

"You sure I couldn't add a little human interest?"

"Naw, it's a simple tunnel and surprise from underneath job. Why don't you go home and take a rest? We'll call you when we need you."

Six months later the Scribe was sitting on a ratty couch in a tenement apartment and watching silverfish battle cockroaches. At least it was quiet, his noisy neighbors having died in successive home-invasion robberies whenever the Scribe didn't have enough K to keep his powers in check. The silverfish seemed to be getting the upper hand when the door opened and a pale woman tottered in on high heels. Her shorts showed a flash of blue panties and her sleeveless T-shirt revealed generous glimpses of breast. When she dropped a wad of cash on the couch, the Scribe didn't even count it before jumping to his feet.

"Bitch!" He slapped her. "There isn't enough money here for my fix."

The woman backed away. The Scribe followed.

"Looking at me like that's not going to save you. I don't have to be a sympathetic character." He raised his hand and the woman flinched. "Get your skinny ass back out on the street and make me some money!"

The phone rang not long after she left.

"Scribe, it's General McAllister. I need your help. A car will pick you up in a half hour."

The Scribe searched the clothes piled on the closet floor for his leotards.

"About fucking time." He tossed dirty panties and faded jeans into the hall. "Motherfuckers finally appreciate...Need me to save their chicken asses."

Finally he found them. His stained leotards smelled of sweat but there was no time to wash them. He suited up and put on his mask. A notepad and pencil riddled with tooth marks would have to do. He'd hocked his tablet computer months ago.

"What the …?" The Scribe paused at the entrance to the general's office and stared.

Many of his colleagues were there. Detective Mukasey paced back and forth. The Lemur hung from the ceiling by the corner. The Mole sat on the couch next to Neutrino Girl who twitched her foot, its toes passing back and forth through the coffee table as if it wasn't there. It had to be something big.

"Thanks for joining us, Scribe." A man he didn't know shook his hand. He was pudgy and wore a tan sports coat, the kind they sell for half price at outlet malls. "We're here because we're worried about you. I'll let your friends tell you why. Mole, how about starting?"

"Remember when we stopped that runaway train? I wanted to just tear up the tracks but you made me dig a canal from the reservoir so the train stopped in the water. I'll never forget how we saved the little girl with the teddy bear and those singing nuns." The Mole wiped his eyes on the back of his claws. "Scribe, we need you. You've got to get clean!"

Each of his friends told an anecdote and made a plea. Their concern wore him down. After the Scribe agreed to enter rehab, he was whisked from the general's office and put on a plane that flew him over the Pacific. Fourteen hours later the plane approached an island that was shaped like a goat's head. As they descended toward the runway by its ear, a green flame shot from one of the nostrils.

"What is this place?" he asked the attendant.

"Monster Island. The Science Patrol runs a rehab facility here that's suited to people with special needs like you."

By the time they landed, the Scribe felt like a thousand invisible hookworms were burrowing into his skin. The methadone they'd given him had helped but it was no substitute for Kryptonite. He wanted to ask the Japanese woman who met him at the gate for something stronger but something in her expression stopped him. She was petite and wore floral scrubs and running shoes. Gray streaks were beginning to appear in her hair but as is common with older Asians the skin on her face remained smooth and unwrinkled. In different circumstances he would have found her attractive if not for the forced smile that betrayed the suspicion in her eyes.

"Welcome to Monster Island. I'm Miss Fukuda, head of the nursing staff." She began scribbling on her tablet computer.

After asking about his superpowers and drug abuse history, Nurse Fukuda led him outside to a golf cart and chauffeured him past a cluster of rounded buildings that looked like something out of a 1960s science fiction movie. They turned onto a deserted road and followed it through the rainforest until they arrived at a charred, concrete blockhouse.

"What's this?" The Scribe got out and followed Nurse Fukuda to the entrance.

"This is the detox facility." She swiped her key card and the steel blast door rolled open. "For your own protection we ask that you begin your stay here. As you know, Kryptonite withdrawal often magnifies superpowers and makes them uncontrollable."

She led him past some kind of control room that was surrounded by thick glass and into a sparsely furnished exam room.

"Please empty your pockets," Nurse Fukuda said.

After he put his effects on the steel table, she handed him a plastic cup and pointed to the bathroom door. Inside he found a robe and assumed he needed to change. After he surrendered the sample and his leotards, Nurse Fukuda ushered him through a locked door onto the ward and showed him to his quarters.

"You'll probably need a day to get over your jet lag. Make yourself comfortable. Starting tomorrow we'll expect you to take part in all scheduled activities." She stopped by the entrance to his room. Inside a bald, pudgy man lay on one of the beds. His glasses were on the nightstand. "Normally we try to room new patients with someone who's nearly completed detox but we couldn't manage it for you on such short notice. After you're settled in, I'll want you to give me all ten inches of your hot, throbbing cock!"

The Scribe stared.

"So sorry." Nurse Fukuda's face grew red. "That was a demonstration of your roommate's superpower. He's called the Ventriloquist." She bowed and left.

The Scribe tried to sleep but sharing a space with his semi-comatose roommate was like being in the middle of a bad radio drama. Voices, sirens, and explosions seemed to come from all directions.

"The murder weapon was a .38 police special."

"Don't ever talk to me that way again!"

"Margaret, I'm having your baby."

When the sound of a pile driver started coming from the wastebasket, the Scribe decided to walk around the ward. Most rooms were empty but one was occupied by someone he later learned was called Doc Quantum. Intrigued by the strange sight inside the Scribe paused to look. A dozen Doc Quantums each varying in transparency filled the room. One sat in the chair. Another lay on the bed. A few paced or stood looking through the bars of the window. Periodically they would coalesce into one violently vibrating person until they split up again.

"Hey!" A woman waved at him from a room across the hall. "You got any K?" Her breasts swelled by about four inches. "I'll suck your cock for some K."

At the mention of Kryptonite the Scribe's knees seemed to buckle. He struggled back to his room, collapsed on his bed, and spent the night sweating and shivering under the blanket. Every time he fell asleep, his roommate's outbursts woke him.

Next morning, dizzy and feverish, he joined the others in the lounge for group therapy. A dozen patients filled folding chairs arranged in a circle. Nurse Fukuda was there as was a muscular, two-hundred pound orderly who carried some kind of electromagnetic rifle with a parabolic antenna where the barrel should have been. He wore a crisp, white lab coat emblazoned with the number one and had his hair styled in the short brush cut of a professional fighter. His face betrayed no hint of sympathy, only the certainty that he'd make you pay dearly if you stepped out of line.

"Let's begin. Shall we?" Nurse Fukuda gave an artificial smile. "I'd like to introduce Mr. Scribe, our newest patient."

"Hey." The Scribe nodded and then looked at his feet to control an attack of nausea.

"Last time we were discussing what made you start using Kryptonite. Why don't we continue?" Nurse Fukuda looked at the green patient on her right. "Chloro Phil, I believe it's your turn."

Waves of fatigue washed over the Scribe as successive patients narrated their dreary histories – problems with love, bosses, trouble with secret identities. He was drowning in tedium. If only there was an argument, some sexual tension, anything to break up the monotony but nothing came. He looked from one boring face to another. It would have been easy to close his eyes and let sleep take him. Somehow his consciousness struggled to remain on the surface. Things got better when the Bronze Skateboarder told his story.

"I first used after an encounter with the shape shifters of Nebulon Five. As you know, they look like a cross between a coyote and an octopus but they can take human form. Anyway, I was chasing a Nebulon who'd stolen the CIA's Perseus encryption key when he ducked into an alley. Soon as I rounded the corner after him, I spotted an old woman carrying a bag. Figuring she was the Nebulon in disguise, I blasted her with my asphalt tsunami." He took off his bronze baseball cap and ran a hand through his copper hair before replacing it. "She wasn't a Nebulon, only an innocent old woman that I turned into meat paste. I started using after that. Guess I wanted to disable my power so I could never misuse it again."

"Yes, Dr. Nakamura of Tokyo University says that superheroes use drugs to hide from the responsibilities of their powers." Nurse Fukuda said. "Who else wishes to tell us how they avoided their duties?"

"Being irresistible to men gets old," the woman who propositioned the Scribe said. "Sometimes I'd take K so I could go to the market without turning heads."

"Thank you, Venusian." Nurse Fukuda gestured to a bald man with icy eyes. "What about you, Mr. Entropy? Please tell us what happened in San Francisco when you were holed up in a K house?"

"If the police had done their job…"

"Mr. Entropy, you cannot progress until you admit your failure. Police or no police, the Komodo Dragon strangled a dozen women when you were high."

"You can't blame that on me."

"Excuse me, please" Nurse Fukuda held up a photo of a blonde woman holding a baby. "Are you saying that saving Marcy Kelly's life was not your duty?" She held up another photo of a girl with braces. "How about Annie Riddle, fourteen-years-old? Was she not your duty either?"

Mr. Entropy's fists glowed red while frost formed on his arms. When he jumped to his feet, a lightning bolt hit him from behind and he collapsed in convulsions to the Linoleum. The orderly lowered his electromagnetic rifle and went to the intercom to call for assistance.

Evidently, Nurse Fukuda didn't consider the Scribe dangerous. That afternoon she let him do work therapy outdoors. The same could be said for his partner, a thin, nonthreatening, black man with graying hair who looked like he was in his sixties. When they met outside the greenhouse, he extended his hand.

"Hi, I'm the Dodge Lion."

"Dodge Lion?" The Scribe shook the man's hand. "What kind of powers does a dodge lion have?"

"Ever hear of an insect called an ant lion? Digs a hole and camouflages the opening. When an ant falls in, he eats it. I'm kind of like that with cars."

"Is there much call for that kind of thing?"

"Just the occasional police chase." He opened the door to the greenhouse. "Come on, I'll show you what we have to do."

The work wasn't difficult. They carried trays of seedlings to the garden and planted them in the rich, dark earth. From his spot the Scribe got a good view of the detox compound and was surprised to see a helipad out back. At the moment it was only being used by Orderly Number One to practice his karate katas. Even in the distance the Scribe could hear the snap of each kick and punch.

If he wasn't so sick from withdrawal, the Scribe might have found the work relaxing but the shivers and body aches made it hard to concentrate. He did the best he could but the tomatoes he planted were definitely not in straight rows. After an hour the sound of a helicopter thudded in the air. The Scribe looked up and saw a camouflaged Blackhawk land. Two orderlies hustled Mr. Entropy on board and the helicopter took off.

"Where do you suppose they're taking him?"

"Iran, North Korea, Afghanistan." The Dodge Lion set down his spade. "Wherever you take a berserker with superpowers."

"But…"

"Nobody pays attention to the old Dodge Lion so I come and go as I please. I've seen things that don't add up. Like how come they dose the most powerful inmates with Kryptonite and then ship them off when withdrawal makes them the most unstable? No sir, something here just doesn't add up."

The Scribe dismissed the Dodge Lion's talk as a fantasy, not that he could do much if it wasn't. At least following the schedule provided a little distraction. He had just about gotten used to the routine when he stopped by a group of patients gathering in the hall.

"It's Mr. Entropy."

"They say he moved all the air to the opposite side of the room and his body exploded."

The Scribe peeked inside Mr. Entropy's room. He wished he hadn't.

"Go back to your rooms." Orderly Number One pushed patients out of his way. "We have everything under control."

The Dodge Lion waited until the next work period to recruit the Scribe.

"A few of us are going to make a break for it. Someone has to get the word out that things are really wrong here. Are you with us?"

"Code one-nine-nine in room sixteen." Nurse Fukuda's voice called out. A crackle of static and shriek of feedback made it sound all the more authentic. "Chloro Phil is having a heart attack!" The Ventriloquist winked at the escapees huddled in the Dodge Lion's room.

Two orderlies rushed out of the control room with a portable defibrillator. Before the door could close and lock behind them, the Urban Chameleon stepped away from the wall, slipped inside, and stopped face to face with Orderly Number One.

"No you don't." He grabbed the Urban Chameleon by the scruff of the neck, tossed him back in the ward, and slammed the door.

Meanwhile the orderlies with the defibrillator arrived in room sixteen. Instead of finding a sick man, they encountered a woman's behind.

"Hi boys." The Venusian looked up from her position on the floor. "I lost one of my earrings. It's got to be under here somewhere." As she turned her attention back under the bed, her ridiculously short skirt hiked even higher on her thighs.

The orderlies set down the defibrillator and leaned against the wall to watch.

"Idiots!" Nurse Fukuda burst into the room. "The patients are escaping!" She yanked the Venusian to her feet and slapped her.

Usually the Venusian took physical acts lying down but she drew the line at assault. With one hand braced on Nurse Fukuda's shoulder for balance she kneed the nurse in the stomach. Both women went to the ground in a wrestling match of scratches and hair pulling. Somehow they managed to lose most of their clothing in the process. Nurse Fukuda, one breast hanging out of her bra, rolled on top and shouted to the orderlies.

"What are you looking at? Go!"

Both men ran toward the control room as a recorded message blared in the hall.

"For your own safety please return to your rooms. For your own safety please return to your rooms."

The orderlies slowed when they came face to face with a thin man in a plaid shirt whose eerie composure made them wary.

"Go back to your room, sir." An orderly stepped forward.

The thin man, known as the Blowfish, expanded his spiny body to fill the hallway and block the orderlies from their destination. By now the other escapees were crowded outside the control room. All were intent on their mission except for the Urban Chameleon whose skin affected a paisley pattern while he held his hurt elbow.

"Guess it's up to you, Doc Quantum," the Dodge Lion said.

Doc Quantum ran toward the door and bounced off with a thud. He tried a second time with the same result.

"Come on, Doc. Third time's a charm."

Encouraged Doc Quantum ran full out toward the door and collided with a sickening crunch.

"Ugh!" the escapees said.

"Hurry up back there," the Blowfish shouted. "I can't hold them back much longer."

Doc Quantum tried once more. This time he passed through the door as if it were smoke.

"We're in!" The escapees rushed inside and halted in front of a half dozen orderlies.

"Execute Plan B," the Dodge Lion said.

While the other escapees fumbled in their pockets, the Bureaucrat stepped forward and began to speak.

"Code of Federal Regulations – Title 21. This part applies to all clinical investigations regulated by the Food and Drug Administration under section 505(i) and 520(g) of the Federal Food, Drug, and Cosmetics act…"

Within seconds the orderlies were snoring.

"Okay!" The Dodge Lion removed his earplugs. "Doc, Bronze, Chameleon, and Scribe, get to the garage. Bureaucrat, stay here in case they wake up. I'll be down by the road preparing a little surprise in case they try to chase us."

"Not so fast!" Orderly Number One stepped out of the shadows with a pair of noise-cancelling earphones in his hand.

"The rest of you go ahead." The Bronze Skateboarder lifted his board in an en guard position. "I'll take care of this."

"Guess we both know how this will end." Orderly Number One tore a steel railing from the wall and twirled it like a sword.

"That's right." The Bronze Skateboarder circled his opponent. "We fight while they make their way to the garage. You nearly beat me but at the last moment I turn the tables allowing the others to make their escape." He lunged at the orderly who parried the skateboard with his length of railing.

The Scribe watched the clash of bronze and steel. The events seemed all too familiar. Could it be that the plot was something cooked up by his overactive mind as it rebounded from Kryptonite withdrawal? The realization came not with a flash and a bang but more like the extinguishing of a fire once its fuel had been exhausted. His aches and fever vanished. The Bronze Skateboarder and Orderly Number One set down their weapons. Nurse Fukuda entered and turned off the warning alarm.

"Mr. Scribe, you're now ready to join the general population." She noticed her chest was exposed and held her torn blouse together.

The Scribe looked at the recovering patients in the room and realized that the drama of his addiction was over if he wanted it to be. All he had to do was live drug free and accept the events of his life as they happened. In a way it was exactly what he'd always wished for. He stood, walked to the podium, and faced the others.

"Hello. I'm the Scribe and I'm an addict."

Pioneer Spirit

Feeling giddy I was up afore the cock crowed. Pa said a boy like me weren't likely to make such a journey 'cept for once in his lifetime. 'Twas true I was about to see sights my schoolmates hadn't – a great continent with its wide rivers, bountiful plains, and gigantic mountains.

My good mood weren't to last, though. Soon as we got to the check-in line, an arrow stuck in Pa's laptop.

"Indians!"

We circled our roll-on bags right there in the departure suite and returned fire 'til we drove them off. Sure was mighty glad we brought along our Winchester repeating rifles. Darn shame them TSA agents confiscated 'em at security. Had to build a campfire in the departure lounge to keep the cougars and coyotes away. Ma fried up some Johnny cakes. Pa set out some snares and came back with a poppy-seed bagel and cream cheese.

About an hour into the flight Ma started to feel right poorly. Pa ain't no doctor but he seen enough sick folks to know a case of swamp fever. We tried to make Ma comfortable with the tiny pillow and airline blanket and all. But when we was over Death Valley, she started begging for water. Only we didn't have no credit cards to buy no beverages or box lunches.

"Hold on, Ma." Pa held her hand.

I tried to cool her brow with a bandanna soaked in urine but it weren't no good. We asked if there was a preacher on board but there weren't none. So Pa said a few words from the Good Book afore we laid Ma's body to rest in the aft galley.

That flight seemed like to last forever what with them tiny seats, Adam Sandler movies, and all. By the time we was over Ohio I'd have rather wrestled a pack of rabid opossums in my long johns that sit through another one. When we made our final approach, we bowed our heads and Pa thanked the All Mighty.

But our trials weren't over. Pa killed a rattlesnake over by the baggage claim and a masked man with a six shooter tried to rob us at the Wolfgang Puck's Pizza. If it weren't for Pa thinking fast and putting back that Caesar salad, we wouldn't have made it out of there.

We rounded up a bunch of drovers to carry our bags but one of the mules got washed away in the torrent from a busted water main on the way to the hotel courtesy van.

I'll never forget my first look at our new home – the Marriott Hotel. It had the prettiest red roof but them big picture windows made us sitting ducks if the Indians decided to attack. Lucky for us there were plenty of trees we could cut down to build proper defenses. Pa said we could do that on the morrow afore planting sorghum on the divider in the parking lot. For now all he wanted to do was set out his bedroll and watch HBO.

Rehab

Life was good. Dick Trout had a well-paying job, wife, and a sturdy car. Arriving thirty minutes before most other employees he parked his gray Volvo 940 in a space only a half dozen car lengths from OmniDyne Defense Systems front entrance. As he walked to the door he counted bumper stickers. It was about even between Bush and Gore but for him politics was only a passing interest. His passion was manufacturing engineering. He lived for his work. Trout owed his success to his early starts and his early starts to standardization. Over the years he'd designed his wardrobe with the same care with which he chose missile components – his slacks khaki, socks white, shirts pale blue, and shoes brown wingtips. The beauty of his system was that he didn't need to spend time selecting. Coupled with his low-maintenance, flat top haircut, he estimated this resulted in a twenty-minute head start each morning.

This day he used that time to begin searching for a replacement for the Jackalope Air-Defense Missile's nosecone material. The initial design specified a beryllium alloy. Beryllium, for God's Sake! How many times had he told the design engineers that it was hard to machine and toxic too? Trout set to work and was deep in the materials handbook when the timer on his computer chimed to remind him of the 9:30 meeting.

"What the …" He set the book down on his desk and removed a voter's guide from his briefcase, something to read while the executives blathered on.

Trout thought better of it, left the pamphlet behind, and headed to the meeting. He scanned the room packed with engineers and technicians until he found a chair next to his friend, Rajiv. If the god Vishnu's avatar were to appear as a brown-skinned Elvis, complete with pompadour and beer belly, the result would resemble H. Rajiv Bandayahadahay. Of course, there was nothing remotely spiritual or even musical about the reliability engineer except possibly the mystery of his first initial. Despite seven years of asking, Trout had yet to learn what the H stood for.

"Yah, so how goes the battle with the designers?" Rajiv asked after Trout sat down.

"You know what they want to make the nosecone out of? Beryllium!"

"Beryllium?" Rajiv raised his eyebrows. "Don't they know it's hard to machine? Toxic too!"

Trout would have enjoyed commiserating further but he was distracted by a smiling, red-haired executive coming down the aisle and glad-handing the employees.

"Hi, Bill Lightner, VP of Operations. Good to see you!"

After a brief introduction by the plant manager Lightner went to the podium.

"There's no easy way to say this," he said. "After careful consideration, headquarters has decided to close this facility."

"Uh oh!" Rajiv turned to Trout. "We're screwed."

Too stunned to think about beryllium, Trout spent rest of the day idling at his desk. He was screwed, all right. Between the defense draw down and the dot-com bust, demand for engineers was at an all time low. To keep his mind off his troubles he read the propositions on the California voters' guide. After an hour wading through the impartial budget analysis, arguments for, and arguments against he stumbled on Proposition 36. Trout jumped from his chair and rushed into the hallway heading toward Rajiv's office. He met his friend coming the other direction. Like him, Rajiv brandished a copy of the voters' guide.

"We need to become..." Trout said.

"Drug-treatment councilors!" Rajiv finished.

"What you say is true." Dr. Fleisher, the bearded psychologist at the Hopeful Horizons Treatment Center, picked up the toy tyrannosaurus on his desk. "If Prop 36 passes a lot more users will be diverted from jail to treatment."

"You'll need more councilors," Trout said.

"Yes."

"And how do we learn to become drug-treatment councilors?" Rajiv asked.

"Well, that's the thing." Fleisher put down the plastic dinosaur. "You could go through the certificate program at UCSD but to be honest most of the people we hire are former addicts."

"So what you're saying is," Trout put away his pen, "we have to get addicted to heroin before you'll hire us."

Trout parked in front of Rajiv's Kearny Mesa ranch house, walked to the porch, and rang the doorbell. In the two months since his layoff he'd sent out hundreds of resumes and made numerous phone calls all with no luck. He'd never seen the job market this bleak, not even in the early 1990s. The only good news was Prop 36. Even though the 2000 presidential election remained undecided, the drug-treatment ballot measure had passed by a wide margin.

A petite woman in a red sari answered the door.

"Rajiv, your friend's here!"

Rajiv came to the door. The huge gut bulging from under his sweater made his body look like a capital D. The two men entered a living room that smelled of spices and tobacco smoke and sat on an overstuffed sofa. Trout kept his jacket on because the room was a bit chilly.

"I put together a POA&M." Trout unfolded a paper and laid it on the coffee table.

"Let's see." Rajiv put his cigarette in the ashtray and took a look.

"Marijuana's the gateway so you'll see on line one that we start with that on November 15." Trout pointed at the paper. "I give us Thanksgiving weekend off. Then we snort heroin on the 29th and enter rehab on the 30th. That way we'll be ready for our new jobs in early next year."

Rajiv's wife entered the room, set down two cups of tea, and disappeared back into the kitchen.

"I don't know if this will work." Rajiv took a drag on his cigarette sucking the ember all the way to the filter. "Who's to say there aren't more stops on the road to addiction? I hear the young people these days take something called ecstasy." He began scribbling on the paper. "And no one will believe we are addicts if we take heroin just one time. We must do it twice. One of those must be by injection."

"True." Trout sipped his tea and tasted cardamom. "But I worry about heroin. Maybe we could try something less addictive. Cocaine perhaps."

"Yah, cocaine is good!"

"It's settled then, marijuana, ecstasy, and finally cocaine. We start Monday."

"Where will we get this marijuana?" Rajiv asked.

"Oh."

Trout picked up Rajiv early in the week because if there was any time party people were bound to be out scoring drugs, it was at 8:30 on a Monday morning. When his friend slid into the Volvo's passenger seat, Trout slipped a Bob Marley's greatest hits CD into the player.

"To get us into the mood," he said.

Rajiv reached over and turned up the bass.

"What are you doing?" Trout turned it back down. "You'll ruin the fidelity of the original recording."

"Not at all. If you examine the frequency response of your speakers, you'll see the gain rolls off around two hundred Hertz."

Trout had to admit Rajiv had a point. So with heads bobbing to the beat of "Jamming" the two drove off to their first stop on the road to addiction and recovery. They'd heard drug abuse was rampant in the public schools. It seemed logical to look for a dealer while parked in front of the Kearny Villa High School. They didn't stay long enough to notice any because a security guard threatened to call the police unless they left.

The two spent the rest of the week staking out schools, head shops, and hydroponic gardening supply stores. Trout had already made an emotional investment with the Marley CD so their lack of success made him even more determined. On Friday afternoon he implemented an all-or-nothing strategy.

The Redemption Store was a tiny, incense-filled space in Ocean Beach filled with cotton skirts, jewelry, and multicolored knit caps. When they entered, the clerk was busy with a customer so Trout examined a red, gold, and green sweatshirt.

"How do I look, mon?" Rajiv modeled a dreadlock wig.

"Irie."

The clerk finished and Trout approached.

"I'd like to buy some herb."

"Herb?" The clerk wrinkled his forehead.

"Yeah." Trout winked. "Ital herb."

"We don't sell any of that here."

"Look." Trout took out his wallet and began laying twenties on the counter. "We're new in town and need to get some." When the clerk didn't respond, Trout added more.

"Okay, come back at closing time." The clerk stuffed the bills in his pocket.

"Are you feeling anything?" Trout took a hit off the joint he'd rolled from the Jamaican herb.

"I don't know." Rajiv inhaled the smoke and held his breath.

They'd been sitting in Trout's parked Volvo a few blocks from Rajiv's home for over a half hour and the sound of Bob Marley was starting to get on Trout's nerves.

"You know." Rajiv opened the plastic bag and sniffed its contents. "This smells like something you'd find on my wife's spice rack."

"Damn!" Trout's fist slammed the steering wheel. "We wasted the whole week and now we're behind schedule." He turned off the CD player to save his car's battery. "I never knew becoming a drug addict would be so hard."

"Accomplishing anything requires persistence, my friend. Call your wife and say you're working late. I have a plan."

Flashing blue lights played over the crowded dance floor at the Lapis Lazuli Club where trendy people moved with enthusiasm to the monotonous, techno beat. Clearly ecstasy had to be powerful stuff to make the dreadful music bearable. Rajiv leaned close and said something Trout couldn't understand before plunging into the writhing crowd on the dance floor. Trout never would have imagined his friend was such a natural dancer, busting moves that would put Bollywood stars to shame. Within seconds he was surrounded by smiling blondes in low-cut dresses who mimed sex acts by pushing their hips against him and opening their mouths in passionate Os.

Trout watched from the sidelines. Most dancers seemed to defer to a stocky woman in a sleeveless T-shirt that exposed generous glimpses of her breasts whenever she stepped and thrust out her arms. She wasn't beautiful and didn't appear to be rich. Why had she been chosen leader?

Trout decided he'd stand out less by moving so he flung his gangly legs and elbows about twitching to the beat of his own drummer, an autistic drummer who tapped with the chaotic rhythm of burst noise on a telephone line. From across the room Rajiv smiled.

Trout gave a thumbs up and made his way toward the woman in the sleeveless T. When he got close, she turned away but he stayed put. Sometime during the night someone placed a pill in his hand. It was an orange, triangular tablet with rounded corners. Trout put it in his mouth and worked up enough saliva to swallow. After another half hour of dancing he began to feel dizzy. The bass seemed to echo inside him as if a pile driver were pounding his very bones. He could see fringes around the lights and the other dancers' movements left trails.

"You okay, buddy?" a guy in a white vest asked.

Trout's legs were pork roasts that had been sewn on his torso. He needed to lie down.

When Trout woke, his tongue felt like one of those packets of desiccant they put in bags of dried mushrooms. He was in some kind of desert, his face millimeters away from the alkaline soil smooth as a missile's tail fin. He scrambled to his feet. Shading his eyes against the cruel sun with his hand, he scanned the distance. There was something out there.

"Hey! Over here!" He waved his arms over his head.

The object changed course and bounced toward him. As it grew closer, Trout made out its shape. It was some kind of rabbit with horns, a jackalope. Within minutes it stood before him.

"Looks like you're in a bit of a jam, partner," the jackalope said in a voice that sounded like Ronald Reagan's.

"Yeah." Trout stepped closer. "I'm sure glad you saw me."

"Hop on." The jackalope pointed his forepaw at a western saddle strapped to his back. "I'll take you back to civilization."

Trout put his left foot in the stirrup, swung his right leg over the animal's back, and planted himself in the saddle. The jackalope began hopping. The ride was anything but smooth. Trout wished for a pillow to cushion his rear end from the hard slap of the leather saddle that rattled his kidneys like a pile driver with every bounce.

"I was out of a job once so I know you must be feeling pretty discouraged about now," the jackalope said. "But you've got to understand that the pain you're feeling is part of the creative destruction that makes our free enterprise system such a marvel."

As the jackalope lectured about the information economy and the growth of the service sector, they passed a Conestoga wagon driven by Barry Goldwater who touched his Stetson in salute.

"Now, some Washington bureaucrats want to interfere with the free market," the jackalope continued. "They want to raise the minimum wage, put tariffs on goods produced overseas, and basically strangle honest business owners with a lot of red tape. They don't realize that taxing the wealthy actually hurts the middle class."

They made better progress than Trout realized. Before long the jackalope stopped in front of a clapboard saloon that had several horses and Ford Pintos tied up outside.

"Well, looks like this is where you get off."

"Thanks for the lift." Trout got down. "Mind if I ask you one more thing? My plan for a new career. Will it work?"

"All I can tell you is that those entrepreneurs, who take the risks, deserve the rewards." The jackalope hopped off into the sunset.

Trout woke in a bathroom stall and pulled his face away from the metal partition he'd been using as a pillow. The room smelled of vomit and urine. He looked down at the pale, skinny legs sticking out of his boxer shorts and ended in a pair of pants that had been pulled down around his shoes. His wallet and keys were missing.

"They probably slipped you a roofy." The policeman was about five foot six and must have weighed over two hundred fifty pounds. He had a thick, walrus mustache and wild, gray hairs zinged off in random directions from his eyebrows.

"Roofy? Is that some kind of drug?" Trout fought the urge to smile now that his plan was coming to fruition.

"Rohypnol, Ketamine, they're what we call date-rape drugs. You have any bleeding from your rectum?"

"What? Rectum?" Trout's hands moved involuntarily toward his back pockets. "No!"

"Because you can't be too careful. Once these creeps get their victims unconscious, they'll do all kinds of perversions. You wouldn't believe the stories I've heard, diseased sex organs squirting their oily jizm deep into bodily cavities, Chlamydia, syphilis, genital warts, hepatitis, AIDS. Why, a victim of that kind of psychological trauma will never recover even after years of therapy."

Trout stared.

"I'll put out a report on your stolen vehicle." The policeman closed his notebook and put it in his pocket. "Wouldn't count on getting your wallet back, though. You need a ride anywhere?"

"No, a friend is picking me up."

"Okay then, have a nice day."

"Why did you abandon me last night?" Trout asked when Rajiv arrived a half hour later.

"You looked like you were having such a good time with that girl, the one with the breasts."

"She drugged me and stole my car."

"Oh."

"Well," Trout smiled, "at least I had a real drug experience. How about you?"

"No luck." Rajiv looked at the floor. "I wasted the whole night with a bunch of dancing Baptists. At 10:00 they asked if I'd accepted Jesus as my personal savior and invited me to a church service."

Rajiv drove Trout home to a wife who became a tornado of suppressed rage in tortoise-shell glasses as soon as he stepped in the door. She began with the four words that strike terror into even the bravest men. "We need to talk."

It went downhill from there. Where had he been? It was bad enough that Trout was out of work but this! What was he trying to prove? Was there another woman? He'd better straighten up. Until he did, she'd be at her parents'. Good bye.

"I don't know if this is such a good idea." Rajiv peeked around the trunk of a eucalyptus tree.

"Can you think of anything better?" Trout looked past the chain-link fence into Hopeful Horizon's Garden of Sobriety. "I don't know about you but my bank account is almost empty."

"How about him?" Rajiv pointed at a man with a pierced eyebrow.

"No, doesn't look desperate enough."

The man went back inside the rehab facility. Trout and Rajiv watched another hour from their hiding place until a thin woman in an over-sized sweater came outside for a cigarette. She was pale and had short, auburn hair. From the dark circles under her eyes and the way she trembled when handling the lighter, Trout knew he'd found his target.

"Psst." Trout stepped out from the trees. "Over here."

The woman walked like a vase that could shatter at any moment.

"We can help you score," Trout said, "for a fifty dollars service fee plus the cost of the drugs."

"I need some meth bad." The woman crossed her arms over her chest. "But I don't have any money on me."

"Pay us when we get back," Trout said. "Should take us about two hours. Now where do we go to get your meth?"

"You've got to look at it this way," Trout said. "We'll more than make up for the damage we're causing her once we become treatment councilors. Besides, she'll probably go back to using once she gets out, anyway."

"I still don't feel good about it." Rajiv turned his 1987 Buick onto El Cajon Boulevard.

"How about this?" Trout said. "We just buy for ourselves and don't bring any back to the girl."

"I like it." Rajiv turned south on 52nd Street and parked across the street from the dealer's house.

"I'm Rajiv and I'm an addict."

"Hello Rajiv."

Sitting on a folding chair in a church basement, Trout watched his friend give his first Narcotics Anonymous testimony.

"I've been drug-free for a month now," Rajiv continued. "My turning point came when I woke up to the sound of an airplane engine. Blood was dripping from my face, my two front teeth were gone, and my left eye was swollen shut. I don't know how I got there."

"Excuse me!" A woman with dyed blonde hair raised her hand. "That's from A Million Little Pieces."

"Well yeah." Rajiv's eyes darted back and forth. "Because the author stole that story from me."

"But didn't you say this happened last month?" the blonde asked. "That book's been out for over a year."

"Yeah!" A bearded man in a denim vest crossed tattooed arms over his belly. "What are you trying to pull?"

"There's a simple explanation." Rajiv stepped around the podium so there was nothing but bad will between him and the audience.

The simple explanation was that they never went through with the drug buy. They'd decided that if lying to one addict was good, lying to several would be even better. So after reading several addiction memoirs like Go Ask Alice, they came up with their own bogus addiction stories.

"You see..." Without warning Rajiv bolted for the door and knocked the podium over as he fled.

Like a passing 747 his sprinting body kicked up a wind that swept pamphlets off the information table by the exit. Everyone sat in stunned silence until the bearded guy began laughing. This allowed the moderator to recover.

"Our next speaker will be Richard." He pointed to Trout. "Are you ready?"

Trout hit the parking lot just as Rajiv's Buick squealed to a halt in front of the doorway. Trout yanked open the door and dived into the back seat. Rajiv stomped the accelerator. The Buick burned rubber and fishtailed between the rows of parked cars. The back door flapped open and shut with each desperate turn. They were doing over seventy by the time they jumped the curb and made it onto the street. The car's undercarriage bottomed out against the pavement sending up a series of sparks that looked like the finale of a Fourth of July display.

"Don't worry." Trout sat up. "There are plenty other NA meetings we can try."

Trout maneuvered his Tata Nano through Bangalore traffic avoiding ox carts and crowded buses. He got on the Salem Bypass, took the familiar exit, and followed Seppings Road until he came to the India Aerospace Ltd. facility. No matter how early he left, the parking lot was always full when he arrived. He took a spot near the fence and walked past rows of new Toyotas and Mercedes toward the entrance.

In retrospect he was glad the drug councilor plan fell through. Just when he was about to give up hope, a distant uncle contacted Rajiv about engineering opportunities in India's Silicon Valley. The pay wasn't great but the cost of living was low and Trout's wife regarded the move as a grand, romantic adventure.

Trout took the elevator to his second-floor office and fired up his computer. He had an e-mail with the preliminary plans for the Maharaja missile. He spent an hour examining the drawings only to pause when he got to the nosecone. The design engineers had specified beryllium.

Strutinsky's Couch

After the poetry festival Seretta invited me to the party.

"You could meet Igor Strutinsky," she said.

"Sorry, I have to visit a sick friend," I reached into my satchel for a booklet. "But you can take these poems I've written. They contain all my thoughts and feelings. It'll be almost like I'm there."

On my drive home on the I-5 I imagined my booklet sitting on the poetry professor's couch with a slice of cheese and making conversation with a woman whose cleavage was as deep as a canyon on Mars. The latter would be difficult because my poems are always tongue-tied around the opposite sex. The next day Seretta called to say my booklet was a huge success and that Strutinsky had invited it to dinner the following weekend. This gave me an idea

On Monday morning I went to the office, propped one of my booklets in front of my computer, and left for the week. To my surprise there was a bonus in my next paycheck along with a note from my boss saying, "Well done."

I began using the booklets as stand-ins for all the things I didn't have time to do. I left one at my girlfriend's apartment because she said I never spent enough time with her. I put one on my pillow so I could always get eight hours sleep even when I stayed up late. The extra time freed me up to master the skills I'd always wanted to try: skydiving, yoga, and Japanese swordsmanship. I went to a few classes but found it easier to send the booklets in my place. Then I came up with the ultimate plan. I left one of my booklets at my writing table with a handful of pens and a stack of legal pads. After that I let things take care of themselves and spent my days at the beach or shopping for fresh vegetables at farmers' markets.

Little did I know my booklet would become more known for writing editorials than poems. One night I turned on Fox News and saw him being interviewed on "Hannity and Colmes." Being shorter than the moderators he was uneasy sitting in the guest chair. Whoever applied the makeup to his cover had done a poor job. It dripped and streaked under the glaring TV lights.

"I'm sick of those sniveling whiners who think the world owes them a living," my booklet said. "I got where I am through hard work. Nobody ever gave me anything."

Next thing I knew, my booklet was running for Congress, saying he was a businessman not a politician, and proposing to run the government like a business. Did I mention that my booklet was a businessman not a politician?

By August my booklet was ahead in the polls by fifteen percent. Then the LA Times broke a story about him visiting a prostitute and paying with a debit card. At first he blamed it all on the liberal media but the evidence was right there on page 23 in a poem titled, "I Visit a Prostitute and Pay with a Debit Card."

Things went south after that. My girlfriend threw the booklet out of her apartment and my boss told him to pack up his effects. Soon my life was back where it had started. I still leave a copy of my booklet at my writing desk, though, because it's such a wonderful thing when a poem writes itself.

Fårö Island

The orthodontists from ADA Local 514 resembled taupe Michelin men in their matching down jackets as they milled about in front of the Acropolis while waiting for the 5:15 bullet train that would take them to Tokyo.

"Is that a Corinthian column or are you just glad to see me?" I asked Dr. Diego Fujimori, who'd invented the diamond retainer made famous by Lindsay Lohan.

The elderly dentist pulled a 9-mm Beretta from his pants pocket and cursed me in Swedish. Why, he wasn't Dr. Fujimori and those men weren't members of Local 514! I surveyed the group for a familiar face and found only my brother Demetrius.

"Let's gö back tö my place för smörgasbörd," Demetrius said, his accent suspiciously laden with umlauts.

We walked past amphitheaters and statues with no arms to the Temple of Zeus, where his Volvo was parked.

"I'm having a crisis of imagination." Demetrius tossed his broadsword and horned Viking helmet in the back seat.

"I hate when that happens." I handed a few drachmas to the blue-faced Krishna guarding the car, and he strolled down the boulevard leading a French poodle.

We drove through the streets of Athens honking at gyros sellers and swerving around falafel stands until we arrived at his residence in Thymarakia. The air inside smelled of roast lamb with garlic and the soundtrack from Cries and Whispers penetrated the thin walls into the stairwell. Demetrius's apartment was on the twenty-fifth floor. Cardboard boxes and partially assembled IKEA furniture were scattered about the living room. Frustrated Nazi war criminals cursed the indecipherable instructions and combed the shag carpet for missing washers.

Olga Olsson lay naked on the Bjustra dining table with Thanatos, the barber, squatting between her thighs and peering up at her through a monocle. With comb and clippers he trimmed her thatch into a rectangle, the lengths of the major to minor sides in direct proportion to the golden mean.

"Cut!" Ingmar Bergman emerged from behind the camera.

Fellini barged through the front door with his key grip and best boy. The Italians began arguing with the Swedes, while Marcello Mastroianni moved the table and looked over the barber's shoulder.

"Gotta run." I snatched a spanakopita, gave my regards to Gunnar Björnstrand, and dashed for the last ferry from Fårö Island to the mainland.

The Breakup

After spending ninety minutes in rush-hour traffic I stumbled through my front door and found my living-room couch standing in the entryway with two suitcases at its feet.

"We have to talk," it said.

"You're upset. Let's go to the living room and discuss this." I circled my couch and tried to take the raincoat off its shoulders.

"You never spend time with me anymore." My couch whirled to face me.

"I've been under a lot of pressure at work. This new project…"

"Work! If it's not work, it's karate lessons, Zen retreats, or poetry readings! And when you get home, you microwave dinner, do those exercises for your sore back, and go to bed. I've hardly seen you in a month.

"I just want things to go back to how they used to be," my couch continued. "Remember how we spent hours binge watching 'The Wire' or how you used to sleep in on weekends and then listen to NPR while drinking Cloud-and-Mist tea?"

"Look, once I get the quarterly reports out, we'll spend a whole Saturday together. I'll get a pizza and one of those Game of Thrones books."

"You're too late." My couch opened the door and waved at the taxi in the parking lot. "I found a two-bedroom apartment in Encinitas. If you don't appreciate me, its tenant will."

From the doorway I watched the driver strap my couch on the taxi's roof and drive away. As the brake lights disappeared into the rainy night, I felt a gnawing suspicion that I'd lost something irreplaceable.

Waggawolla

After winning a hundred dollars at the horse races Jack Econski drove his VW Beetle north on Pacific Highway. About a half hour after maneuvering his VW past Coffs Harbor, he felt a beer shit coming on. There was no way to hold on until he made Byron Bay, so he searched for an exit. What he saw on the green and white freeway sign was as welcome as an angry landlord on the third of the month. Waggawolla! Jesus, he hated Waggawolla!

Econski took the exit and saw a bar not far from Waggawolla Land the amusement park he'd vowed never to enter. He drove around looking for a place to park and got more desperate every minute. Finally he found a spot under the purple glow of a mercury vapor light on an abandoned side street. The bar was mostly deserted except for a few hard-core regulars, who'd traded careers, lovers, and dreams for glasses of cheap whiskey.

"Hey!" the bartender yelled. "Restrooms are for customers only!"

"Give me a beer, then!" Econski muscled through the men's room door. His beer was waiting on the bar when he returned.

"That'll be nine bucks," the bartender said.

"Nine bucks for a beer?" No wonder Econski hated Waggawolla.

After taking the money, the bartender disappeared into a back room. Econski had planned to drink up and leave, but after paying nine dollars he decided to stay and drink in the atmosphere to get his money's worth. It was a quiet place except for the crunching of ice and sound of breaking glass coming from the back room. No one wasted money on the jukebox glowing in the corner. The woman sitting in a booth by the door could have been pretty, if alcohol and bitterness hadn't made her features brittle. Econski smiled at her. She stubbed out a lipstick-smudged cigarette and turned her back.

A large wombat dashed through the door. He wore a tuxedo and a big stupid smile. The wombat's eyes darted back and forth and settled on Econski.

"Hey buddy, can you hold these for me?" He tossed Econski a plastic bag and ran for the bathroom.

A policeman entered moments later. "Anybody see a short guy with long, digging claws come in here?"

The woman pointed toward the back, and the cop gave chase. Econski opened the bag. It contained a half-dozen pink pills shaped like wombat heads. He swallowed all of them and washed them down with beer.

"He's the one!" The giant marsupial led the policeman to Econski's stool. "I saw him selling drugs to the children outside the Gum Tree Forest."

"Let's see what's in the bag." When the policeman found it empty, he grabbed the wombat by the scruff of the neck and hauled him outside.

The bartender returned from the back room.

"You get many five-foot wombats in here?" Econski asked.

"What are you talking about?"

Econski shrugged and ordered another beer. By the time he finished it, he was beginning to feel strange. The pills made the colors brighter and the room seem flatter, as if drawn on an animation cell. The woman by the door now wore a long black dress and a gold crown. Econski made his way outside.

"Hey, watch where you're going!" A kookaburra shoved past and stepped on Econski's foot in the process.

Econski wasn't sure he could find his car. He wandered past castles, wicked stepmothers their smiles dripping venom, and singing platypuses. A group of kangaroos looked in dumpsters for bottles and aluminum cans to stuff in the garbage bags slung over their shoulders. Some guy had a mermaid in the alley. He'd gotten her top off but didn't know what to do with the rest of her. When Econski finally made it to his VW, the wombat and a goose in an ANZAC hat were waiting.

"I think you have something that belongs to us, mate." The wombat tapped a cricket bat against his palm.

"I ate them. I had to when you ratted me out to that cop."

"Then you owe us fifty bucks," the goose said.

"Buzz off!" Econski reached for the car's door.

He heard a whoosh and ducked. The cricket bat whistled past his head and dented the car's roof. Econski spun, knocked the bat away, and grabbed the wombat by the balls. Strangely the wombat's scream was no more high-pitched than his speaking voice. Econski heard an agitated honking, sidestepped, and caught the charging goose under the bill with an uppercut that knocked him off his webbed feet.

Econski stepped over the unconscious cartoon animals and reached for the car door. He felt a shock and a pain, as if a hundred cherry bombs had gone off in his skull. He hadn't seen the six-foot koala come out of the shadows with a tire iron.

A fly buzzed and tickled his cheek. Econski brushed it away, sat up, and opened his eyes. The sunlight made his head hurt. He was sitting in an alley behind a green dumpster. A used condom lay by his left foot, and the air smelled of rotting fish. Econski struggled to his feet and patted his pockets. The hundred dollars he'd won at the track was missing. He bent over, vomited, and wiped his mouth with the back of his hand before stumbling out of the alley. Waggawolla! He hated Waggawolla!

The Seven Labors of Sir Gordon

Long, long ago in the land of Nor, there lived a beautiful princess. In all the surrounding kingdoms no princess had rosier cheeks, blonder tresses, nor more orchid-like hands. As news of her beauty spread, visitors came from miles around to glimpse her loveliness. Naturally, some were suitors who wanted to make Princess Isadora their own. These brave knights greeted her with courtly phrases like, "Care for a beer?" or, "Wanna hook up?"

So many suitors came that Princess Isadora couldn't tell them apart. She found the courtly dating scene tiresome especially after that last jerk she went out with. The chambermaid was just getting a stain off his codpiece indeed! More than anything Princess Isadora wanted to take a year off to start a jousting apparel business but her father, King Stanley, reminded her that at nineteen her biological hourglass was ticking. She needed to get busy and make him some grandsons before the last grain of sand fell. So with his help she devised seven labors to test her suitors' worthiness. The first knight to complete these tasks would claim her hand in marriage. Many tried and many failed. After three years not even one had completed the first labor. It seemed Princess Isadora might die an old maid, her orchid-like hands caressed only by support gloves.

Then Sir Gordon arrived at the palace after making the long journey from Glendale on his Marxist-Leninist horse, Che. Gordon, whose friends called him Gordo, laid eyes on the princess as she was combing her blonde tresses with her orchid-like hands and was immediately smitten. He'd never seen tresses so blonde nor hands so orchid-like, and he vowed to do whatever it took to hold those orchid-like hands in his own.

"Do you like Roxy Music?" Princess Isadora asked. "'Cause I just love Bryan Ferry and all that music from the 70s, especially glam rock. There's something really sexy about a man dressed in drag. Don't you think? Have you ever been to a gay bar? 'Cause we could go if you want." She picked up her dog, a Bichon Frisé, and set him on her lap.

King Stanley cleared his throat. "The test."

"Oh, that's right!" Isadora slapped her forehead in a very un-princess-like manner. "If you would claim my hand in marriage, you must first complete seven labors to prove your worthiness. The first is to defeat Randy the Dragon who has made us most unpleased lately. Good luck, then. Guess I'll see you back here when you're done." Princess Isadora kissed her lap dog. "Who's momma's favorite boy?"

King Stanley, who sometimes wondered if his daughter was really management material, cleared his throat.

Isadora looked up. "Oh yeah! My personal assistant will give you Randy's contact information."

Randy the Dragon lived in Gundeson Hall at Nor State University's Dunsmuir Campus. Rather than putting up with the inevitable diatribe about oppression of the working class, Sir Gordo left Che at the palace and booked a red-eye carriage at Pig Offal Station. He arrived the following morning just as the students in Dr. Wilson's 7:30 Siege Machines 101 class resumed work on the trebuchet outside the physics building. In addition to the sound of hammers there were several not-so-rosy-cheeked coeds to distract him, but since their hands were more clover-like than orchid-like, Sir Gordo ignored them and went looking for breakfast at the student union building. Once there he ordered some Mac Gruel and curled up in a corner to get some rest. Unfortunately, the sword fights and banging of tankards made quite a din so he decided to get on with the day's slaying.

After locating Gundeson Hall and climbing five flights of sticky stairs that smelled of stale beer, Sir Gordo knocked on Randy's dorm room door. It took longer than reasonable for anyone to answer. In fact, Sir Gordo would have thought the room was deserted were it not for the sound of "Love is the Drug" coming from inside. Finally, a blonde man wearing a sleepy expression and a pair of NSU gym shorts answered. He took one look at Sir Gordo's sword, turned back inside, and said, "Dude, it's for you."

"Another one?" Randy coughed and came to the door.

Except for a slightly green pallor and a bad smoking cough, Sir Gordo could see no reason for Randy to be called Randy the Dragon. Nevertheless, he issued his challenge.

"Randy the Dragon, on behalf of the fair Princess Isadora, I challenge you to mortal combat."

"Yeah. Yeah." Randy cleared his throat. "Meet me at the octagon at 7:00 PM."

"Is that the octagon on 13th Street or the one by the stadium? 'Cause if it's the one on 13th, there's this great barbecue place…"

"The stadium!" Randy's outburst triggered a coughing fit. "Let me give you some advice, champ. First, never fill up on pork before a cage match. And second, if you end up dating Princess Herself Adora, never bonk the chambermaid no matter how long it's been since you've had any of the princess's attention. Now get out of here. I have to study for my 1:00 art appreciation class."

Sir Gordo spent the day at Dunsmuir Monastery pouring over the illuminated manuscripts of Randy's previous fights. By 7:00 he entered the octagon confident that he could win.

"In the blue corner, weighing 165 pounds, Sir Gordon of Glendale. And in the red corner, weighing 182, Dunsmuir's own Randy, the Dragon, Donnaghee!"

Even though the crowd had come to see the main event between Sirs Shamrock and Couture, they gave Sir Gordo and Randy a hearty cheer. The fighters touched gloves. Sir Gordo raised his hands into a high guard, looked at his opponent through the gap in his hands, and noticed the dragon tattoo on Randy's bicep. The two danced around the ring maneuvering for distance. Randy threw jab, hook, and roundhouse kick combinations to keep Gordo off balance. Gordo knew that merely reacting to Randy's moves would lead to his defeat. He had to take the initiative so he threw a flurry of punches at Randy's head. When the Dragon raised his hands to block, Gordo dove to the mat, captured a leg, and took his opponent down in classic Saxon Jiu Jutsu style.

Gordo scrambled on top but not before Randy wrapped his legs around his torso. Then came the long, slow struggle for advantage. Gordo needed to disentangle himself from his opponent's legs. He hit Randy's head with fists and elbows but the close range prevented him from getting in a solid strike. Muscles strained as he struggled to stay in control of his opponent's sweaty body. The match had lasted only a minute but Gordo was already exhausted. He prayed for it to end but knew taking risks for a quick victory would lead to defeat. Better to bide his time, cinch his opponent up inch by inch, and wait for him to make a mistake.

As Gordo drew back for another punch, Randy lifted an elbow catching him in the teeth. Blood sprayed from Gordo's mouth as he struggled against his rage. Gordo continued working free of Randy's legs. Suddenly Randy reached for him. Gordo sprang like a rattlesnake, securing Randy's free arm between his shoulder and chin, and using both hands to put pressure on Randy's elbow. Randy the Dragon pounded the mat in submission. Sir Gordo was victorious.

"We are much pleased with your victory over the vile Randy and present you with this token of our esteem." Princess Isadora handed Sir Gordo a poster of David Bowie as Ziggy Stardust. "You have earned the right to attempt the next labor, which will enhance respect for women everywhere."

While Princess Isadora spoke, Sir Gordo wiggled a tooth that was loosened in the fight with his tongue. If the princess's cheeks seemed a little less rosy, perhaps it was because he was thinking of his upcoming root canal.

"You must ensure that all toilet seats in our kingdom remain down."

"Excuse me?"

"Toilet seats!" the princess said. "Down!"

"Right."

"When I was young, we didn't bother with toilets," King Stanley said. "We just squatted behind a bush. I guess that's not good enough for people, today. Bunch of spoiled pissants!"

As Sir Gordo left the palace, he performed a quick back-of-the-parchment calculation. Factoring in the population and a reasonable time to get to each privy, he concluded it would take forty-five years for him to visit each one in the kingdom, and there was no guarantee that subsequent patrons wouldn't return the seats to their upright positions.

Clearly he needed a different strategy. But what? Distributing public-service leaflets with the princess's picture would run afoul of Nor's chronic toilet paper shortage and Sir Gordo preferred grassroots campaigns about issues that really mattered such as disease or world hunger. No, the best he could do was nail down the toilet seats in the palace, ignore the rest, and hope the princess didn't notice.

A week after his root canal Sir Gordo sent word to the palace. Princess Isadora granted him an audience in the throne room. King Stanley lay on a litter in the corner and moaned about the spear stuck in his groin.

"It's your fault, daddy," Princess Isadora said. "I told you to wear your safety gear but you had to go jousting with Mohammedans without it."

As his reward Princess Isadora allowed Sir Gordo to watch "The Way We Were," starring Barbara Streisand and Robert Redford, with her. It might as well have been another of his labors. Sir Gordo had to resist clawing his eyes out every time the princess gushed over the young Redford. To make matters worse, her gay yapper dog bit him and then dashed to safety behind her legs.

"Your third labor is to help me, uh." Princess Isadora glanced at her injured father for guidance. When none came, her lip trembled. "To help me buy a new party dress. Let's go shopping!"

She whisked him to a waiting carriage and before you could say, "I'm feeling a bit of the plague coming on. Perhaps I'd better go home," they arrived at the Duke of York shopping mall. An eternity of tedium followed: dresses, shoes, and endless waiting in the women's section while Isadora was in the changing room. Sir Gordo thought of all the better things he could be doing with his time, like having another root canal. When Isadora finally emerged, her cheeks seemed a little less rosy and her tresses a little less blonde, though they were still the rosiest and blondest Gordo had seen.

They stopped at a night club for dancing and mead shooters on the way back. Sir Gordo showed off his latest moves: the Salterello, Black Nag, La Spagna, and Maltese Branle. Circling, spinning, the intricate weave of partners, he had a marvelous time until Princess Isadora criticized his stepping. But that was soon forgotten when she decreed his fourth labor. He was to show her a good time on the British Riviera over the long Saint Olaf's Day weekend. She dropped him off at his barracks so he could get some sleep and be back at the palace at 8:00 AM sharp.

When Sir Gordo awoke, the little hand on his sun dial was almost on the VIII. Furious with himself that he'd forgotten to set his squire, Gordo struggled into his chain mail cutoffs and dashed outside to his trusty, Marxist-Leninist horse.

"Let's get a move on, big fellow. I'm late."

"Don't think that using an affectionate term absolves you from exploiting my labor," Che, the horse, said. "How would you like it if I sat on your back?"

"Please."

"Oh, all right."

They galloped through muddy streets avoiding peasants, penitent monks, and landlords throwing offal from second-story windows. On arrival at the palace, Sir Gordo parked Che in the short-term lot, rushed inside, and found Princess Isadora bent over an open suitcase.

"Now, where did I put that chastity belt?"

Sir Gordo sat down to wait. His stomach growled. Isadora went back and forth between the closet and her suitcases. Shadows shortened. Flies performed an aerial version of the Black Nag. Gordo's stomach rumbled some more. After two hours Princess Isadora closed the lid on the last of her twelve suitcases. As Sir Gordo hauled the eight-stone bags, one after the other, to the carriage, he noted that the princess's dainty hands seemed not to resemble orchids as much as devil's clubs. Princess Isadora strolled down the stairs after he'd finished loading the carriage. Sir Gordo held the door open closed it after her.

"You're not coming?" she asked.

"I think I'll ride along outside on my trusty, Marxist-Leninist horse, Che."

As they made their way through the teaming cesspit of humanity that was downtown Nor, Che asked, "Something bothering you?"

"It's Princess Isadora. After performing those labors, her cheeks no longer seem so rosy nor her tresses so blonde." Sir Gordo swallowed. "I'm beginning to think that women and I have incompatible needs. How can I ever live with one? How can I live with anyone?"

"What do you want to do?"

"If I had my way," Sir Gordo glanced back at the carriage, "I'd abandon this whole quest."

"Why don't you?"

"Because it would violate the whole mythic structure."

"I don't follow." Che sidestepped a leper lying in the road who was then crushed under the carriage's wheels.

"A knight's quest follows a basic narrative pattern. He overcomes difficulties along the way to achieving his noble goal. At the end he triumphs over an internal crisis as well as the ultimate obstacle and attains that goal. If I abandon my quest at this point, I'd be letting down the team. I'd be ashamed to call myself a knight."

"That's just what the feudal power structure wants you to think." Che paused and let the carriage pass. "The Man's been laying that guilt trip on you, since you were a boy, to make you do his bidding. It's time to reject his indoctrination and just say no."

"There may be something to what you say." Sir Gordo stroked his chin. "But what would I do without a quest?"

"How about dedicating yourself to a new goal, world socialism?"

"Or maybe I could go on a quest for self."

"We could go to Bolivia and fight for workers' rights." Che's ears perked up like they always did when he talked about the workers' revolution.

"No, my friend. You go ahead. I release you to follow your dream. As for me, I'm enrolling in a solitary meditation retreat. I can't be with people until I work on myself. It's a cliché but the only one who can make me happy is me. After three years, three months, and three days I'll see if I'm ready to rejoin the human race."

Did Sir Gordo find happiness? We don't know because no one ever heard from him again. We do know that Princess Isadora got back together with Randy the Dragon. They married and had a little girl named Amy. Isadora was happy for a few years until Randy left her for the Duchess of Luxembourg. After divorce lawyers bankrupted the kingdom, Princess Isadora was forced to start that jousting apparel company to keep up with the alimony she had to pay. She found she had a better head for business than for princessing. Now her company's logo can be seen on armor from Aragon to Byzantium.

A Cautionary Tale

The poet woke in a granite-walled room and inhaled stagnant air that smelled as if undisturbed for millennia. Despite the motionless sun blazing outside the window, he felt no need to remove his cable-knit sweater. He sat up on the cot and ran a hand through his shock of white hair. What had happened? The last thing he remembered was gasping at the dinner table while his wife looked on in horror.

"Are you ready?" a being with a man's body and a falcon's head asked after entering the room. "You can start by telling me why you deserve eternal life."

"I published poems in all the major journals like ONTHEBUS, Rattapallax, and such." The poet somehow found it natural to relate his publication record to the Egyptian god he'd never believed in. "I even placed one in Poetry."

The god Horus led him into a chamber where jackal-headed Anubis sat before a golden balance scale. Like Horus, Anubis wore a white linen robe that left his right shoulder bare. A crocodile and a baboon squatted in the corner playing Snakes and Ladders.

"This is the judgment in which we compare meaningful words to empty ones." Anubis withdrew the words spoken by the poet at public readings from a calfskin bag, placed those from poems on the balance's right pan, and placed the ones from poems' introductions on the left.

By intuition the poet realized that if the scale tilted to the right, green-skinned Osiris would embrace him with eternal life and lead him to the field of reeds. As the indicator needle wavered, the poet prayed for all his iambs and clever metaphors to gain weight but it was no good. The scale's needle swung left.

"Condemned!" The baboon wrote the verdict in a notebook.

The crocodile lunged and tore the poet's heart from his chest. In the moments of consciousness before entering oblivion a final regret seared the poet's mind. If only he'd skipped the bloated intros, his poetry would have lived for eternity.

Arugula

Her balloon floated through the living room leaving a trail of entropy in its wake, the blue propane blasts from its burner interrupting conversations of high government officials and captains of industry. And though we bent our heads in Ls to view her cherry-bowl panties, she never stepped from the gondola except to set foot on a dash-built bridge of denial by the coleslaw.

From overhead she complimented the missile plans I'd spread on the buffet table and speculated on the warhead the Pentagon would choose, a bomb of a conservative opinion, no doubt. She was the only woman who'd ever grasped the genius of my Diet Coke and Mentos propulsion. So when she asked that my head snap off and follow her to Paris for several months I took a job as a Salade Niçoise in a Montmartre café. I was happy for a time next to the onion soup on the checkered tablecloth but something in the French dressing was not Italian. I sensed that she was unhappy too. Offended by the ostentatious display of forks, she fasted and poured her Chianti into the bowl of a Jack Russell Terrier with a drinking problem.

"Pig dog! Pig dog!" the customers chanted. "Rouge!"

The terrier dashed out of the café and returned moments later with a can of red latex house paint.

"Pig dog! Pig dog! Jaune!"

He brought back yellow.

"Pig dog! Pig dog! Blanc!"

The terrier returned with a can of paint swinging from the handle in his jaws and set it by the bartender.

"Non, c'est ivoire."

Head held high with Gallic pride the pig dog turned his back on all the free drinks and stalked out into the Paris night. Sensing my salad days were over, I followed and eventually took up residence under the Pont Neuf where I lived off fish, baguettes, and radicchio from the River Seine. After a time I found that I could move through the rushing water like a snake except for the snakes head and snake's body, which I found unappealing, especially when they were in the water with me.

I never saw her again though I heard she had a daughter with a Cambodian zeppelin designer who, despite helium being the second most common element in the universe, could not get his business off the ground. He died at a Phnom Penh karaoke bar in a tragic Michael Jackson impersonation. Some say it was suicide.

After that mother and daughter lived a weird Jungian fairy tale in Lakehurst, New Jersey. The girl developed a severe case of agoraphobia. After high school graduation she married a man named Jack Russell and moved to an abandoned missile silo in Minot, North Dakota. The couple lived happily underground with their bilingual terrier, raising hydroponic vegetables and emerging once a week to take the dog to his AA meetings.

And me? I came down with a bad case of tobacco mosaic virus, no doubt from a broken heart. It was touch and go for a while but the doctors say that with daily topical application of oil and vinegar, I'll make a full recovery.

The Adventures of Non Sequitur Man

Using his amazing powers to stun the mind, Non Sequitur Man protects Jupiter City from criminals and terrorists alike. When we last saw our hero, the evil Kohlrabi had rendered him unconscious with knockout gas. Our story resumes in Kohlrabi's hideout.

"It's no use struggling, Non Sequitur Man." Kohlrabi twisted the tips of his green mustache. "Your shackles are unbreakable and once my henchman Dwayne lowers you into that pit, one hundred thousand hungry earthworms will turn you into compost. Ha! Ha! Ha! Ha!"

Dwayne waved and then turned to Kohlrabi. "Hey boss, shouldn't you explain your evil plan?"

"Why should I explain my evil plan to him? He's about to pass through the alimentary canals of one hundred thousand hungry earthworms."

"Because it's traditional."

"Very well." Kohlrabi struggled with Windows 8 to bring up a computer graphic. "Where's the damn start button? Oh never mind. I'll just use this icon here..." Kohlrabi paged through a Power Point presentation to the figure he wanted. "Once you're out of the way, I'll send weekly boxes of organic produce to every man, woman, and child in Jupiter City. They'll be so busy trying to figure out how to cook the stuff that Dwayne and I will waltz right in and take over. There!" Ignoring Dwayne's desperate gestures Kohlrabi then asked, "Do you have any last words before you die?"

Non Sequitur Man looked into the gaping maws of one hundred thousand hungry earthworms and said, "No parking between 9 AM and 3 PM Tuesdays due to street sweeping. Violators will be towed."

"Ah! Ah!" Kohlrabi grabbed his head with stalk-like arms. "That makes no sense! I gave you a perfect, dramatic scene and you reply with that. Unless..." He began pacing. "You mean that my plan will be foiled by some unforeseen parking violation."

"But boss, he is called Non Sequitur Man, after all."

"No, you fool! A non sequitur is a term in logic that describes a conclusion that does not follow from the premises." Kohlrabi waved his stalks. "You know, like all men are mortal. Socrates is a man. Therefore Socrates hates Swiss cheese."

Jon Wesick

"I was referring to a non sequitur used as a literary device." Dwayne pulled up a Wikipedia page describing Theater of the Absurd on Kohlrabi's laptop.

"Give me that!" Kohlrabi snatched the laptop from Dwayne's hands but try as he might, he couldn't get Windows 8 to do what he wanted. "Damn piece of …" While attempting to throw his laptop against the wall, Kohlrabi tripped and fell into the pit. "Ahhh!"

Later while police packed Kohlrabi's remains into yard bags, Detective Kobo Dashiki expressed the thanks of a grateful city.

"Well Non Sequitur Man, looks like Mayor Kardashian owes you another one."

"Thanks, Kobo." Non Sequitur Man pointed at the detective's colorful outfit. "Damn, that's one hell of a shirt!"

"You like it?" Dashiki beamed. "I got it in West Africa on my way back from Mount Koya."

"Bake at three hundred fifty degrees for thirty minutes or until browned."

"What the…?" When Dashiki realized the joke, he punched Non Sequitur Man in the shoulder. "You idiot!"

Jon Wesick's *Arugula* Publication Credits

Story	Where Published
Moon of a Divided Heart	*Tales of the Talisman*, Vol. 3 Issue 4, March 2008.
Political Correctness	*Bracelet Charm*, Vol 5, No 40, August 2009.
The Slender Thread	*Clockwise Cat*, November 22, 2013.
Quest	unpublished
Necessary Precautions	*Writers Post Journal*, April 2005.
Angola	*Tabard Inn*, Issue #3, March 2008.
Golden Delicious	*Sangam Magazine*, Volume 1, Issue 1, Spring 2009.
A Christmas Story	*CC&D*, (scars.tv website), November 4, 2011, also *CC&D* print version, volume 239 December 20, 2012.
The Divine Parody	Space and Time. Issue 108, Fall 2009.
Confessions of a Wallflower	*Zahir*, Issue 11, Winter 2006.
Menace II Your Arteries	*Words of Wisdom*, Vol 25, No 3, July 2007, p. 63.
Operators are Standing By	*Samizdada*, February 2007.
The Long, Bad Good Friday	*Berkeley Fiction Review*, Issue 32, 2012.
Radiator Dog Saves the Day	*The MiniMAG.com*, Issue #3, March 2004.
Sundaes Will Never Be the Same	*Hipster Fight*, Issue 3, October 2012.
Missionary Position	*Missing Slate*, November 2011.
Fox Slapping	*Contemporary World Literature*, Issue 5, February 2011.
Middle Class Man	*Jersey Devil Press*, Issue 43, June 2013.

Postmodern Adventures of the Scribe	Unpublished. I was accepted for the *Static Movement Gifted Anthology* but the publication disbanded.
Pioneer Spirit	*Everyday Weirdness*, June 14, 2010.
Rehab	*Contemporary World Literature*, Issue 2, November 2010.
Strutinsky's Couch	*Hot Air Quarterly*, Number 19, Summer 2011.
Faro Island	*Journal of Experimental Fiction*, 37, 2010.
The Breakup	*Clockwise Cat*, November 22, 2013.
Waggawolla	*Smashed Cat*, July 8, 2014.
The Seven Labors of Sir Gordon	*Cynic Online*, Volume 14, Issue 9, September 2012.
A Cautionary Tale	*Medulla Review*, Volume 1, Issue 2, March 2010.
Arugula	*Binnacle*, Spring 2014.
The Adventures of Non Sequitur Man	*Clockwise Cat Strikes Back Episode XXXII*, Fall 2015.